"Every cop in the state is after you, and you're worried about my ankle? What do you really want from me?" she asked.

"For now, all I want is for you to get in that bath."

Liar. Marco knew what he wanted. Just once he wanted her to look at him like he was something other than a drug-stealing scumbag. He wanted her to look at him like she had the last time he'd been in her apartment, the night they'd made love.

"I won't help you again," Paige said. "Why don't you just go away and leave me alone?"

"I can't do that."

"What is that supposed to mean?"

"It means that I'll be going, all right, but I won't be leaving you alone. I'm taking you with me."

Dear Reader,

There's so much great reading in store for you this month that it's hard to know where to begin, but I'll start with bestselling author and reader favorite Fiona Brand. She's back with another of her irresistible Alpha heroes in *Marrying McCabe*. There's something about those Aussie men that a reader just can't resist—and heroine Roma Lombard is in the same boat when she meets Ben McCabe. He's got trouble—and passion—written all over him.

Our FIRSTBORN SONS continuity continues with *Born To Protect,* by Virginia Kantra. Follow ex-Navy SEAL Jack Dalton to Montana, where his princess (and I mean that literally) awaits. A new book by Ingrid Weaver is always a treat, so save some reading time for *Fugitive Hearts,* a perfect mix of suspense and romance. Round out the month with new novels by Linda Castillo, who offers *A Hero To Hold* (and trust me, you'll definitely want to hold this guy!); Barbara Ankrum, who proves the truth of her title, *This Perfect Stranger;* and Vickie Taylor, with *The Renegade Steals a Lady* (and also, I promise, your heart).

And if that weren't enough excitement for one month, don't forget to enter our Silhouette Makes You a Star contest. Details are in every book.

Enjoy!

Leslie Wainger

Leslie J. Wainger
Executive Senior Editor

Please address questions and book requests to:
Silhouette Reader Service
U.S.: 3010 Walden Ave., P.O. Box 1325, Buffalo, NY 14269
Canadian: P.O. Box 609, Fort Erie, Ont. L2A 5X3

The Renegade Steals a Lady

VICKIE TAYLOR

INTIMATE MOMENTS™

Published by Silhouette Books

America's Publisher of Contemporary Romance

This book is dedicated to the loyal canines who serve our law-enforcement agencies and military everywhere.

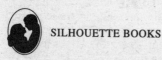 SILHOUETTE BOOKS

ISBN 0-373-27174-3

THE RENEGADE STEALS A LADY

Visit Silhouette at www.eHarlequin.com

Printed in U.S.A.

Books by Vickie Taylor

Silhouette Intimate Moments

The Man Behind the Badge #916
Virgin Without a Memory #965
The Lawman's Last Stand #1014
The Renegade Steals a Lady #1104

VICKIE TAYLOR

has always loved books—the way they look, the way they feel and most especially the way the stories inside them bring whole new worlds to life. She views her recent transition from reading to writing books as a natural extension of this longtime love. Vickie lives in Aubrey, Texas, a small town dubbed "The Heart of Horse Country," where, in addition to writing romance novels, she raises American quarter horses and volunteers her time to help homeless and abandoned animals. Vickie loves to hear from readers. Write to her at: P.O. Box 633, Aubrey, TX 76227.

Prologue

Paige Burkett arched in her lover's arms. Beneath her palms, his shoulders shuddered like a locomotive, straining for that first forward inch under a heavy load. Paige's head tipped back. Her mouth fell open in a silent gasp and she hung there, eyes closed, suspended in the moment like a fly in amber.

The curtains above the bedside window parted, exhaling a breeze as hot and humid as a human breath. Overhead, the lazy spin of the ceiling fan circulated the smells of summer—the tangy brine of the Texas Gulf Coast, sweet rosemary from the pots lining the porch below, and sweat. Warm, moist flesh entwined with warm, moist flesh.

"Open your eyes," the man above her commanded, and she complied, helpless to deny him.

Moonlight flowed like mercury over his glistening olive skin. Black hair, half an inch overdue for a trim, curled damply on the back of his neck. A twelve-hour shadow framed the sensuous curve of his mouth.

But it was his eyes that drew her attention, as they had

since she'd first caught him watching her almost a month ago. The eyes of an angel, she'd thought then. Not the innocent orbs of some winged cherub, but the deep soulful wells of a mortal creature, torn between the heavenly aspirations of the divine and the sins of the damned. Dark, beckoning, full from their first glance of the inevitability of this moment, his eyes had called to her. Drawn her in even when better judgment warned her away.

Three years. For three years she'd denied herself this closeness. Told herself she didn't need a man. Didn't want one. Then one look from him, and she'd wanted nothing else.

Damn Marco Angelosi and his angel's eyes.

He must have sensed the change in her mood. "Paige?"

She turned her head aside, away from his eyes. "It's all right."

"No." Clasping her chin between his thumb and forefinger, he nudged her face toward him. His black eyes probed deep inside her, to the root of her secrets. "It's not."

A subtle shift by him broke the fledgling bond their bodies had formed. His absence left her bereft, a hollow outline of the woman she had been. Anger flourished in the empty space.

It had to be all right. Marco might have started this thing between them, watching her all the time with those haunted eyes, but she was the one who had invited him inside tonight. Invited him to her bed.

She needed this. Needed him. Needed to feel like a woman again, if only for one night.

Paige surged up. A soft chop cut the arm he'd been leaning on from beneath him, and she flipped him easily to his back. Straddling his chest, she pinned his wrists above his head. "Then you're just going to have to make it all right, Angelosi. Because I'm not letting you go until you finish what you started."

He took stock of her for another long moment. Apparently he was satisfied with what he saw. A smile ghosted around the corners of his mouth, then disappeared, gone before it ever really materialized. With a flick of his wrists, he reversed her grip so that it was he who held her captive.

Her breath caught as he pulled her close. The hair on his chest fired erotic shocks where it grazed her aching nipples. His lips hovered over hers, close but not touching. Gently he wound her arms around his waist.

"Then hold on tight, Burkett, because I plan to make it a lot better than *all right*."

The promise tingled like a shower of tiny meteors on her skin. She reached for his face, but he was gone, working his way down her throat, touching, licking and kissing as he lowered himself. He paused to settle his mouth on her left breast, pulling the breath from her chest as his cheeks hollowed, suckled.

Cool air teased the slippery trail he left behind when his lips wandered along her ribs. He wriggled his hips between her splayed knees, sliding down the bed on his back. Pausing again, his tongue delved into her navel, then dipped lower.

Sharp sparks of pleasure darted from her core. She swayed, falling forward until only a white-knuckled grip on the headboard kept her upright. Electricity arced around her, through her. Her skin grew unbearably tight. Unbearably hot. Her blood thickened until the cells pulsed through her veins in great, throbbing knots.

"Now, Marco," she groaned. "Oh, now." Releasing the headboard, she clutched at his hair.

He pulled her down, rolled, and covered her with his hot, damp length. Perspiration beaded at his temples. Sinew corded in his neck and he bared his teeth, stark white against a swarthy complexion. Lacing his fingers with hers above her head, he pushed their hands against the mattress, levering his upper body away and driving his lower body inside.

Filled at last by his hardness and heat, Paige mewled her approval.

"Ah, that's better." That not-quite-there smile crossed his lips again, pure male satisfaction, she was sure.

Gradually adjusting to his thick intrusion, she stroked her hands down his smooth back, marveling at the power of his gathered muscles and the tremble of need, barely contained. Cupping his backside, she pulled him closer, taking his full measure.

"Much better," she agreed.

His smile disappeared as he groaned. He eased away from her, then rolled forward, a thick wave tumbling heavily ashore. Again and again he moved over her, as rhythmic as the sea. And as deep.

The current of his passion dragged her under. She'd never felt more alive than she did at that moment, yet she was drowning. In him. The deeper he took her, the more intensely she felt the onrush of something even more dangerous, something as powerful—and unstoppable—as the tide.

Dark eyes bid her surrender to the flow.

Fear clutched at her from the shadows. Head thrown back, she gasped for air, for coherence. Her fingers bit deep into his shoulders.

His body pierced hers furiously. Seductively. Enticing her to match his pace. "Come on, let go."

"I can't."

"You have to."

No, she mouthed soundlessly, her head thrashing from side to side.

Yes, his eyes commanded.

Gulping down her panic at the consuming void she felt approaching, she squeezed her eyes shut.

Growling, he interrupted his rhythm. With his teeth bearing down on the flesh of her neck, he wedged his hand between them, his fingers touched her where all her nerves joined together. Swirling. Spiraling. Creating a riptide of sensation.

She pushed at his shoulders. Cried out once.

And gave herself over to the vortex.

Wonder cascaded over her like moonlight on the crest of a whitecap. One by one the molecules of her body disassembled into pure energy and danced in the beam. Marco pulled back and thrust once more, then his back went rigid. He cried her name, guttural and raw, as his body pulsed inside her.

Paige held on to him as if he was the last life preserver on a sinking ship. She clutched with arms, legs, body, while the surge swelled around them, lifted them. She held him so close their hearts beat as one, their minds connected, both tumultuous.

It wasn't until he gently kissed the tip of her nose and the creases of her eyelids that she realized the maelstrom had passed.

Still dazed by the intensity of what they'd shared, she rolled to her side, tucking her hands beneath her cheek. Without a word she waited for the shift of the mattress that would signal Marco's exit from her bed, but Marco didn't leave. Instead he wrapped his arms around her. He held her securely, almost possessively. One of his firm thighs insinuated itself between her knees and his beard stubble razed the back of her head as he smoothed her hair with his cheek.

Seconds, then minutes, ticked away. The flush gradually cooled from her skin. She shivered, and Marco pulled a blanket up and tucked it around her shoulders.

"Sleep," he murmured.

But surprise—and the warm current of his breath behind her ear—held sleep at bay. She wasn't sure what she had expected tonight, but it certainly hadn't been this. A joining that transcended sex into intimacy in its purest form.

He'd known exactly how to touch, how to move, to elicit her response. Like master and puppet he'd pulled her strings, and she'd danced for him. She'd held nothing back. She couldn't have stopped the shattering climax he'd wrung from her even if she had wanted to—which she hadn't.

No man had ever affected her so deeply. Touched her on such an elemental level. Had he summoned her very soul, she would have answered his call.

And that frightened her.

Marco possessed a will few men could match. He was intense. Driven. Obsessive in the pursuit of whatever—or whomever—he went after. Compulsive in the protection of anything in his keep. He would want too much from a woman, a lover. Demand too much.

More than she was willing to give.

Three years ago she'd given everything she had to a man. So much that when he walked out, there'd been nothing left of herself for *her.*

She'd worked hard since then to take charge of her life, to regain her independence, her self-respect. She didn't plan to give it up to another man.

Not even a man with a sinful body and angel's eyes.

The grandfather clock downstairs chimed twelve bells. Midnight. Appropriately, heralding both a new day and a time come to an end. For her first night with Marco Angelosi, she vowed, would also be her last.

Morning dawned in shades of gray instead of the pink and orange hues more common to coastal Texas. Paige welcomed the dull skies. A full-strength August sun would have been murder on her irritated eyes. She hadn't slept much last night.

Despite the gunmetal canopy hanging overhead, she jammed on a pair of aviator sunglasses before stepping out

of the Battan Industries warehouse she and her canine police partner, a German shepherd named Bravo, had just
wasted another morning searching. This raid hadn't turned
up anything more than the last five.

Gulls screeched and circled above the nearby docks. A
sea breeze toyed with the hair around her face. She tucked
the yellow locks behind her ears and surreptitiously
scanned the parking area for Marco.

Not that he had any reason to be here. He hadn't been
appointed to the multiagency task force assembled to investigate the influx of a new cocaine derivative called
''Magic'' into the area. But then, he hadn't had a reason
to be at any of the other task force busts, either, yet he had
shown up at each and every one.

Department gossip rumored he was jealous. As Port
Kingston Police Department's best narcotics detective, he'd
been the leading candidate to head up the task force. But
for reasons unknown, his name had been left off the final
postings.

Paige didn't believe he was jealous. Marco was too much
his own man to worry about office politics. She suspected
his reasons for showing up where she was working were
more personal. Or at least they had been. Today he had no
personal reason to be here. Not after the way they'd parted.

Standing in her kitchen doorway at dawn, her bare feet
chilling on the checkerboard tile floor and a terry robe
wrapped around her like a suit of armor, she'd told him she
couldn't see him again.

He had taken her rebuff stoically, but something disturb-
ing had simmered just beneath the black slate surfaces of
his eyes. Something volatile and yet vulnerable. Not quite
frightening, but not terribly comforting, either.

For a moment she'd thought he might argue. For a moment she'd wished he would. But Marco had apparently
been raised to listen when a lady says *no*. In the end, his

only rebuke had been a clipped goodbye and an unsettling look from eyes turned cold and hard as polished obsidian.

She'd spent the quiet morning hours afterward convincing herself that she'd done the right thing.

Outside the bedroom, men like him had little use for women like her. In their eyes, she was a lowly canine patrol officer, young, blond and petite, and therefore naive, witless and weak.

He was a renegade narcotics detective. Seasoned. Some might say jaded. Not to mention tall, dark and devastatingly handsome, his near-perfect Mediterranean features flawed only by a nose slightly bent in the middle, and an attitude to match. His station-house poodle jokes about the canine squad were legend in the department.

Despite the way it had felt between them last night, he would never see her for the cop—or the woman—she was, and she wouldn't let herself be used by a man who saw her as anything less. Not ever again.

She slammed the steel door of the warehouse, but the noise made her jerk as if she'd been jarred from a dream— or a nightmare. Bravo thumped his tail against her thigh and whined. Rubbing his favorite spot behind his ears, reassuring them both, she set out across the parking lot.

A dozen or so officers and agents milled around in windbreakers emblazoned with Police, DEA or Customs in big, block letters. A few of the men waved. Not in the mood for conversation, she fluttered her hand as she passed by. With any luck, she could make a getaway before one of them hailed her.

"Well, Officer Burkett," Assistant District Attorney Jarvis Bickham chirped from behind her. Paige would have known it was Bickham even if she hadn't recognized his voice. The parrot beak he called a nose cast a long shadow in front of them as he fell in step beside her. "How are you this fine morning?"

Grinding her teeth in an effort to crush her annoyance,

she cut him a hard look. "Frustrated. Just like all those other cops over there." She waved toward the cluster of men. "Where's the Magic your source keeps promising us?"

More and more of the drug had been turning up on the streets of Port Kingston and nearby cities every day. So far, the task force had had no luck in tracing it despite the A.D.A.'s snitch, who was supposed to be feeding them information. As if created by the sorcery it was named for, the Magic seemed to appear from nowhere.

Supercoke, the users called it. It was a form of cocaine, ultrarefined and baked into hard bricks fifty or sixty times more potent than standard coke. Its potency meant smugglers could import smaller quantities—thus eluding detection more easily—and earn the same or greater payout.

It also meant death for the uninformed kids who didn't properly dilute the stuff before they smoked it.

Bickham tugged at his tie uncomfortably. "There were drugs, right where my source said they would be."

She gave a derisive snort. "A few kilos of low-quality marijuana, just like last time. It's probably worth less than the cheap pottery it was stuffed in."

Cheap imported flowerpots of thick ceramic, glazed in colorful geometric patterns, to be exact. Five of them. But the shipping label said six. One was missing, along with the marijuana that had probably been in it. A payoff to one of the customs agents, maybe. Or stolen by a warehouse worker.

She made a mental note to check the employee roster later, and to double-check the packing slips from the other low-yield busts the task force had made this month. It was possible this wasn't the first time they hadn't gotten all of the dope.

"Look," the A.D.A. said a bit too brightly, as if glad to find an excuse to change the subject. "There's Detective Angelosi."

Paige's heart lurched. She stopped. At her side, Bravo automatically sat. Lowering her sunglasses, she squinted at the figure hovering around her car. It was Marco, all right.

"Maybe he's feeling a bit more optimistic today than you," Bickham said.

Paige shrugged noncommittally. "I doubt it." Not after the way he'd looked when he'd left her place this morning.

Her stomach fluttered. She jammed the glasses back on her face. Maybe she'd go chat with those Drug Enforcement Administration guys, after all.

"Why don't we just go see?" Before she could slip away, Bickham hooked his arm around hers in a grip so tight it pinched, and dragged her forward. "Angelosi?" he called.

Marco looked over his shoulder. Paige caught a glimpse of deep blue circles under reddened eyes. Sagging cheeks. An unshaved jaw. He looked just like she felt—like hell.

He scanned the lot to see who'd called. She tensed, waiting for the jolt she always felt when that dark gaze landed on her. But the jolt never came.

His gaze cut across her as if she didn't exist, then he walked away, his shoulders hunched and his forearms guarding his middle as if his stomach hurt.

Anger pooled in her gut. The brush-off shouldn't have surprised her, she supposed, given the way she'd treated him this morning.

But this was work, not her bedroom. She was a cop, dammit. He would show her the respect she deserved. On the job, at least.

She exploded after him. Halfway across the parking area, she caught him with Bravo at her side, Bickham on her heels and in full view of the dozen officers and agents standing around. A couple of the others gathered closer, probably sensing something was wrong in the way she reached for Marco's sleeve and spun him to her.

"Paige, no—" he started, then stopped. For a moment,

his eyes held the same vulnerability she'd seen this morning in her kitchen, and then regret, bone deep.

Bravo whined. The dog's tail thumped on Paige's leg as he stepped forward, sat in front of Marco and barked, then scratched at Marco's foot.

Paige's face wrinkled as if she'd aged decades in the span of a second. The task force officers formed ranks behind her, recognizing Bravo's "hit" signal, the sign that he'd found drugs.

"Marco?" she whispered. The tightness in her chest prevented her from speaking louder.

Marco's eyes went blank. Carefully, painfully blank. Sighing, he let his hands fall to his sides. His jacket opened, and the packages he'd been hiding beneath tumbled out.

"Marco..." Her voice trailed off as she stared at the five kilos of marijuana piled at his feet.

At least she needn't second-guess her decision this morning to end their affair. Nor her presumption that he would only have used her.

Because he already had used her. He'd been using her all along, apparently, her and Bravo both, to find his drugs.

So he could steal them.

Chapter 1

Six months later

*M*idnight. Fitting, Paige thought, checking the luminous hands on her watch as she ran.

Midnight, moonlight, the bay of hounds muffled by a chilling mist—what better backdrop for a manhunt? Especially when the man being hunted was Marco Angelosi. Marco was a man of shadow and light, comfortable in the dark and as hard to get a handle on as a fistful of fog.

At one time he'd been a good cop. Dedicated. Driven. Although his methods were sometimes unorthodox, he'd had the best arrest record on the force, and his cases stuck.

But that Marco had been an illusion. What was fog, anyway, but a trick of the light?

Thin air.

As thin as the sharp, frosty air she couldn't seem to pull enough of into her heaving lungs as Bravo, nose deep to the ground, pulled her along the rocky terrain of Lake Rowan State Park, fifteen miles north of Port Kingston.

"Break, Bravo." She pulled the dog to a stop and listened, but the howling of the other canines had long ago faded into the night behind her.

Her sergeant would have her cleaning kennels until Christmas when he found out she'd broken off from the grid search and circled the lake on her own. Eventually he'd forgive her, though. He had to; he was her brother.

Besides, Sergeant Matt Burkett and the others were barking up the wrong road. She knew Marco Angelosi. Knew him intimately. She knew the confidence he had in his body.

He wasn't on the highway.

She looked back at the black lacquer surface of Lake Rowan. That's where Marco had gone. He'd swum the lake.

Never mind that it was February and the water temperature couldn't be sixty degrees, or that the narrowest crossing from shore to shore spanned better than a mile.

Marco wouldn't take the easy way.

Bending over against a stitch in her side, she raised her head to get her bearings. The shifting fog glowed around her, reflecting the light of the three-quarter moon and limiting her visibility to twenty or thirty feet in front of her. Curse this weather. It was making the job ten times harder than it should have been, and the job was hard enough already, emotionally and physically.

She shivered. Bravo let out a high whine.

Her hand automatically fell to the pleasure spot behind the dog's ear and rubbed. "It's all right, B. We'll find him."

No matter what, she added silently.

Marco couldn't just walk away from a prison van wreck and pick up life where he'd left off. She *would* find him.

And then she would send him back.

Her fingers clenched around Bravo's leash. Apprehending Marco wasn't just her sworn duty as a peace officer; it was a matter of dignity.

After his arrest, Paige had quietly resigned from the task force. She didn't deserve the post. She'd made a mistake, allowed her objectivity to be compromised and because of it the entire investigation could have been compromised. The combined agencies working the case still hadn't found the source of the Magic, but at least no more evidence had disappeared from the drug shipments they *had* found.

Bravo's nose twitched, turned into the breeze, snuffling. He had a scent. Marco?

Her skin tingled at the mere passing of his name through her mind. Like some genetically programmed reaction, the feeling was intense, instinctive and unstoppable. For a moment he was there, touching her again, his broad fingertips skimming expertly over her breasts, her belly, the insides of her thighs.

A moan rumbled up her throat, but she snatched it back, tamping down the surging warmth inside her by concentrating on the cold of the night. The chill seeped under her jacket and she felt the charge in the air. Her nostrils flared.

He was here; she felt him.

They'd been together only that one night, but oh, what a night. Chemically, electrically, she was still connected to him. She feared she always would be.

Bravo strained at his collar, eager to get back to work. Her breath less labored now, Paige stamped her boots in the fallen leaves, forcing circulation to her toes, and motioned Bravo forward with a flick of her hand.

The dog tugged her along as he picked up speed. He whined again and his tail thumped Paige's thigh as she scrambled for footing on the slippery ground. He snuffled the base of a rocky hill, not terribly tall—twenty, maybe twenty-five feet high—but steep. On another night, another search, she might have taken Bravo around. But not tonight. Not when it was Marco she was after.

Her own heartbeat reflecting Bravo's near-giddy excitement, she let go of the leash, urged Bravo on and scrambled up the hillside. Her fingers scratched at soil and rocks, clinging even where there were no handholds.

Finally she dragged herself over the top edge and, puffing hard, propped herself against a narrow trunk in a stand of pine.

Her first thought was for Bravo, loping up the trail ahead. The dog wouldn't wait for her. He'd follow the scent, as he'd been trained, unless she called him back. It was up to her to follow him, which, in this fog, wouldn't be easy.

Her second thought wasn't a thought at all, but a pain, like a hand wringing dry her heart. On the hillside above her, a rock outcropping burst through the mist. On that rock stood the figure of a man.

Fog wafted across his outline like ribbons of silk, making him appear magical, ethereal. Prisoner's coveralls plastered his figure like a bright orange second skin, detailing every curve, every bulge of a muscular physique she knew too well.

Her skin zinged. The temperature seemed to warm ten degrees in as many seconds, or at least the cold no longer mattered.

She'd found him.

Or had he found her?

He was looking right at her. He couldn't possibly see her through the fog, in her little stand of trees, yet she felt certain he knew she was there. Could he feel her presence the way she felt his? The possibility set her blood pounding even harder.

His head snapped to his left. Brush crackled and twigs popped.

Bravo? Had he caught up to Marco already?

She moved from behind the tree trunk to call instructions

to the dog. As she did, Marco leaped into a clump of scrub around the base of a cottonwood tree.

A few bushes wouldn't protect him from Bravo. She ordered her feet to run. Heading out along the edge of the precipice, she opened her mouth to yell.

The words never had a chance to form in her throat. She saw the muzzle of a gun flash from the spot where Marco had disappeared. Instinctively she skidded to a halt, bracing for the impact of the bullet even before she heard the shot.

Her feet slipped on the rocks. She flailed her arms, struggling madly to regain her balance. A puff of air breezed by her temple. She wasn't sure if the bullet hit her or not, because she was already falling.

She grasped at branches, at roots, but couldn't hold on. Down she fell, tumbling, twisting, bouncing along the slope until there was nothing but the pounding of her body on rock, the snaring of her clothes and skin on brush.

Her last thought before darkness overcame her was of Marco, not as he'd looked on the rocks in prisoner's garb, but as he'd looked in her bed. Naked. Virile.

And hungry.

Lying in the brush behind the man he'd just choked into unconsciousness, Marco forced himself to ease his forearm off the shooter's throat just short of killing him.

The bastard had shot her. Shot Paige.

Pushing the man's prone body away, Marco jumped up to run, but spared one last scathing glance for the limp form at his feet. He needed to get to Paige, but if he was going to make any sense of what was happening to him, to them, Marco needed to know who this man was.

That evening, while working on a prison crew cleaning up litter from the side of the highway, another prisoner, Tomas Oberas, had picked a fight with Marco, getting them both sent back to the lockup early. At the time, Marco had wondered what was going on. He'd never had a problem with Oberas before. On the way back to the prison, he got his answer.

The fight was a setup. Someone had wanted Marco on that van, with only one guard and no other prisoners except for Oberas. They'd wanted him there because they'd wanted *him*. And they'd nearly gotten him.

He'd barely escaped alive when they'd forced the van off the road. Then this man, and others like him, came after Marco. If it hadn't been for the dense woods and nightfall, he would never have evaded them.

He hadn't escaped them, yet, he thought, reminding himself not to get cocky. They were a determined group. He wasn't sure what they wanted from him, but whatever it was, they wanted it badly.

Counting each precious second wasted, Marco dug his toe under the man's shoulder and flipped him over. Whoever the guy was, he wasn't the one behind all this, of that much Marco was sure. Arranging a prison break took money. More money than a man wearing a stained sheepskin jacket, faded camouflage and boots with cracked soles would have.

He was just a hired gun. But whose?

Most likely the same person who had hired the other prisoner, Tomas Oberas, to pick a fight with him. Marco's being on that van tonight hadn't been a coincidence any more than the wreck had been an accident.

Fingers fumbling in his effort to hurry, Marco bent over and checked the man's pulse. Steady and strong, but he'd have a headache when he woke, not to mention a sore throat. Next he pulled the man's wallet out of a pocket. Kind of the shooter to bring credit cards along—those might come in handy. Another valuable moment flew by while Marco glanced at the driver's license, memorizing the name—Lewie Kinsale—then holding the cards in his teeth while he ejected the rounds from the man's rifle and flung the bullets as far as he could.

As long as he was helping himself, he shimmied the man out of his coat. Marco figured he needed it worse than this guy did. Skinny-dipping in the lake had nearly turned him blue. He'd known the water would be cold, but he hadn't figured on the swim taking twice as long as it should have. On a good day he could swim the mile in less than twenty minutes. But today was definitely not a good day.

Knowing he would need dry clothes to prevent hypothermia when he reached the other side, he'd held his jumpsuit out of the water with his one good arm. With the other arm, the one he'd wrenched in the wreck, he'd pulled himself along as best he could, glass shards grinding inside his shoulder with every movement. For the last ten minutes of his swim, he hadn't been sure he'd ever see the far shore. The cold, black bottom of the lake had seemed almost inviting.

Marco shivered at the memory. He hadn't given up then and he wasn't about to give up now.

He gave the sheepskin sleeve a final yank and clutched the coat to his chest. Pulling the man's belt out of its loops next, he fashioned a pair of makeshift handcuffs to slow the man down in case he woke sooner than Marco predicted. Finally, urgency battering his chest like a jackhammer, he turned to run.

He hadn't taken the first step before he had to pull up short again. He froze, face-to-face with the most intense whiskey eyes he'd ever seen. Familiar eyes. And familiar lips, peeled back to reveal two rows of teeth. Very long, very sharp teeth.

"Bravo," he finally managed to say, pushing the childhood horrors out of his mind. "Hey, boy."

Bravo growled, low and deep.

"Long time no see." The dog's diesel rumble kicked up a gear. Marco swallowed. Hard. "You know who I am, don't you? You remember me. You've been looking for me."

Bravo took a menacing step forward. It took all the will-power Marco possessed not to step back. God, he hated dogs. Especially big ones like this—giant furry bundles of claws and fangs and eyes that locked on like laser-guided missiles.

Bravo swung his head around to check the trail behind him, a whine intermixed with his growls. Marco recognized the dog's confusion. Hopefully he could use that uncertainty to his advantage. Slowly he wrapped the sheepskin coat around his left forearm, just in case Bravo wasn't as confused as Marco thought.

"What'sa matter, boy? Don't know what to do without Paige here to tell you?"

Marco took a brave step forward. The dog's attention snapped back, but he didn't attack. Marco's confidence soared. He could do this. Bravo knew him. Marco had watched Paige handle the dog enough times. Had worked crime scenes with them. He even knew a few basic commands.

Paige had insisted on introducing him to Bravo up close and personal when he'd come into her house, despite Marco's reluctance to be in the same room with the dog. Bravo was trained to protect her, she'd said. He needed to know Marco wouldn't hurt her.

Marco had agreed quickly enough then. God knows he hadn't wanted Bravo to mistake the, uh, gymnastics with Paige as a struggle. Not with the most vulnerable part of his anatomy attracting trouble like a lightning rod.

He'd sweated all the way through his brief Police Dog 101 course, but he had survived. Now that training was paying off in a way he'd never imagined. Bravo knew him as one of the good guys. The dog wouldn't bite him.

He hoped.

"Paige isn't coming, boy," he said reassuringly. "You're going to have to figure this one out on your own."

Marco eased forward another step. Bravo barked a warning, shifting his weight from paw to paw.

Marco stopped. His heart spiked every time the dog blinked, much less barked. Dammit, he had to get past that dog. What was the matter with him? It was just an animal, a dumb mutt.

A dumb mutt with three-inch incisors and more schooling than most people with college diplomas.

He took a deep breath. He didn't have time for this.

Paige had told Marco that looking a dog in the eye was tantamount to a challenge. Sort of like staring a man down, direct eye contact established dominance…to the survivor.

Swallowing his fear, he looked down at Bravo. Unblinking, he held the dog's gaze.

"Sorry, boy, but I've gotta go see about Paige." He stepped forward, ignoring the foam dripping from the corner of Bravo's mouth, or at least trying to. "You're really just a big, prissy poodle, aren't you?" Picturing Paige's protector with a big frou-frou haircut bolstered Marco's confidence again. "You're not going to bite me."

He moved past the dog, turning sideways but never releasing the dog's stare as he passed. Bravo barked harshly, a decidedly unpoodlelike warning.

Determined not to show fear, Marco took another step. A twig snapped under his heel. Instinctively he jerked his head toward the sound.

Bravo lunged, taking Marco's break of concentration as victory. And to the victor go the spoils, as they say. Marco just hoped the spoils didn't include his jugular.

Bracing against the attack, he flung the arm he'd wrapped in sheepskin out in front of him. Long teeth sunk deep into the coat. At first there was only intense pressure, like a vise closing on his arm. Then the coat slipped, and Bravo's teeth sunk through the sheep's hide and into Marco's. Into flesh and sinew.

He stumbled backward, fighting his panic as much as the

pain. All he could think was *Don't go down. Don't let him get you down.*

His back hit a tree. He used the solid trunk to regain his balance. Bravo tugged with all his weight, sitting back on his haunches and pulling. Fire streamed through Marco's arm, then ice. Then nothing. Numbness.

Okay. No more poodle jokes, ever. I promise.

With his free hand, he groped for the leash dangling from the dog's collar and jerked. The German commands Paige had taught him came back in a rush and he reeled through them, searching for the right one. *"Aus!"* he commanded. *Out.*

The dog twitched, clearly confused by this man who was both master and prey. Marco repeated the command twice more, yanking on the leash until the dog reluctantly released his padded arm.

Ignoring the slide of blood down his palm, Marco pulled the dog close, all his attention on the ninety pounds of quivering canine at his side.

"Foos," he ordered. *Heel.*

Unmoving, the dog glared at him like a rattler ready to strike. Matching glare for glare, Marco put all the breath he had into his voice. "Give it up, big guy. I'm in charge."

The dog's ears sloped back. A good sign, he thought.

"Now, *foos!*"

Bravo spun around Marco's legs to sit at his heel. Marco smiled. Almost.

Flexing his fingers painfully, he unwound the punctured coat from his forearm and pulled it on.

"All right, let's go."

He jogged away, slowly letting out his breath when Bravo trotted along beside him instead of chewing his leg off.

Marco thought he'd have another showdown when they reached Paige's crumpled form. Bravo circled his fallen mistress, whining and batting at her with his paw as if to wake her. Marco was beyond caring about the dog. The hounds of hell couldn't have scared him more than the sight of her body folded on the cold ground.

Hardly breathing as he knelt at her side, he brushed the dirt and leaves from her face and uttered quiet thanks when her breasts rose visibly with her next breath. Her pulse bounced steadily off the fingertips he pressed to her carotid.

Bravo let out a low, moaning howl. All hint of aggression disappeared from the dog as he lay down at Paige's side as if he knew she was in trouble.

"It's all right, boy," Marco reassured the dog. "She's going to be all right."

Bravo lapped his tongue over Marco's ear.

"Thanks," Marco said, wiping his face as he restarted his heart. "I think."

Laying Paige's head gently on the ground, he worked his hands over the length of her body, probing carefully. There was no sign of a bullet wound, thank God. The shooter had missed. Either Marco had tackled him in time to ruin his aim, or Lewie Kinsale wasn't a very good shot. Marco didn't care which; he'd take *alive* any way he could get it.

The sight of the abrasions on her face and the reddened areas that would soon be bruises sobered Marco quickly. A bullet wasn't the only way to die out here. The cliff over his shoulder climbed some twenty feet up, its sharp slope made even more treacherous by jagged rocks, protruding roots and brush. It must have been a rough ride down.

The thought of spinal injury worried him most. But as he checked her out, she shifted her arms and legs restlessly. That was a good sign, he hoped. And the Kevlar vest she wore under her uniform would have offered some protection to her vital organs.

Lightly massaging the scalp beneath her full, blond hair, he found a gash on the crown of her head. The cut oozed blood steadily, but didn't appear deep. All in all, he figured she'd been lucky, until he got to her left ankle.

She groaned when he wiggled her foot. He muttered a curse. The joint was already swelling. He couldn't tell if the ankle was broken or just sprained, but either way she wasn't going anywhere under her own power for a while.

Tamping down a feeling of impending disaster, Marco gently settled her foot back on the ground, raised his head and looked around. He needed to put some distance between himself and those hunting him. The night was deep and dark now, but it wouldn't be for long. When the sun rose, he'd be an easy target.

As would Paige, if there were more like Lewie Kinsale prowling around these woods.

He looked down at her pale face. As it did every time he looked at her, every time he thought about her, his heart gave an involuntary twist.

Guilt. He'd made his mistakes.

Shame. He'd endured the humiliation his actions had brought about. More.

Frustration. He'd had heaven at his fingertips and let her slip away.

Six months in prison hadn't taken any edge off those emotions.

Desire. If anything, being away from her had only made him want her more. So much so that he wondered if, at this point, the woman could live up to the fantasies.

And somewhere deep inside, below all the other feelings, stirred the strongest sentiment of all.

Anger. The cold sting of rejection.

She didn't want to see him again. It was a mistake, she'd said the morning after they'd made love.

If that was true, it had been a damn costly one. Because of that one night with her, he'd lost his job, his freedom, and now very nearly his life. All for a woman who wanted nothing more from him than a single night's pleasure.

At least that's what she'd said.

He couldn't help feeling there was something else holding her back. Something she was afraid of. He just couldn't figure out what it was.

Her lashes fluttered. She was coming around.

As she struggled for coherence, he relieved her of her sidearm, shoving the pistol into one of the big pockets of the sheepskin coat, and tossed her crushed police radio into the woods.

"Welcome back," he said when her eyes found focus on his.

Her back stiffened. Her face twisted, whether from pain or outrage, he couldn't be sure. She raised a hand as if to strike him, but he easily blocked the blow and held on to her wrist to prevent her from trying it again.

She rolled away from him, scrambling to her hands and knees, but he rolled with her, pinning her beneath him. They came to rest in a tangled heap of arms and legs, her back to the ground, her chest heaving up to meet his with each laborious breath. With some difficulty, he managed to trap her arms above her head before she scratched his eyes out.

Her eyes spit venom.

"You're under arrest," she hissed.

Chapter 2

A burst of laughter warmed Paige's cheek, but Marco's eyes held no humor. Nor did his appearance.

His hair was shorter than when she'd seen him last, the cut almost utilitarian. She supposed simplicity took precedence over style in prison.

His haircut wasn't the only thing about him worse for wear, she thought, her head still muzzy as her gaze trailed down over his face. He still had the eyes of a dark angel, but now one of them sported a blue bruise underneath. An abrasion marred his square jaw and blood coagulated over a split lip.

He looked like he'd been in a train wreck.

Her head cleared with the suddenness of a rifle shot.

Wreck. The prison van. Escape.

Oh God, he'd shot her.

She squeezed her eyes shut, blocked out the sight of him, the pain in her head and ankle, the singing of her traitorous nerves at the feel of him draped over her, his heart pounding and his body pulsing.

"I mean it," she said. "I'm taking you in."

He laughed again, then flexed his arms slightly, pressing his heat even closer. His body felt all warm and supple, and she was cold. So cold.

"You have no idea how good that sounds right now," he said.

Her cheeks sparked like roadside flares. At least the fire chased away the cold. By God, whatever he did tonight, he was not going to make fun of her. She was a cop, and he was going to respect her for it, this time.

She reached for her holster, but her hand came away empty.

He smiled down at her, saying nothing.

"Bastard."

His stony silence continued. He didn't deny. Didn't defend himself. Just like in court.

He'd been sentenced to four years for theft and evidence tampering. He could have gotten less if he'd offered some explanation for his actions, or shown some remorse. Instead he'd let the charges pass with a single comment.

Guilty.

She still wore the word, as if he'd stamped it on her soul.

Though she'd found the drugs on him herself, she and Bravo, she'd watched every minute of his trial, hoping for some explanation before the judge. Until it was over, and his sentence pronounced, she hadn't really believed he'd done it. Hadn't wanted to believe it.

Hadn't wanted to believe she'd been used again.

A small sound of distress escaped her throat. She was at a loss for what to do next, how to get away, until Bravo whined beside her.

Slowly she raised her gaze to Marco's.

"Don't even think about it," he said.

Confidence in her partner added substance to her words. "Bravo will rip your throat out if I tell him to."

"I don't think so." Marco let go of one of her wrists

and lowered his arm until she could see his bloodied sleeve. "The poodle and I have already reached an understanding about who is alpha male around here."

"He bit you?" That wasn't possible. No man got away from an attack by a well-trained police dog, and Bravo was the best. "What happened? How did you get him off?"

Levering herself upright, Paige grabbed at his arm, examining the bite.

Marco hissed and jerked away. His fingers looked like five fat sausages. "I guess he found me as distasteful as I find him."

Bravo promptly disproved that theory by scooting up to Marco, tail wagging, and laying a big, fat smooch on the offended arm. Marco reared backward as if he'd been burned.

Paige was still trying to puzzle out both man's and dog's odd behavior when Marco, apparently recovered, clambered to his feet.

"We've got to get out of here," he groused. "We're losing time."

A shudder scuttled up her spine. "We?"

He scooped her into his arms, answering that question. "You didn't think I'd just leave you here, did you?"

She pushed against his left shoulder and he flinched. A weak spot, she noted. Maybe one she could use against him, later. She was going to have to wait for the right time, and opportunity, to have any chance of escape.

"I think you'd better," she said, forcing herself to be patient. "Or you're going to be facing kidnapping charges."

"Not if they don't catch me."

"There are fifty cops out there looking for you. How do you think you're going to get away?"

He flicked his dark gaze down at her. "You're going to help me."

Her breath stopped cold. "Like hell."

"You'll do it." He headed into the woods at a quick walk. "We're going back to your car, and you're going to drive me out of here."

"I'll scream my head off at the first cop I see."

He stopped. His breath crystallized in front of his face like miniature storm clouds. "No you won't."

Shifting her weight onto one arm, his good arm, with the other he raised the pistol he'd taken from her to her cheek. The gun's gleaming steel barrel chilled her flesh. She tried to turn away, but that put her face against his chest.

She preferred the gun.

"You won't scream," he continued in a voice more suited to seduction than intimidation, "because you don't want another cop to go down with a bullet from your gun. The gun I took away from you."

She almost laughed hysterically when she realized she'd been about to say that Marco wouldn't shoot a cop.

He'd shot her, hadn't he?

Damn him. Losing a gun, someone else getting hurt with it, killed with it, was every cop's nightmare, and he knew it.

She gulped in a mouthful of air as sharp as knife blades, glaring at nothing over his shoulder. "I don't need another cop to take you down. I'll do it myself, when the time is right."

He put the gun away, hefted her securely against him and set out at a jog. "I'm sure you'll try."

Marco had been running for nearly an hour and still couldn't find a shred of rhythm. Each step landed harder and jerkier than the last. His lungs burned under the ribs Tomas Oberas had pounded. The forearm Bravo had bit throbbed. Paige's weight in his arms, slight as it was, drove needles in and out of his bad shoulder.

Since he'd been a teenager, he'd used running as a way to leave the physical pain behind, the way his friends in

Oklahoma had taught him. By concentrating on the exertion and the hypnotic beat of his step, he could go outside his body, outside his troubles, and more recently, outside the prison walls.

Yet tonight, when he tried to picture the red rock canyons of Oklahoma he once ran with his friend, Toby Redstone, and the other Caddo Indian boys, all Marco could see was Paige's head lolling against his chest. When he tried to visualize a thunderstorm gathering over the tall grass of the plains, he saw only her hair fanned across his shoulder. Hair that reminded him of warm honey.

She'd cut it since he'd seen her last. A multitude of in-triguing layers now fell around her cherubic face, curling in at the ends to cup her high cheeks and support her fine-boned jaw.

He definitely approved.

And the smell…

He breathed deep. Her hair smelled just the way he re-membered. Like he'd dreamed about. Pure, clean baby shampoo.

Every night these last six months, he'd buried his nose in the single, thin pillow allotted for his bunk, inhaled a breath that shouldn't have held the scent of anything except industrial detergent and the odor of too many men in too close quarters, and smelled baby shampoo instead.

Sometimes it infuriated him that he couldn't get her out of his head. Sometimes he was glad to have the memory to hold on to. Either way, sleep was lost in the wanting and the regret.

He'd learned to live on the edge of exhaustion, which was a good thing, because he was beyond exhaustion now.

One foot in front of the other, he told himself. Inhale four beats. Exhale four beats. Focus on the rhythm.

But no amount of concentration blocked out the con-stricting pain in his gut when he felt her shiver in his arms.

She was cold. He held her closer and forced himself to

evaluate more than the proud rise of her cheekbones and her perfectly pitched eyebrows. Her eyes were closed, but he knew she was conscious.

She just didn't want to see him.

He supposed he couldn't blame her.

She was pale, but not deathly so. Instead of their usual red-wine color, her lips were light pink, and parted slightly as if she wanted to be kissed.

The urge to do just that took him with the force of a freight train. He could put some warmth back in those lips. Color back in her cheeks.

His heartbeat tripled and blood surged to the center of his body. The sharp pangs of regret troubling his gut softened to sweet hunger. Then he stumbled, caught himself and cursed, his breath sawing harshly through the quiet night air.

He should be watching where he was going, not eating up the sight of her like a starving man at a king's banquet. She hadn't wanted him even before she'd caught him stealing drugs from her bust. She surely didn't want him now.

What they'd had was not to be repeated, regardless of any false hopes rising in his traitorous body. In fact, if she got her hands on her gun anywhere in his presence, he might never have to worry about that particular discomfort again.

She was a good shot, and she had reason to hold a grudge.

Up ahead, an engine came to life. Paige's eyes snapped open. Her body tensed in his arms, but she said nothing as he pushed on.

Beyond the tree line, radios crackled. Hurried footsteps scuffed across gravel. This was it, the search command center.

In the fog, the parking lot looked like a sea of cop cars. Dozens of vehicles, many more than he had counted on, were strewn in front of him in no particular order. County

Sheriff, Department of Corrections, City Police, Texas Highway Patrol—they were all in attendance.

All looking for him.

He couldn't see Paige's truck, but it must be nearby.

Throwing her a warning glance, he zipped out to the closest car and ducked behind the rear bumper. Bravo followed like a ghost, the slight click of his toenails on rock the only proof he was more flesh and blood than spirit being.

Zigging and zagging from vehicle to vehicle, the three of them crossed the lot. Marco chanced a look over the hood of their latest hiding place, reorienting himself and searching for Paige's canine-equipped Ford Expedition.

"Where did you park the thing, New Mexico?" he grumbled.

He spotted her truck before she could answer. Not that she would have answered, anyway. Apparently she found satisfaction enough in glaring at him.

A few yards closer, and he could see the wire barrier behind the front seat that sectioned off the dog's compartment.

Good.

He glanced cautiously at the mutt. Bravo hadn't offered him any trouble since their showdown in the forest, but Marco would feel better when he got that animal and its fangs back in a cage. The arm he'd bitten hurt like a—

A car door slammed to Marco's right. He hit his knees behind the front wheel well of a highway patrol souped-up Ford. The trooper was close.

Too close! Jesus, he could see the man's shiny black shoes on the other side of the car. The feet were broad and the steps sluggish, like a man overweight and out of shape.

Marco flattened himself against the car door, holding Paige to him tightly. He did the best approximation of the "down" hand signal he could manage. Thankfully, Bravo dropped to the gravel despite Marco's limited command of doggie sign language.

The trooper's steps led around the front of the car. Marco's heart shot into overdrive. His brain screamed for oxygen, but he didn't dare breathe. He fingered the gun in his pocket.

Hell, if it went down like this, it was going to get ugly. Paige's fingers curled in the collar of his jumpsuit. Her eyes implored him.

Looking away from her, he brought the gun to his side, his fingers stiff with dread.

The trooper stopped just short of coming around the corner of the Ford where he could see them. Another man, lighter on his feet, joined him.

They were so close Marco could smell the smoke of the cigarette one of them lit. The smoldering match landed just inches from Marco's hand.

For the first time in a lot of months, Marco prayed, silently but fervently.

"Getting here kinda late, aren't you?" The question came from the trooper's position.

"Had to find a sitter for my little girl," the other man grumbled. *Riley Townsend.* The voice was unmistakable, disgruntled as it was. Riley rounded out the Port Kingston canine squad at three, with Paige and her brother, Matt. If he got his dog out of his car, it was all over.

"It's supposed to be my night off," Riley finished, sounding no happier than he had before.

Marco didn't blame the man. He'd seen Riley's daughter, Alyssa, at a department picnic once. If he'd been called away from a kid like that to traipse around the woods all night, Marco wouldn't have been too happy about it, either.

Paige recognized the voice, too. Marco felt tension spiral through her. It must have been hell for her, knowing help was so close, and not being able to call for it.

He pushed away his empathy for her. Help came in a lot

of forms. A lot of packages. Sometimes people didn't recognize it.

After a moment's silence, Riley asked, in a make-peace tone, "So what's the deal here? Anybody got a trail yet?"

"On your boy Angelosi? Nah. But we'll get him."

"He's not my boy," Riley said. "And you sound like you're enjoying this."

"To tell the truth, some of us are right looking forward to ridin' him down. Don't like what he did. One bad cop makes us all look like a bunch of thievin' dopeheads, you know?"

There was a pause. Paige's gaze turned up to Marco's and he looked away, choking on the tattered remains of his pride. It was bad enough to hear condemnation like that. Worse to have to look in her eyes as she heard it, too.

"He was a good cop, once," Riley said.

"Well, he ain't no cop no more, is he?"

Riley's pause was shorter this time. "No. I guess not."

The trooper rocked heel-to-toe. "Damn straight. He's just a con on the run."

Riley snorted disgustedly. "He's a minimum security walk-away. Nothing to get your shorts in a wad about."

The trooper went still. "You didn't hear the squawk?"

"What squawk?"

The trooper's weight eased back as if he'd lifted his head or squared his shoulders. Marco heard him tap out another cigarette. "Got a light?" Shiny Shoes asked.

"Those things'll kill you," Riley answered. "What squawk?"

Sweat chilled along Marco's spine, that and apprehension making his skin crawl. He needed to get out of there. Get Paige out of there. But he also needed to hear what the police were saying about him. He had a feeling it wasn't good. Cops didn't tell stories without milking them for all they were worth. The bigger the buildup, the better the punch line.

This one was getting a pretty big buildup.

The trooper hitched up his pants. A second later, Marco heard the strike of a match. A sulfurous scent mingled with the crisp fog. The trooper puffed, then blew out a slow breath. "Your boy Angelosi walked away, all right. Walked away from a burning van with a guard and a driver still pinned inside."

Paige jolted in Marco's arms. This time he couldn't look away. In her eyes, he saw the horror, the flames she must be imagining. In his mind he smelled the smoke.

Heard the screams.

Dull blades of pain tore through him at the memory.

"They're dead?" Riley asked.

"Uh-huh," the trooper said. His voice bubbled with hatred. "Don't know about you canine types, but for us troopers, that makes Angelosi a murderer."

Paige's nails dug into Marco's chest. Her pulse galloped beneath his fingertips. Even in the near dark, he could see the sheen of revulsion in her eyes. She was going to call for help. Despite the danger to herself, she was going to give him up.

Her lips parted. The urge to press his own mouth over them hit him like a bolt from the heavens.

Her body arched as she pushed against him. The soft mounds of her breasts pressed against the hard planes of his chest. She pulled in a deep breath, ready to scream.

Aw, hell.

Just before the sound welled out of her, he crushed her to him and stopped the noise.

Paige's lungs burned with the need for air. When her head began to swim, she bit the hand Marco had clamped over her mouth. He flinched, but didn't let her go. His other hand caressed the nape of her neck, stroking maddeningly.

A promise, or a threat?

Two sets of footsteps crunched across the gravel behind

her, then receded into the darkness. A car door thunked, and an engine roared to life. Paige slumped back to the ground at the grind of tires over rock, headed the other way. Dully, she recognized the noise as the sound of hope pulling away. Dignity. For as Marco carried her to her truck and sat her behind the steering wheel, she realized she had none left.

He was going to use her again, and there was nothing she could do about it.

Yet.

Marco put Bravo in the back, then circled to the passenger door, climbed inside and handed her the keys.

"Get on the radio," he said. "Tell them you're leaving."

She reached for the microphone with an unsteady hand. "Matt won't buy it."

"Make up an excuse. Make it good." Marco shifted her Glock in his hand, an unsubtle warning. "You don't want your brother coming after us, do you?"

Her breath shuddering at that thought, she did as Marco said. "Adam four-niner," she said, giving her call sign. "I'm ten-six to the vet's office. Sorry, guys."

"Adam four-niner, S-six. Where the hell have you been?"

"Ah…" She looked at Marco. "I must have slipped out of my grid. Got a little lost."

"Why weren't you answering calls?" Matt asked, sounding suspicious.

Paige poured confidence into her voice. She couldn't live with herself if Matt was hurt because of her. "My handheld went on the fritz. I'm in my vehicle now."

There was a moment of silence, then Matt's deep voice rumbled across the radio again. "What's up with Bravo?"

"S-six, he stepped on some glass. I don't think it's serious, but I'm going to have it checked out."

Matt sighed. "Roger, four-niner. Get him back out here later if he can work. We need all the help we can get."

"Will do." Paige returned the microphone to its clip with more than a little relief pouring through her.

Until she looked at Marco.

He smiled at her sickly. "Piece of cake." Shoving the Glock back into his coat pocket, he said, "Let's go."

As soon as they cleared the search perimeter, Marco insisted on pulling over so that he could drive. They were twenty minutes down the highway before either of them spoke again.

"Where are we going?" she asked, rolling her forehead off the passenger-side window to look at him. The green lights of the dashboard gave his face an eerie cast.

"You still have the Miata?"

"Yes." Her head ached too much to see any advantage in lying.

"Then we're going to your place."

He turned his eyes away and was quiet, his expression strangely serene, given the circumstances. She wondered if he was remembering, as she was, the first time he'd ridden in her bright blue convertible, the night they made love.

She'd been aware that Marco had been watching her off and on for nearly a month when they'd ended up working a narcotics bust together. Marco had been cuffing a prisoner when the man pulled an ice pick from beneath his belt and slashed Marco's hand, then ran. Paige and Bravo gave chase, with Marco gaining ground behind them, bloody palm and all, yelling for her and her "poodle" to back off.

Determined to make the collar herself, to show the almighty narcotics detective what the poodle squad could do, she followed the suspect up a hay elevator and into a dilapidated barn. She'd pounded ten feet across the loft before realizing the floor was only half there.

Bravo had his man already, standing over him in the corner.

Breathing hard, Marco had rushed into the barn below her. "Don't—"

She didn't. But the floor collapsed, anyway. A second later she found herself sprawled across his chest, chaff from ancient bales of hay dancing in the sunbeams all around them.

"—move," he'd finished dryly.

He needn't have worried. She couldn't, paralyzed as much by the feel of the muscled male body beneath her and the dark eyes boring into her as by the fall.

That night, as she lay in bed with a mystery novel, trying to banish the memory of his heat and the sudden, searing connection between them, she'd heard a tap on her window. Angelosi had stood outside throwing pebbles like a teenager, for goodness sake.

She'd met him in the driveway, her aqua-colored robe locked around her like a suit of armor. He was leaning against her new Miata, an indulgence, the first nonsensible thing she'd bought in years....

"What," she asked sharply, irritation mixing oddly with excitement in her voice, *"are you doing here?"*

"This yours?" He stroked the hood, and her mouth turned to cotton.

She nodded.

"Put the top down and let's take her for a spin. See what she can do."

"It's late."

He laughed. "Yeah, and the breeze is warm and the stars are out. So what's the problem?"

She fingered the neckline of her robe. "I'm not dressed."

Leaning close, too close, he fingered her robe just the way she had, picked it back just far enough to see the lacy edge of her nightgown curved over the mound of her breast. "You look fine to me."

Her breath caught at the rough edge to his voice. She jerked back, her mind spinning. She must be crazy. Insane to even consider this. At the moment, though, insanity—in the form of a tall, dark Italian-American looking at her like

*the wolf must have looked at Little Red Riding Hood—
sounded pretty appealing.*

*"Give me five minutes," she said, and ran to the house.
She might just be crazy enough to go driving with him in
the middle of the night, but she wasn't lunatic enough to
do it in her nightgown.*

*They drove out of the city, to the rural ranching counties.
The stars glittered overhead like a mirrored ball at a dance
hall as they streaked down country lanes that smelled of
fresh-cut hay and livestock.*

*"Faster," Marco urged, and she couldn't say why, but
she found an empty stretch of road and pressed the accel-
erator down until the wind whipped tears into her eyes and
she felt like she was flying.*

*Far from being afraid, Marco threw his head back and
laughed.*

*Breathless and exhilarated, she pulled back into her
apartment complex just before midnight and invited Marco
in, where he laid her down on her wide four-poster bed
and took her for a ride every bit as breathtaking....*

Her night with him had been a learning experience. A
discovery.

Not that she hadn't been with other men. She'd dated.
Been intimate on occasion. Safe, mediocre sex with safe,
mediocre men.

Nothing about Marco Angelosi qualified as safe.

Or mediocre.

He was wild. He was wicked. He scared her to death.

And he'd ruined her for other men.

From the moment she'd first gazed up into his angel's
eyes, she hadn't wanted anyone else. She hadn't wanted
anyone else even after she'd sent him to prison. And Lord
help her, she wouldn't want anyone else even after she sent
him back.

But she *would* send him back.

Chapter 3

"**Y**ou okay?"

Marco's voice sounded faraway. Paige jerked herself out of her reverie and glanced at the rearview mirror. She was surprised, for a moment, to see him so close—just across the seat from her. She was even more surprised to realize her cheeks were as wet as they had been that magical night in the Miata.

Must be due to the head injury.

As unobtrusively as possible, she wiped her nose with her sleeve. "Fine."

He looked grim. "Your face is as pale as a baby's bottom."

"I've been shot at, fallen off a cliff and I'm being kidnapped. How am I supposed to look?"

His only answer was a frown. Or maybe it was a scowl.

She rubbed her sleeve harder across her face. She had to get her act together. She was a cop. They were almost to her house. She had to talk Marco into giving himself up.

"You won't get far in the Miata," she reasoned. "It's too easy to spot."

"Not if no one is looking for it."

It was Paige's turn to frown as Marco pulled her Port Kingston PD Expedition into a parking spot in front of the steps to her second-floor apartment. He had to know every cop in the state would be looking for her car within minutes after he left.

Unless there was no one around to tell them he'd taken it.

She shivered, sure that her blood temperature had dropped five degrees in the last five seconds. She didn't even realize Marco had moved until the car door next to her swung open. One of his hands slid behind her shoulders and the other caught her behind the knees.

Her heart seized up like a bad bearing.

She studied the hard lines in his face, the bruises, the shadows under his eyes. This wasn't the Marco she knew. This man was a stranger. A murderer, the state trooper had said, and she had no reason to disagree. He'd shot her. Kidnapped her.

For the first time since she'd known Marco, she was afraid of him—truly and deeply afraid. Each step he took with her in his arms added to her anxiety. Her fingers curled to fists on his back. Forget convincing him to turn himself in. She just wanted him to leave.

The thought twisted her pride. She was a cop. She had a job to do. But she was also a woman, alone and vulnerable, and she was hurt.

Bravo followed them up to the apartment entrance and ducked around Marco as soon as the door swung open. Marco followed him to the laundry room. A creature of habit, Bravo went straight to his kennel and stood over his bowl. She always fed him when they got off work.

Standing well back, Marco swung the gate to the dog

pen closed with his foot. The clank of the closing latch signaled the loss of Paige's last best hope for survival.

As she watched Bravo nose his empty bowl, whining, Marco carried her out of the room.

In the bedroom, she scanned frantically for potential weapons. Her thoughts raced with her heart. If he put her on the bed, there was the lamp. If he set her on the chaise in the corner, she might be able to reach the scissors in her sewing basket. If—

He walked right through the bedroom, into the bathroom, and plunked her down on the toilet lid, then promptly turned, dropped the stopper in the tub drain and twisted the faucets on full.

Her jaw hung slack. "What are you doing?"

He'd left the tiny bathroom before she finished the question, but he called back, "Get out of those clothes."

Like hell. The image of her naked body swimming in a crimson tub, her wrists slashed, shimmered in her vision. Would he try to make it look like suicide?

The absurdity of the thought wiped the vision away a second later. The bruises and abrasions on her body would make suicide a tough sell. She wasn't sure what he was up to, but whatever it was, she didn't like it.

Growing more frantic, she scanned the cluttered bathroom counter for something to use as a weapon. The facial cleansers, perfumes and assorted hair products within her reach weren't much of a match against the 9 mm Glock Marco had taken from her.

But they would have to do.

Keeping one eye and one ear turned toward the bedroom, Marco dumped ice from Paige's freezer into a plastic bag. He'd taken the phone out of the bedroom, but he didn't dare leave her alone for long. He didn't think she was ready to give up yet. Not by a long shot.

Ice pack in hand, he hurried back through her room, refusing to let the wide, pine bed he passed mean anything to him. What was past was past. He wouldn't dwell on it.

Yeah, right.

He was still trying to shake himself out of the daze brought on by the sensory assault of her bedroom when he walked into the bathroom. Too late, he realized he should have been more careful.

Through the steam, a pair of dark service blues lunged at him. Instinctively he threw his hands up. Her forearm collided with his and he grabbed on to her fine-boned wrist.

He heard a hiss, but didn't identify the sound until it hit him.

Aerosol.

Fire ripped through his eyes. Tears streamed down his cheeks, but did nothing to douse the flames. Only the edge of the counter that caught his hip kept him from going to his knees.

He swiped at his face with his free hand, the pain shooting back from his eyes into his brain. Paige tried to jerk away, but he tightened his hold on her wrist and yanked her toward him, growling, "No!"

The hair-spray can clanked to the floor. Paige fell forward. Her sharp cry pierced the curtain of pain blinding him. He pried his eyes open long enough to see her huddled on the floor beside him, grasping her leg. He must have pulled her weight onto her sprained ankle.

Grunting, with one eye cracked open just wide enough to be sure she didn't have any more tricks up her sleeve, he lifted her from the floor back to the toilet seat. "Don't move," he warned.

As soon as she settled back, he fell over the vanity and splashed cold water in his face. The wash cooled the fire in his eyes pretty quickly. The fire in his blood took a little longer. He gave himself a few more seconds. Then, when he had himself under control, mentally and physically, he straightened up, shutting off the faucets and drying his face with the rose-embroidered hand towel hanging over the counter.

"Good try," he said tightly. "But not good enough."

"This time." She angled her chin defiantly, but the tremor in her chest ruined the effect.

"There won't be a next time." He bent to scoop the ice he'd dropped back into the plastic bag.

"Why don't you just get it over with then, and get out of here?"

"Get what over with?"

"Are you having trouble building up the courage, or are you just dragging it out because you're enjoying torturing me first?"

He stared at her, trying to figure out what the hell she was talking about. Understanding gradually dawned. His throat tightened. "I'm not going to hurt you."

"You *shot* at me," she said.

"If I'd shot at you, you'd be dead."

She had to know that. He was the Port Kingston Emergency Response Team's best marksman. At least he had been, once. But that seemed like a lifetime ago.

"You couldn't afford to kill me. You needed me to get out of the park," she said.

The cords in his neck pulled so tight he thought they might snap. A headache beat at the back of his skull. "And now I don't need you so I'm going to kill you?"

A heartbeat passed. Enough time, even for Marco's watery eyes, to read the confusion etched onto her features. To feel the genuine fear radiating from her. For it to twist through him like a corkscrew in the heart.

His jaw turned to granite. "You know me better than that."

She turned her limpid gaze up to him. "I don't know you at all. Not anymore."

"That's a lie."

Mesmerized by the melted-honey swirl of confusion in

her eyes, he stepped forward. When he reached out to cup her chin, she flinched—the final blow to his tattered pride—but he wouldn't let her turn away. He brushed a wayward curl off her cheek, let the myriad feelings inside him boil close to the surface.

"You know me," he said, reveling in the way her pulse kicked up where he stroked the soft underside of her jaw. "You know every inch of me."

A tide of color flooded her cheeks. Suddenly disgusted with himself, he dropped his hand.

The water in the tub had nearly run over. Fixing his gaze anywhere but on hers, he pushed past her and twisted the faucets off. Mentally he shut down the flow of his emotions, as well. He couldn't afford to feel anything toward her. Not anger, not lust and certainly not sympathy.

"If you didn't shoot me, then…" Her voice trailed off as if she forgot what she was going to say. Her eyelids sagged as if she didn't have the strength to hold them open. "Then who…?" She swayed left, then right on the toilet seat.

Marco crossed the room in one long stride, cupped the back of her neck and pushed her head between her knees.

"Breathe slow," he said, squatting down next to her. "Deep."

Damn. He didn't think she was concussed, but he didn't like this dizziness.

After a few moments, she raised her head slowly. Some of her color had returned, but not much. "Oberas? The other prisoner? Was he the one who shot at me?"

"Get in the tub," he said in place of confirmation or denial.

"Why?"

"How should I know why someone would want to shoot you?" he said, more harshly than he'd meant to.

She looked at him strangely. "I meant why do you want me to get in the tub?"

He sighed, propping his hands on the tank behind her and looking her straight in the eye. "The warm water will keep you from stiffening up after that fall, and some of those cuts and scrapes are deep. You need to clean them out." He handed her the bag of ice. "You can prop your foot up on the side and put this on your ankle."

"Every cop in the state is after you, and you're worried about my ankle? What do you really want from me?"

"For now, all I want is for you to get in that bath."

Liar. He knew what he wanted. Just once he wanted her to look at him like he was something other than a drug-stealing scumbag. He wanted her to look at him like she had looked at him the last time he'd been in her apartment, the night they'd made love.

Dragging his hand through his hair, he lurched to his feet. He couldn't think straight when he was that close to her.

She stood, balancing on her good foot by holding on to the towel bar, and motioning for him to turn around with her other hand. He complied. He could leave her that much dignity, at least.

One by one he heard the pieces of her uniform swish to the floor.

"I won't help you again," she said.

He resisted the urge to look over his shoulder, but he couldn't stop himself from cutting his eyes to the mirror beside him. The steam put a soft haze over the image, but didn't completely obliterate the pale curve of her shoulder, the tantalizing taper of her waist or the swell of her hip.

Despite the humidity in the room, Marco's throat dried up. "I'm not asking you to help me."

She glanced back at him, angling her naked body toward the mirror. He locked his eyes onto hers in the last clear spot on the glass. *Only her eyes.* Admirable restraint, he told himself. Not to mention self-preservation.

"I'm just asking you to take a bath."

Marco closed the door behind him and leaned his head against the wood, waiting. When he heard water sloshing, he retreated to the kitchen. He needed to get away from the bathroom. Away from the thought of Paige's lithe body sliding into a warm, wet bath, and the memory of his body sliding into a warm, wet Paige.

Every time she'd opened her mouth in there he'd turned a hundred and eighty degrees, from cursing her to wanting to kiss her, and back again.

Not that what he wanted mattered. He was all too aware she didn't want him. Never would.

Hardening his heart to the loss of something he'd never really had, he mentally listed the things he would need from the apartment. In the hall closet, he found Paige's extra ammo, along with another prize—a man-size sweatshirt and jeans.

An unwelcome pang of jealousy shot through his gut until he unfolded the sweatshirt and saw the Port Kingston PD logo. From the multicolored spatters on both the shirt and jeans, he'd guess Paige's brother, Matt, had helped her do some painting.

After a quick change, Marco collected food in a cardboard box, along with towels and soap, blankets, a flashlight and matches. On his way out to stash the goods in the trunk of her car, he spotted a book on the couch. Sue Grafton's novel *O is for Outlaw.*

Prophetic, he thought. And kind of sad.

He tossed the novel in the box with the other goodies. Maybe it would entertain her over the next few days.

Realizing what he'd just decided, he stared at the book as if it had bit him. Until that point, he hadn't let himself think about where he would go from here. What he would do. He'd just concentrated on getting himself and Paige out of the woods alive.

Now his course seemed clear.

Six months ago he'd cut a deal that had landed him in prison. Tonight his *partners* had reneged on the agreement.

So much for honor among thieves.

He was sorry Paige had to be involved in this, but whether she knew it or not, she was a player in the game. A pawn to be sacrificed for the higher goal.

Him.

Marco couldn't afford to give them that advantage. There was only one way to keep them from using Paige against him.

And that was to keep her *with* him.

Pawns could be played both ways. Used for offense as well as defense. She'd already helped him escape once. She might prove useful yet again.

Paige wasn't going to be happy about being his hostage, he realized. In fact, she was likely to make the next few days pure hell.

He would have to watch himself every minute around her. She was a cop and a woman, and he'd managed to offend her on both levels. She knew how to fight dirty, and he was too easily distracted in her presence. Six months was way too long for him to be without a woman.

Without this woman.

If either one of them was going to survive this, he was going to have to stop thinking about how perfect her breasts were and how long her legs were and how good it would feel to get between them again. Instead, he needed to concentrate on avoiding those who were after him, cops and otherwise, while making sure Paige didn't put a bullet where it would do the most damage the first chance she got.

He could do that.

Sure.

Still trying to convince himself, he stopped by the kitchen for more staples and loaded the supply box into the trunk of her car. As he walked back inside, he stopped to listen. All was quiet in the bathroom.

Too quiet.

Cursing his own stupidity, he took the hallway in a dead run.

Paige heard Marco coming. She swung her legs over the faux-wrought-iron railing of her balcony, ready to shimmy down to the ground floor, but another wave of dizziness assailed her. The concrete below rippled like moving water. Her vision closed to a narrow tunnel.

A pair of strong arms snagged her waist.

"Are you trying to break your neck?"

"I'm trying to save it!" She squirmed in Marco's grasp, her fists landing ineffectual blows on his hips, his shoulders.

"Then get in here."

"Let me go!"

"If I do that, you're going to splatter your pretty little brains all over that parking lot down there."

All the writhing and motion made Paige's stomach turn. Her limbs softened to rubber. She moaned.

Marco scooped her up and lifted her over the railing. She felt the warmth and strength of his hands even through the cotton T-shirt and bike shorts she'd put on while he'd been in the kitchen. Hating the weakness that left her incapable of fighting, she sank against the strong, broad wall of his chest.

He plopped her down in the bathroom again, this time in front of the toilet instead of on it. He lifted the lid.

"I am not going to be sick," she said between clenched teeth.

"Good." He wet a washcloth and pressed it to her forehead. She pushed his hand away, holding the cool compress in place herself.

Somehow, she held her stomach. Spite, she figured. She

wouldn't give him the satisfaction of watching her vomit. After a few minutes, he took the washcloth from her and eased her into the tub.

She had to admit the warm water felt heavenly, even with all her clothes on. Sinking back, she closed her eyes. Marco fished her injured ankle out of the water and propped it on the side of the tub, then laid the ice pack over the swollen joint. The odd combination of hot and cold made her skin tingle. Her breasts pulled tight.

She opened her eyes and realized the bathwater wasn't the only thing making her tingle. Marco's dark gaze wandered lazily up her body from her toes to the tips of her ears.

He was squatting next to the tub, a tube of antiseptic cream in his hands and something much more sinister in his flinty eyes. One hand dipped into the tub and tested the water. "Too hot?"

Way too hot. The water he stirred lapped at her chest. Her breasts grew heavier. The T-shirt she wore stretched across her nipples, chaffing, confining. She followed the trail of his gaze to the dark aureoles showing through the wet fabric.

Why in heaven's name did a white T-shirt have to be on top when she'd reached into her dresser for something to wear?

She was still pondering that when he began to dab at her with the antiseptic, his expression impassive. He cleaned up her head wound first, then worked on the various cuts and scrapes, which seemed to be everywhere. He dabbed a little antiseptic on the side of her neck, like cologne.

A second later it started to burn. She hissed. Leaning forward, Marco blew on the wound. The cool stream of air pulled her skin tight. Her eyelids drifted shut.

She heard, felt, him swirling his hand in the water again. "You feel it, too, don't you?"

"No." She would *not* feel anything for this man, attraction or otherwise.

"It was different between us. Special."

Her heart knocked against her hands, which she'd folded across her chest. "It was a mistake."

"Maybe." He pulled his hand from the water, rose and stepped over to the sink, where he cleaned his own wounds, starting with the bite on his forearm. "Maybe not."

She had no idea what he meant by that. Wasn't sure she wanted to know. She was tired of his riddles.

She opened her eyes. Modesty be damned. She was getting out of here. Grimacing, she pushed herself up on one foot.

"Careful," he warned. "Not too fast."

Holding on to the wall for support, she tried to hop out of the tub. She might have made it, if the floor hadn't suddenly tilted and her stomach hadn't raised up into her throat, blocking her air. The room went as dark as if someone had turned out the lights. Then starbursts exploded behind her eyelids. The swaying floor tossed her off balance and she fell.

Right into the last pair of arms she wanted to catch her.

"What happened?" she asked when her vision cleared. The steady thump of Marco's heart—maybe a notch faster than it ought to be—comforted her cheek.

"You fainted," he replied roughly.

She straightened. Carefully. "I don't faint."

"Okay." He sat her on the rim of the bathtub. "You took a little nap standing up—or falling down, rather—in the tub."

"I mean it. I don't faint."

"I said okay." He'd wet another washcloth for her forehead. Once he'd applied it, he tilted her head back and stared deeply into her eyes. This time there was nothing sensual about the gaze. "Maybe you've got a concussion, after all."

She pulled the cloth from her forehead. "I'm fine."

"You don't look it."

"Why don't you just go away and leave me the hell alone?"

"I can't do that."

"What is that supposed to mean?"

"It means—" he pulled a towel off the bar and snugged it around her shoulders "—that I'll be going, all right, but I won't be leaving you alone."

Shock raised gooseflesh on her arms as his meaning registered. He couldn't— He wouldn't—

One look into his shuttered black eyes, and she knew with dead certainty that he could. Most certainly would.

"I'm taking you with me," he said.

Chapter 4

"This is a felony!" Paige twisted her fingers in the sweatshirt beneath Marco's open coat.

Purposely withholding his gaze from hers, he set her down on her good foot in the shadows outside her door and fumbled the key into the lock. Inside, Bravo barked like a maniac at being left behind.

Bravo, however, wasn't the reason Marco didn't look Paige in the eye. She had damned near passed out again when he'd told her he was taking her with him. Since then her eyes, the pupils large and dark, had held such stark animosity that he hadn't been able to look at them.

"It was a felony the minute I forced you to drive me away from the search area," he said, as much to convince himself as her.

"You've always been a renegade, but this is going too far. You can't just…steal me away as if no one will notice. You're making it worse for yourself, Marco."

"How much worse can it get?" With the door locked, he hefted her into his arms again. Even through the thick down of her navy-blue ski jacket, he could feel her heart race like a startled rabbit.

"People could get hurt," she insisted, kicking her blue-jean-clad legs and almost wiggling out of his grasp. One of her sneakers bounced off his hipbone.

He gritted his teeth. "No one is going to get hurt if you cooperate."

"*Cooperate?* Is that what you think I'm going to do? Just give up? Be a good little hostage and do whatever you tell me?" She flung her fists at his back as he started down the stairs.

"No," he said, flinching as she landed a blow on his sore shoulder. "I suspect you're not going to do a damned thing I tell you."

"Then why are you doing this? Why not just leave me here?"

He stopped. "Because I can't," he said simply, but his gaze, now that he'd finally looked at her, must have said more. He felt the pull between them, the memories their bodies shared even when their minds refused to acknowledge their past, and he knew she felt it, too.

Color flooded her cheeks. Far from being unsightly, the blush added to her sensuality, her vibrancy. He found the look infinitely appealing. He always had.

Slowly he peeled his gaze away.

She looked over his shoulder toward the door, where Bravo's barking had dissolved into long consonant howls. "Wh-what about Bravo?"

"What about him?"

"You can't just leave him."

"Watch me."

"But—but… He knows something's wrong. That's why he's howling. And he's hungry."

"Someone will come looking for you soon. When they find you gone, they'll take care of him." He started down the stairs again. Starving a dog would be the least of his sins before this was over.

"Marco!"

"Forget it, Paige—"

She surged halfway out of his arms, nearly knocking him off balance on the stairs. "So help me, if you take one more step, I'm going to scream."

He scowled at her. "Don't do this here, Paige. Too many innocent people could get hurt."

She raised her chin. "Then get my dog."

"No."

"If you're lucky, that excuse I gave Matt about taking Bravo to the vet will buy you a couple of hours. Maybe a little more," Paige said. "But if he keeps up that ruckus, one of my neighbors is going to complain. When they see the Expedition here, but can't get me at home, they'll call the police station, and you're going to lose half of that time."

Bravo's howls hit a particularly shrill note. Marco's skin prickled like someone had scraped fingernails over a blackboard.

"You could shut him up."

"I could, but I won't." Her eyes narrowed. "And don't you even think about hurting him."

Marco almost grinned. She had a backbone of steel. He knew that. It was one of the things he liked about her. All that strength in such a small, pretty package. She wasn't going to back down, and she was right about Bravo's barking costing him time.

Still, he'd rather walk over burning coals than take the poodle with him. At the moment, though, he didn't see where he had much choice.

He gave Paige a long-suffering look. "You're really going to make me take the dog, aren't you?"

She smiled smugly. "Are you going to just stand here

all night, or are you going to get Bravo so we can get out of here?''

He studied her curiously. "Let me get this straight. Now you *want* me to take you with me?"

Somehow, even while he was carrying her in his arms, she managed to look down her nose at him, wearing an expression of regal superiority that would have made Queen Elizabeth proud. "As long as I'm *with* you, I haven't *lost* you."

He almost laughed. Backbone of steel, indeed. More like titanium. "Still figure you're going to take me in, huh?"

"I know it."

"And you aren't the least bit worried about your safety?"

"How many murderers do you know who put antiseptic on their victims' scrapes before they kill them?"

Marco couldn't afford to let her think like that. "There's a lot of ugly territory between murdered and safe," he said.

She was still looking down her nose at him, but her haughtiness was shallow now. Wariness ran much deeper. A wariness he'd sensed in her before. Not just tonight, but going all the way back to the night they'd made love.

More specifically, the morning after. Her words had been brave, but her eyes had held that same deep-seated fear.

It hadn't done much for his ego then, realizing she was afraid of him. It didn't feel any better now.

Maybe having lost the battle over the dog wasn't such a bad thing. If having the poodle along took the edge off her panic, it would be worth the embarrassment that Marco would more than likely suffer.

He started back up the stairs to her apartment. "Let's just get the dog and get out of here."

"Make sure you keep him out of my face," Marco warned as he set her in the car.

Paige smiled brightly. With Bravo nearby, she felt like

a cop again, not a woman being kidnapped. A victim. "That's going to be tough to do with all three of us packed into a two-seater Miata."

It proved damned near impossible.

"You sit in the middle," Marco ordered. "Make him stay by the door."

"How am I supposed to do that?"

Marco hefted her over until her rear was on the console, then motioned the dog into the car before he hurried around to the driver's side. While he was climbing in, she wriggled around to situate herself more comfortably. It was a good thing she was a size four. Otherwise they never would have all fit in the tiny car. Bravo sat with his hind end on the floorboard, his front paws on Paige's thigh. His head hung practically in Marco's lap, but far from being in protection mode, the big lug stared at Marco like the man was a god.

"Damn car," Marco complained. "Couldn't you have bought something bigger than a cracker box?"

She didn't recall him complaining the last time he'd ridden in her car. "Put the top down, there'll be more room."

"Yeah, that'll be real inconspicuous. Me, you and a grizzly bear all jammed into a sardine can with the top rolled back for everyone to see."

"Why are you getting testy? I'm the one being kidnapped, remember?"

Marco nearly ran into a Suburban when Bravo leaned across the seat and licked his hand as he was pulling out of the parking spot. He slammed on the brakes, sending all three of them careening into the dashboard. "I told you to keep him out of my face."

"He wasn't in your face." Paige straightened and helped Bravo rearrange himself as best she could. "He likes you, can't you see that?"

Lord knew what her dog saw in the man, but she'd never seen the German shepherd take to anyone like he had to Marco. The dog must be sick.

Yeah, right. He had a serious case of hero worship.

"Just let him say hello," she suggested. "Then he'll leave you alone."

"No." Marco leaned toward the driver's door.

"Oh, what's the matter with you?" Paige asked. "I thought you said the two of you had worked out who was alpha male."

"We did."

"Then what is your problem?" Couldn't he see the dog wouldn't bite him now even if she ordered him to?

Rolling her eyes, she pulled Marco's hand toward Bravo's head. If Marco would just pet him once, the dog would settle down.

Marco snatched his hand back. "Dammit, Paige. I'm afraid of dogs."

She did a double-take. "Af-afraid?"

He squeezed the steering wheel until his knuckles went white, staring straight ahead. "When I was a kid, the old lady down our block had a Great Dane. Damn thing used to terrorize me. Knock me down and hold me there until one of the neighbors would finally hear me screaming and come to rescue me."

"He bit you?"

"No," Marco admitted. "He just stood on my chest so I couldn't get away and...licked me."

"He...licked you." Paige smiled, despite the seriousness of her circumstances. A giggle threatened. "Well, I can see how that would leave psychological scars."

"It's not funny."

"Of course it's not." She bit the side of her lip to keep herself from laughing.

"I was just a kid."

"I understand completely." A snicker tittered out of her.

Marco growled. "Just get the dog settled." He pulled the car onto the street. "And keep him out of my face."

"He won't hurt you. I promise." To prove the point,

Bravo leaned across the seat and slopped his tongue up Marco's cheek.

Marco almost drove into the ditch.

Paige's snickers burst into raucous laughter.

Paige gritted her teeth as the truck Marco had somehow acquired hit another pothole. The heavy-duty suspension bounced her off the seat and jostled the foot Marco had insisted she keep elevated by propping it on the dashboard. It would help with the swelling, he'd said. She pulled her leg down, anyway. Swelling be damned. The jostling was killing her. Darts of pain speared up to her knee.

Sticking with Marco until she could take him into custody or convince him to surrender himself had sounded like a good plan three hours ago, but already she felt like she was losing her grip on her nerves. She hated having no control over what was happening to her. She hated being used.

Just after sunrise, he'd cruised her Miata slowly past a truck rental agency. A few minutes later, parked behind an abandoned building a block away from the rental place, he'd left her handcuffed to the car door—with her own handcuffs, yet—and disappeared. While she was still trying to take the car door apart using a paper clip, he'd pulled up behind her in a box truck.

She wasn't quite sure how he'd managed to rent a truck, since he had only the paltry two hundred dollars in cash he'd taken from her house, and no ID that she knew of, but he had accomplished it somehow.

That wasn't the end of his tricks, either. It only got better when he opened the back of the truck, pulled out tire ramps and drove the Miata inside.

They'd been heading south ever since.

"Where are we going?" she asked.

"Mexico."

"Mexico?" She straightened up. "You'll never get across the border."

He smirked at her from across the seat. "I'm a narc. I know ways across the border."

Mexico. She sank back in her seat, a new nervousness taking hold of her gut. Did he plan on taking her with him?

She fiddled with a torn piece of piping on the edge of the cracked vinyl seat. "It's not too late," she said after a few minutes had passed. "We can still find a police station and walk in nice and peaceful. End this without anyone getting hurt."

Marco's grin fell. His fingers tightened on the steering wheel. "I'm not going back to prison, Paige. I can't." The bruises on his cheek and jaw served as ample explanation why. Her heart swelled with an uncomfortable sympathy. It couldn't be easy for a cop—ex-cop—in prison.

"Your sentence was only four years," she said, trying to rationalize. "You'd have been paroled in less than half that. Why go on the run, Marco? It doesn't make sense. Why spend a lifetime as a fugitive when you could be free, legitimately, in a few years?"

When he turned his head to her, he looked more tired than she'd ever seen him. Fatigue rounded his shoulders and pulled at the skin beneath his eyes. "Every day in that place was like a lifetime," he said quietly.

A blast of guilt sheared the breath out of her. She shored herself up with logic—and self-righteousness. She wasn't responsible for his prison term; he was the one who had stolen the drugs.

She clenched fingers in Bravo's fur. "You won't get away with this," she said. "You don't have a chance."

Marco just turned his gaze down the road and kept driving.

Less than an hour later, Paige was forced to admit his chances were improving.

He was good. Very, very good.

Within sight of the Mexican border, he stopped the truck, unloaded the car and drove it up to an outdoor automated teller machine. There he parked in clear view of the ATM's security camera and ordered her to max out her card. She refused, of course, so he tried it on his own until the machine finally swallowed the card for exceeding the allowed number of invalid PIN attempts.

"They'll trace that here, you know."

"I'm counting on it."

Looking very pleased with himself, he drove a quarter mile farther down the road and pushed her car into a ditch.

"They'll find the car when they come to check out the ATM report," she said incredulously as he carried her back toward the truck. "They're going to think we crossed the border."

"Yup."

"But we're not going to, are we?"

"Nope."

The plan was crazy. And brilliant. "You're a snake."

He grinned. "Yup."

A cold sweat made her skin prickly. Her chances of getting help from the outside were next to nil now. Rescue efforts would be concentrated along the Mexican border and in the little towns just on the other side. The political mess alone could slow down the search by days. Meanwhile, he could take her anywhere. No one would be looking for the truck. No one knew to look for it.

"You're enjoying this, aren't you?" she asked sourly.

"No." But there was no denying the spark of pleasure that lit his eyes. He blew out a deep breath, some of the fatigue seeming to lift from his shoulders as he cranked up the truck and pointed out the windshield toward the long stretch of open road and blue sky before them. "But I'm enjoying that."

* * *

Marco rolled his head around his shoulders for what must have been the thousandth time in the seventeen hours he'd been driving. Even his whiskers ached.

The springs in this old truck weren't helping, poking and prodding him in all the wrong places, but he'd been afraid to rent anything fancier. He didn't know how much expense Lewie Kinsale's credit limit would bear without setting off alarms.

What nerves Marco had left were being methodically scraped raw by the static on the radio. He switched it off. Hadn't been able to get anything but gospel since they'd hit the arid West Texas desert, anyway. Peace and quiet suited him just fine.

He glanced over at Paige. Slumped against the far door, her hand resting lightly on Bravo's head, which was in her lap, she'd been quiet since dark had fallen a few hours ago. She looked so peaceful in her sleep. Fragile and almost childlike. So opposed to the strong, sensuous woman he knew her to be.

She'd surprised him in the last—he checked the clock on the dashboard—nearly twenty-four hours now. Despite everything he'd put her through, she'd laughed this morning. He'd been waiting all day to hear it again, that rich, from-the-heart laugh of hers, but she hadn't said a word, or smiled, since they'd headed north.

He couldn't blame her. With every mile they traveled, everything she knew—family, friends, safety—fell farther and farther behind.

He looked her way again, his gaze ensnared by the contrast of the seductive curve of her full mouth and the child-like way her hands were folded beneath her cheek.

Looking at her, he felt something shift in his chest. The rest was good for her, he thought. She'd had a tough day. So had he. He could sure use a little rest himself. His eyelids were getting heavier by the hour. Minute. Second.

Man, it was quiet. Too quiet.

"Paige?"

No answer. He reached over and touched her shoulder.

Bravo rolled his eyelids open and thumped his tail on the floorboard once, but Paige was still.

He shook her a little harder. "Paige?"

"Whaa—?" She jolted, banging her elbow on the truck door as she reached for the hip where her holster would be if she'd been in uniform. "Oww!"

"Sorry," he said, when she'd stopped hissing.

Her head fell back against the seat. "What do you want?"

"I, uh, I just thought I should, uh, make sure you were okay."

She looked at him like he'd lost what was left of his mind.

"Head injuries," he explained. "You're supposed to stay awake."

"I don't have a concussion."

"You can't be sure of that."

"I'm sure."

"Fine." He squinted at the black void ahead as a pair of oncoming headlights momentarily blinded him. "I was just trying to help."

Bravo sat up, yawned, then whined, his tail beating the truck floor again. Marco stiffened reflexively at the sight of too many teeth.

"You want to help?" Paige said, drawing his attention from the dog. "Pull this truck over and let me and Bravo out."

Marco tightened his grip on the steering wheel. "Sorry. No can do."

"You better do. Bravo has to take care of business again."

"He'll have to wait."

Paige crossed her arms. "I have to take care of business again, too."

''We've only got a couple more hours. We'll stop when we get there.''

''Where?''

He bit the inside of his cheek and pulled the truck onto the shoulder. Maybe the quiet hadn't been so bad, after all.

''Here you go.'' He carried her out behind a scrub mesquite and stepped a few feet away as he had during their previous pit stops. It wasn't like she was going to run off on that ankle. ''Look out for prickly pear and make it quick.''

She didn't—make it quick, that is—but he'd expected no less. While she and the dog diddled around, he paced beside the truck, restoring circulation to his nether regions and trying to wake himself up. Thirty-six hours without sleep and still counting. Not good. A man's brain could get seriously fogged going that long without sleep. He could say things, do things he wouldn't consider when his mind was sharp. Especially when the only thing his mind seemed to be able to focus on was a woman.

Paige.

He rubbed his palms on his borrowed jeans and settled her back into the cab of the truck when she called him. None of this had anything to do with his feelings for her; he had to keep telling himself that. She was just a mistake he'd made six months ago. Nothing more. Never would be.

Back in the truck, the hum of the tires on blacktop was hypnotic. Logically, he knew that the yellow lines on the road were straight, but by the time he and Paige crossed the Oklahoma border, they seemed to be slithering like snakes across the asphalt.

Another hour, he told himself. Two at most. Then he could rest.

When he looked into two bright lights and it took him three full seconds to decide if they were headlights or if the sun was rising—and had multiplied—he knew he wasn't going to make it that long. Not like this. The blast of the semi whose lane he had been in, and the driver's rude gesture as he passed, helped convince him.

"Paige?"

"What now?" she answered without lifting her head. Her eyes were closed. He was glad. That meant she hadn't seen their close call.

"Unless you want us both to wind up in a ditch with two tons of truck on top of us, I think you'd better talk to me."

She sat up, frowning, and studied him. Whatever she saw must have convinced her he was serious. "Why don't you just pull over?"

He shook his head. "It's too open here. Besides, we're almost there."

"What do you want me to say?"

"Just talk to me," he said hoarsely. "Tell me something like…do you ever wonder what it would have been like if you'd just let me be that day at the warehouse? What would've happened to us if you'd walked away, instead of coming after me?"

"I assume I'd still be your task force patsy and you'd still be stealing drugs from my busts."

"No," he said. "I mean what would've happened between us."

Her shoulders stiffened. "Nothing. It was over. *We* were over."

"Because you said so that morning in the kitchen?"

"Yes."

"You really think I give up that easily?"

"It was a mistake. You admitted it."

"Some mistakes just have to be made." His eyes darkened. "And made again, and again, and again."

"Is that why you're doing this, Marco? Revenge?" she chided. "Because I told you I didn't want to see you anymore? Is that why you stole the drugs from my bust in the first place? Because you were angry at me?"

"No." His jaw turned to steel. She hadn't hit the bull's-eye yet, but she was zeroing in on the target.

He had been angry that morning. He was still angry.

"Five kilos of marijuana isn't enough to throw away a career for, much less risk jail time," she said. "There had to be some other reason."

He refused to look at her. He'd had enough of this damned discussion. He didn't want to hear any more.

"Were you just trying to make the task force look bad? Was that it?"

"Why would I do that?" he said, despite his resolve not to participate in this conversation.

"I know you didn't like it that the little lady cop with the big dog was assigned to the team while you were left sitting on the bench."

"Oh, that's rich," he retorted. "You think I stole the dope because I was jealous?"

She didn't have to answer. Accusation shone bright and clear in her mutinous expression. But she had it all wrong. All wrong.

"I wasn't mad about not being on the task force, sweetheart," he snarled. "I *was* on the task force."

"What?" Confusion rippled across her face. "I would have known—"

Marco felt himself being dragged over a line he hadn't meant to cross. "Not if you weren't supposed to know."

"Why wouldn't I be told?"

Marco knew he should back off, but it was too late now. Even if he didn't tell her, she would figure it out soon, if she hadn't already. There was only one reason cops withheld information from other cops.

"Because I was assigned to the task force to investigate you," he confirmed for her.

Chapter 5

"**W**hat the hell do you mean, *you were assigned to investigate me?*"

"Come on, Paige—all those piddly little busts when a major new smuggling ring had moved into the area? You know as well as I do that something was wrong on that task force."

"And they assigned you to find out what that was? Isn't that a little like asking the fox to guard the henhouse?"

"The chief asked me to dig around a little."

"Is that what you were doing with me? *Digging around?*" Her throat constricted. Mortified by the tears that sprang into her eyes, she turned her head.

"No." He beat his palm against the steering wheel and winced. He'd smacked the arm that Bravo bit.

"But you did single me out. You weren't just investigating the task force in general." She couldn't believe that he would think she was capable of cooperating with drug dealers. "I know you don't think much of the canine squad, or the job the dogs do, but I'm a good cop, dammit!"

"I know you are!"

She had opened her mouth to curse him out. Instead her jaw hung slack. "You do?"

Sighing in exasperation, he said, "I already explained my problem with the dogs, and as for you, hell, I think you'll be running the whole department one day if you decide that's what you want. But there were rumors about you."

"What kind of rumors?"

"The kind that can ruin a career. Someone had to prove they weren't true."

"And you were first in line to volunteer."

"I knew I would give you a fair shot. Not railroad you into anything, like some of the others. I was trying to protect you."

"You didn't even know me."

When he looked at her, his eyes were flat black. "No, but I wanted to."

She crossed her arms over her chest, buoying her indignation while heat slowly suffused her cheeks. Surely he didn't think she'd believe he'd had his eye on her even before he'd been asked to investigate her.

If he'd been assigned to investigate her.

What he'd said couldn't be true. This story was just another way to manipulate her.

"If you were investigating me, then why risk getting involved with me?"

Her eyes dry now, she studied him, but his gaze was inscrutable. His defenses impenetrable. "I guess that's the sixty-four thousand dollar question, isn't it?" His jaw squared as he stared into the darkness. "When I figure it out, I'll be sure to let you know."

In truth, Marco knew exactly why he'd gotten involved with her. Because he'd seen her and her dog track suspects through condemned buildings that a city rat wouldn't go into without a thought for her own safety. And he'd seen

her haul foul-mouthed, drugged-out kids from those buildings, playing tough cop in an attempt to scare them straight
one minute and calling social services to get them to the
top of the list for a rehab program the next. Paige intrigued
him like no other woman. The range of her attributes, from
the height of her intellect to the depth of her compassion,
had fascinated him. Her commitment to justice, balanced
by an uncommon capacity for forgiveness, had lured him.
The pent-up passion that brewed just beneath her unpreten-
tious surface had bewitched him.

Bewitched him still.

Now if he could just figure out what to do about it,
maybe he could get her out of his system and get on with
his life—shambles as it was.

But the more he tried to figure out how to break the pull
she had over him, the more confused he got. Tired as he
was, all he had to do was look at her to feel it. To feel her,
her soft breath on his neck, her body frantically clasping
his as he moved inside her.

He groaned.

Sleep. He needed sleep.

He pulled the truck over and shut off the engine at the
end of the dirt track he'd followed into the hills. His final
destination was still almost an hour away, but they'd have
to make the rest of the trip on foot. Which meant he'd have
to carry Paige.

Tomorrow. After he'd had a few hours sleep. No way
could he manage another hike through the woods tonight.

Paige raised her head from the side window. Her liquid-
gold eyes were soft and sleepy in the moonlight. Blood
pooled in his groin. His libido seemed to be the only part
of him that wasn't exhausted.

She asked, "Why are we stopping?"

"I've gotta get some rest," he said roughly. "You can
crash in the back of the truck."

As he carried her into the cargo compartment, she stared

out the door behind his shoulder. When he had her settled on a blanket, he turned to see what she saw.

A tapestry of stars glittered in the night sky. A breeze, cold but gentle, swayed the tops of the evergreen trees beneath them. Marco breathed deeply, the smell of pine and clay and Paige bringing him the first measure of peace he'd felt in six long months.

"It's pretty here," Paige said. "Where are we?"

"Home," he answered honestly.

Embarrassed by his sudden surge of sentimentality, he turned to leave. Paige twisted her fist in the sleeve of his sweatshirt. "Where are you going?"

"Up front."

She swallowed hard.

"You'll be safe back here." From him, among other dangers.

"You—you won't go off and leave me?"

His chest constricted. He doubted it was the lack of his company that she was afraid of. She just wanted to be sure he wouldn't abandon her out here where she might not be found for weeks. Months.

He tucked a sprig of golden hair behind her ear, but it slipped right back to her cheek. "I won't leave you. I promise."

Gently he eased her fragile hand from his shirt and warmed it between his rough palms. Her fingers were cold, but it was their trembling that was his undoing.

"I don't want to be alone," she said, half-breathless. Fear sparkled as brightly as the starlight in her eyes.

"But you don't want to be with me, either."

She parted her lips as if to argue, but no words came out. She couldn't deny the truth.

Breathing raggedly, he lurched to his feet. "Bravo will keep you company," he said.

This time when he left, she made no move to stop him. With Paige safely contained—and out of his reach—

Marco stretched his legs out on the cold vinyl seat and closed his eyes. He pushed aside the image of the pale, bleak look the moonlight had highlighted on her face as he'd closed the truck's cargo door.

She'd be fine back there. She had bottled water, a box of food, blankets and her dog. Morning was just a few hours off, and then they'd move on. Until then, she'd be just fine.

"Marco?"

His eyes popped open. Her voice sounded close. As if she was right next to him. She must be leaning against the forward wall of the truck. "What?" he asked.

"Don't you want some of these crackers? You haven't eaten much."

"No."

He let his eyes fall shut. The vinyl creaked as he shifted, trying to find a comfortable spot where there was none. His elbow banged against the steering wheel.

"Marco?"

"Go to sleep."

"It's awfully quiet here."

"It's like that in the country."

"What are we doing here?"

"Sleeping," he said, more sharply than he meant to.

A muffled thump sounded behind him. Hopefully that meant she'd lain down.

"Marco?"

His teeth ground. "What?"

He could tell by her long pause that the frustration in his voice hadn't gone unnoticed. "I'm cold."

He'd expected some stinging remark. Sarcasm, maybe. Not a reedy half plea. What did she really want?

His head began to pound. "Curl up with Bravo. He'll keep you warm."

A few more moments passed. Blessed silence. But he couldn't sleep. A small figure, all curves and secret places, haunted him when he closed his eyes. All he could see was her huddled in the dark, curled up with a dog for warmth.

"Marco?"

"What?"

"You're really not going to leave, are you?"

Smoky tendrils of suspicion curled in his mind. That pleading tone of voice wasn't like Paige. She was up to something. He knew it. But still it tore at him that she thought he might abandon her here. "I won't leave."

Another heartbeat passed.

"Marco?"

This time he didn't answer. He wouldn't. She was getting to him and he was sure she knew it. This had to be a trick. He would damn well *not* answer her again.

"It's..." Her voice was so quiet he could hardly hear her. "It's dark back here."

He clapped his hands over his face. His eyes shifted left, to the flashlight on the floorboard beside him. It went against every bit of good sense he had, but he climbed out of the truck. And he took the flashlight with him.

Victory trilled through Paige when she heard the truck door open. He was coming. Quickly she spread the blanket across her lap and folded her hands beneath.

For a moment she almost felt guilty, using his compassion against him. What kind of kidnapper showed compassion for his victim, anyway?

Before she had time to answer her own question, the cargo door swung out. Moonlight poured in. Marco stood outside, his broad shoulders backlit by the stars and the silhouette of tall pines. He made an imposing figure, shoulders square despite the fatigue he had to be feeling, hands propped on lean hips and feet planted.

The sight of him sent a strange excitement coursing through her. The same excitement she always felt around him, a dangerous mix of adrenaline and something much more intoxicating. It made her bold. Brazen. Unafraid, even now. Especially now.

She finally had him. All she had to do was get him inside.

She sat perfectly still. Even if she couldn't see his eyes, she knew he'd be watching her every move. He might have fallen for the little-woman-who's-afraid-of-the-dark act, but he wasn't stupid.

The flashlight snapped on and its beam bore down on her, making her squint, then arced over the walls, the floor, the ceiling of the tomb he'd buried her in.

After he'd checked out the truck, he rolled the flashlight to her. "Here."

"Wait!" she cried as he turned away. "The batteries won't last. I can't leave this on all night."

He paused with the door half-shut.

"And it really is cold." She shivered for effect.

"What do you want me to do, build you a fire?"

"Maybe I could sit up front with you?"

"No."

"We could run the heater. Just for a little while."

"No." He sounded gruff, but also more than a little guilty.

"You...you could handcuff me to the door. Anything would be better than freezing back here. Alone." She tucked her chin to her chest and looked up at him beguilingly. "In the dark."

He let his head tip back. His chest rose and fell silently for several long breaths. "Put the flashlight down," he finally said. "I don't want any weapons in your hands when I come get you."

Clicking the light off, she complied gladly. The darkness would hide both her trap and the smile she couldn't keep from her face.

She rose on her good leg, leaving the blanket on the floor

where she'd lain. He climbed inside. Took one step toward her. Two.

He stopped, maybe sensing that something was wrong.

She leaned over to pick up the blanket. "Don't want to leave this behind."

He took another step. She dropped the blanket and yanked the long, webbed cargo strap she held beneath it. Tied to the far wall of the truck, then looped through a hook on this side, the strap pulled taught, neatly tripping Marco.

He sprawled face first onto the floor, swearing.

Paige dived toward the door, barely evading the arm Marco hooked out to snag her. A stake of pain drove through her when she hit the ground outside, but she fought the blinding agony, turning back to the truck. "Bravo, *hier!*" she called, but it wasn't Bravo's figure looming over her when she looked up. Her heart lurching to her throat, she slammed the cargo door closed just as Marco's body crashed into it. The sound of fists pounding on steel alternated with Bravo's choppy barks.

Hands shaking on the bolt that would guarantee Marco wouldn't get out until she let him out, Paige paused. Bravo! She couldn't just leave her partner. But she couldn't get him out without giving Marco a chance to escape, too.

"Paige! Open this door! Don't do this!" The tempo of Marco's pounding increased. So did Bravo's barking.

She couldn't blame the poor dog. She wouldn't want to be trapped in there with a madman, either.

"Dammit, Paige, let me out."

"No."

"Don't do this. Do you hear me?"

Paige sucked in a deep breath, squaring her shoulders. "I hear you. I'm just not *listening* to you. Not anymore."

Marco went crazy. It sounded as if he was flinging himself against the door. Bravo's woofs grew deeper, more aggressive.

"Paige?" Marco shouted. "Don't leave me in here with this…animal."

"He's not an animal, he's a dog. And don't you dare hurt him."

"Me hurt *him?* Are you crazy? He's going to eat me alive. Let me out of here."

The fear in Marco's voice sounded genuine. As genuine as the rage. Paige considered what is must be like to be locked in the dark with one's worst fears. Much to her annoyance, a thread of compassion wound its way through her thoughts. "Just stop making so much noise and he won't bother you. You're agitating him."

"*I'm* agitating *him?*" Marco said, his voice a full octave higher than its usual timbre. A line of curses colored the air, but the pounding stopped.

Bravo's ruckus faded to a few low growls, then whines, and the sound of his paws scratching at the door.

"He wants out, Paige." Marco's voice was much more reasonable now. More persuasive. Manipulative.

"I can't."

"You don't know what you're doing. Just open the door."

"I know exactly what I'm doing," she snapped. A deep breath steadied her as she slid the bolt shut. Marco wasn't going to talk her into giving up her chance at freedom. All she had to do was drive to the nearest town and park in front of a police station. She could get Bravo out when she had about forty armed cops at her back. Her partner would be fine until then. Marco wouldn't hurt him—he wouldn't dare try.

"I told you I was a good cop, Marco. Hold on back there, because I'm taking you in."

"You're going to have a hard time doing that without the keys."

She hopped to the driver's door. Sure enough. Locked. Hell, he must have the keys with him.

Her eyes welled hotly again. "If I can't bring you to the authorities, then I'll bring the authorities to you."

"We're miles from the nearest town. You'll never make it on that ankle."

"No? Just watch me." Fire streamed through her blood. He thought she was weak. Helpless. An easy mark. But she'd show him.

She surveyed her surroundings—what she could see in the dark. The ground was rocky, the terrain hilly. The road they'd been traveling wasn't a road at all, but two deep ruts in the dirt. And the ruts ended here. At least that narrowed down the choices on which way to go. Back the way they had come seemed to be the only option.

She was the one in control now.

Paige didn't remember driving this far on the uneven dirt trail before they'd stopped last night. But then, she'd been pretending to be asleep, her mind all wrapped up in Marco's claim that he had been assigned to the task force.

To investigate her.

Why did that upset her so much? Because someone suspected her of wrongdoing? Or because his interest in her had just been part of a job? Nothing personal?

She was so absorbed in her thoughts that she didn't watch where she placed the walking stick she'd found earlier. It wobbled off the top of a rock and she took a misstep, coming down hard on her sprained ankle.

"Ow!" Hot needles shot through that leg. Every muscle contracted, then went limp. She flopped on the ground like a caught fish. Her foot was so swollen she could feel her heartbeat in her toes. She wouldn't be able walk much farther.

Tears filled her eyes. She wished Bravo were here. She should never have deserted her partner. A new fear crept over her. She shivered uncontrollably, but not from the cold.

What if she couldn't make it? It could be days before anyone found the truck. Marco and Bravo didn't have enough food and water....

Rolling to her side, she levered herself upright. She had to go on. She couldn't leave them in the truck. Leaning heavily on her walking stick, she took another step. Grimaced. Took another step.

She stumbled, caught herself, bit her lower lip to keep from crying out. Through eyes blurred with tears she looked ahead, and nearly collapsed again, this time from relief.

Headlights shone against the dusky pink backdrop of dawn.

She hobbled down the trail with new energy. A battered tan pickup—maybe it had once been yellow—rumbled toward her. There appeared to be two men in the cab and two more standing in the bed, pointing her way.

She waved frantically. The truck skidded to a halt.

Relief flooded her system with warmth, but her smile fell as the clouds of dust around the pickup settled. Suddenly the rising sun seemed uncomfortably warm. The men in the back of the truck had long dark hair and wore faded denim.

They held guns. Rifles.

She couldn't see the man in the passenger seat, but the driver leaned out his window, giving her a long look up and down, then spat a wad of tobacco from the side of his mouth. A bear claw tattoo on the back of his hand dripped red-ink blood.

"Well, well," he said. "I been huntin' these hills for twenty years. But I ain't never caught me one of these before."

Chapter 6

Marco woke with a start, cursing himself as soon as his eyes opened. How could he have been so stupid? Never mind. He knew exactly where he'd made his mistake. He'd let a pair of honey-gold eyes blind him to the devious, sneaky little waif behind them. He'd let her worm her way under his skin.

As if she hadn't already been there for months.

Now she was gone. She didn't have her dog for protection, and since he hadn't heard her smash a window, he assumed she hadn't got her hands on the gun he'd tucked under the front seat, either.

Bravo growled, low and edgy. The dog's ears pricked forward. A second later Marco's ears pricked up, too.

An engine. Someone was coming.

Paige? Even though it had been several hours since she'd left, he doubted she could have made it far enough to get help and come back already.

Rising carefully, silently, he listened. Tires ground to a halt on the rocky earth outside. Footsteps crunched toward the truck. His heart pumping like an eight-cylinder engine, he backed into the corner behind the door and waited.

The door latch rattled. Blood rushed in his ears. Hinges squeaked. He held his breath. Sunlight slashed through the dim interior, and Marco made his move. Driving his shoulder into the half-open door, he pushed it wide, knocking back the man on the other side and sending them both crashing to the ground.

Black shoes and khaki trousers kicked in the dirt near his head. Twisting, Marco grappled with the man's legs to hold him down. A big fist locked in his hair, pulled up his head. Then Bravo was there, growling, hunched like a rattler ready to strike, lips pulled back, teeth gleaming.

Marco's opponent froze. So did Marco.

"Easy boy," he said, not knowing if the dog would be particularly picky about which man he made his victim if he decided to attack. "Easy."

"What the hell is that thing?" the man he'd been fighting asked roughly.

The words drove what breath Marco had left after the fight right out of his lungs. He knew that voice.

Forgetting the dog, he turned to the man tangled on the ground with him. "Toby?"

Bravo growled again, jerking Marco's attention back. "Go find a fire hydrant or something, would ya? Get lost," he said firmly.

To his surprise, Bravo's hackles settled back into place and he trotted off toward the woods. Apparently a tree was as good as a fire hydrant.

"Why didn't you call out?" Marco asked, turning back to his friend. "Let me know it was you?"

"You should have felt my presence, brother."

"Feel the force, Luke," Marco said in his best Obi Wan Kenobi voice, then added more than a dollop of sarcasm. "Cut the voodoo Indian magic. And I'm not your brother."

"Not in blood, maybe, but in spirit."

When Toby had brushed off the dirt and combed the stray leaves from his hair, Marco stepped into the arms of his childhood friend.

"What are you doing here?" Marco asked.

"Looking for you."

"How did you know I'd come?"

"I didn't," Toby answered immediately. "But I hoped."

"Why? So you can get your name in the paper for taking me back in?"

"So that I can help you, you idiot."

Marco straightened up and gave Toby Redstone a long look. His friend's dark eyes sported a few more laugh lines than when he'd last seen him. His black hair flowed a few inches farther down his back. But the strength of character that lay beneath his Native American features hadn't changed. Neither had the integrity shining in his clear, blue Anglo eyes.

Ashamed that he'd been suspicious of his friend even for a moment, Marco dropped his arms from around Toby's shoulders and shook his head. "I'm sorry," he said.

Toby was one of the few people Marco unconditionally called friend, but aiding and abetting was a lot to ask, even from a friend. "But you shouldn't be seen with me. It'll cause trouble for you and your people."

Toby just laughed. "You are one of my people. Have been since you were fifteen. And I don't have to be seen with you to help you, do I?"

Marco's breath slowly leaked out, a measure of his tension with it. Whether he liked it or not, he couldn't deny he needed Toby's help. "No, I guess not." Then Marco's eyes narrowed. "How did you find me?"

"I've had men out looking for you since I heard you'd escaped."

"Men? Toby—"

"Don't worry," his friend cut in quickly. "Only a few and only those I trust completely."

Marco didn't like involving still more people in this, but what was done was done. "Then call them back in. We need to change who they're looking for."

Toby arched one eyebrow.

Marco met his friend's gaze directly. "I need to find a woman. She's out here somewhere, alone and on foot. Hurt. We've got to find her."

"This woman," Toby said, clapping Marco on the back and turning him toward the four-wheeler he'd arrived on. "She wouldn't be about five-foot-four, blonde, hazel eyes, mad as hornet?"

Marco looked at his friend incredulously. "You've seen her?"

"No, but I've heard an earful about her." Toby grinned. "She weighs, what? Maybe a hundred pounds? And she overpowered you and left you locked in this truck here?"

Marco stopped and pulled his friend around to face him a little harder than was necessary, but it wasn't his friend he was angry at. It was himself. "Do you know where she is, or not?"

Toby's expression sobered. "Don't worry, little brother. She's in good hands. One of the groups I had out looking for you found her. They took her to Doc's."

Even as he groaned at the fact that the whole damned Caddo tribe must be involved if Paige was at Doc's, an odd mixture of hot rage and cool relief washed through Marco. She was safe with his friends; he was glad for that. He was also furious at her for worrying him.

Quickly they camouflaged the box truck in a thicket of scrub and climbed onto Toby's four-wheeler. Marco called for Bravo, who trotted out of the trees and up to the all-terrain vehicle.

Toby studied the dog curiously. "I thought you didn't like dogs."

"I don't."

"Then what are you doing with this one?"

"Mostly trying to keep him from eating me alive."

Toby laughed. Marco pointed down the trail. "To Doc's, Toby. Now."

Paige gritted her teeth, ready to scream. Despite their dubious introduction, the men who'd found her turned out to be perfect gentlemen. Well, almost perfect.

They'd helped her into the truck without so much as laying a finger where it shouldn't have been. Given her water from their canteen. Responded to every question with "Yes, ma'am" or "No, ma'am." But they completely ignored her every time she insisted they take her to a law enforcement office. Instead, they'd brought her to a little frame building on what appeared to be the main street of a tiny Native American neighborhood. The sign out front read simply Doc Redstone.

The people inside the clinic had been as friendly—and as unresponsive—as the men in the truck. A young girl had given her a mug of spicy-sweet tea. An elderly man with a braid of gray hair that hung to his waist—she assumed he was the doctor—had gently kneaded her ankle, probing all the tender spots, but not really hurting her, and declared it not broken. She might have questioned his judgment if it hadn't been for the Harvard Medical School diploma marked *Summa Cum Laude* hanging on the examination room wall right next to what she assumed was an authentic collection of hand-hewn arrowheads framed in a shadow box.

She'd been sitting in the examining room for close to two hours now, she guessed. Every few minutes, a young boy with the flawless burnished skin of a Native American and the pale blue eyes of an Anglo peered at her from around the door frame.

Making sure she hadn't escaped, Paige was beginning to think.

Meanwhile the buzz of activity in the waiting area had

grown louder. She cracked the door open and counted heads again. The crowd had grown by five or six. Either she'd landed in the middle of an epidemic, or something was going on.

"Excuse me," she called to no one in particular. The buzz of conversation stopped. Two dozen pairs of black eyes turned toward her. A toddler in a denim dress hid behind her mama's skirt. "I need a phone."

A woman with high, arching cheekbones and silver bangle bracelets that matched the color of her hair took hold of Paige's elbow. Like the boy who had stood guard over her, the woman's eyes were crystal blue. His grandmother, Paige suspected.

"I'm Kia," the woman said. "Let me help you."

"I've been kidnapped," Paige explained firmly. "I have to contact the police." She searched the crowd for a sympathetic face. They all looked sympathetic. The problem was, no one stepped forward to help.

Something was definitely wrong here. Pulling free from the older woman and hopping forward, she discovered what. Like the sea before Moses, the crowd parted.

Marco stood across the room.

Bravo loped to her in a bouncy stride, tongue lolling happily. At the sight of the dog, the little girl behind her mama's skirts overcame her shyness. She waddled toward Bravo. "'uppy!"

"No!" Paige exclaimed. Bravo wasn't vicious, but he was trained to protect her, and in his excitement to get to her, she couldn't be sure how he would react to a child in his path. Paige lurched forward, but couldn't get her leg under her. She fell to her knees a foot short of the child and dog.

Then Marco was there, scooping up the baby.

"'uppy!" the little one called again, more demanding this time. She puffed out her lower lip and scrunched up her face.

Bravo reached Paige's side without incident and sat, but his whole body wiggled in his excitement at seeing her. Absently, she stroked the dog behind the ears, her attention focused on Marco.

Marco grinned and swung the toddler up on his shoulders. "No, no puppy." He bounced the little girl up and down. "Horsey ride."

The little girl giggled, then laughed outright when the horsey "bucked."

Dumbstruck was too mild a word for the way Paige felt. Mouth gaping, she watched as Marco plopped the girl, who had by then forgotten all about Bravo, in her mother's arms. Paige had never seen Marco look at a child, much less play with one. At least, not in real life. In her imagination she'd pictured it—Marco wrestling in a game of tickle with a kid. Their kid.

They hadn't used protection the night they'd been together—they'd both been too far gone to think of it—but the timing hadn't been right.

A sudden sense of loss knocked the air out of her.

Marco patted the toddler on the back, grinned at her mother and walked slowly toward Paige, the smile replaced by two brows hovering low over shuttered eyes. Stopping in front of Paige, he reached a hand down to her.

Still on her knees, she lifted her head and looked past him. "Someone call 911." Her authoritarian cop's voice didn't have much effect, probably due to the very unauthoritarian waver in it. "This man is wanted."

He lowered the offered hand.

"He's an escaped convict!"

The woman named Kia stepped forward, moving with a grace befitting a Civil War era Southern belle. "The tribe is the law here," she said softly, but proudly. "And the tribe has no quarrel with Marco."

One by one, the faces turned away. Kia shooed everyone out of the cramped office.

Paige clenched her fists, turning a glare on Marco. "You won't get away with this."

Squatting down next to her, he looked over his shoulders at the departing crowd. "I already have."

The old doctor shuffled up behind Marco. "We must talk."

Marco spoke over his shoulder. "I can't stay."

"We will talk, Walks-in-Moonlight," the doctor said in a no-nonsense tone. The tone a parent might use with a contrary child. "In my office."

Marco grimaced. "I'll be right there."

When the doctor scooted away in his bowlegged gait, Marco held out his hand again.

Paige pushed to her feet without his help. "I can walk."

"Not as long as I can help it." He scooped her into his arms as easily as he'd picked up the child a few moments ago. He plopped her into a plastic chair and glanced back down the hallway where the doctor had disappeared.

"Don't worry about me," she muttered sarcastically. "I'll be waiting right here."

As if she could do anything else.

She hated the control he had over her. He could just pick her up, sweep her here or there. Her will didn't matter. She didn't matter. He was in control. He was using her. Hell, he was using a whole people. Only they didn't seem to mind.

The fact that he'd ensconced himself in their midst didn't change facts. He was still wanted, and she was still a cop. Her duty was to return him to custody. If these people wouldn't help her, she'd find another way. In the meantime, she would watch and listen.

Maybe she would learn something that would help her.

"Does she speak the truth? Did you bring her here against her will?" Doc's voice was stern, but his eyes were kind. As kind as the old man's hands had been when he'd cleaned and bandaged Marco's bitten arm.

Marco seesawed between the honesty he owed his friends and the need to protect them. He'd never meant to involve them in his problems. The more they knew, the more criminally liable for his presence they became. And yet to lie to them would be to disrespect them.

He settled on words that were neither lie nor the full truth. "She's safe with me."

"Does she know this?" Kia's lilting voice piped in. As Doc's wife and the unofficial Caddo matriarch, Kia's opinion would carry a lot of weight in how the people here responded to Marco's presence. Whether or not they notified the authorities.

He met her aquamarine eyes steadily. "She wouldn't believe me if I told her."

Kia wrung her hands once, then folded them quietly on her lap. "What will you do then?"

"It's best if you don't know."

"We are your friends," Doc argued.

"Family," Kia corrected. The hurt on her face crawled inside him, twisting like an eel in his belly.

"That's why it's best if you don't know," Marco said softly.

He rose.

"If you need us..." Doc said.

"If we can help in any way..." Kia's eyes were as glossy as her husband's.

Marco smiled, his back already half turned to them. "I know."

Toby stopped him on the other side of the door, yanked him into an exam room with a worn black table in the middle and a jar of tongue depressors on the counter. "What was that crap? Why won't you let us help you?"

"I got myself into this mess. I have to get myself out."

"And her?" Toby nodded toward the waiting room where Marco had left Paige.

"Her, too."

Toby rolled his head back on his shoulders. "You are one sorry, pigheaded white boy, you know that?" He blew out a breath, then jerked his head down and slapped his palm against the wall behind Marco's head. "She's not just a hostage, is she? This is *her*."

"Who?" Marco asked calmly.

"The woman who's had you tied up in knots for months. The yin to your yang. The cat to yo' dawg." Toby leaned close. "The woman you went to jail for."

Marco pushed Toby's arm down and stalked toward the door. "I went to jail for stealing evidence."

"You might fool some people with that, but you can't fool me," Toby said to his back. "I know you're headed up to the cabin. What're you gonna to do, handcuff her to the bed? That why you brought her along? A little something to ease the pain while you're on the run?"

Even though Marco knew Toby was baiting him, he bit. Bit hard. He had two fistfuls of khaki shirt and Toby's back against the wall before either of them could blink.

The veins in his forearms bulged between them. Damn, he didn't want to do this. Didn't want to fight with the only man he'd ever really called friend. Didn't want to turn his back on Kia and Doc.

"If I was in trouble," Toby said softly, "would you stand by and let me walk away?"

Defeat washed through Marco in frigid waves. He unwound his fingers from Toby's shirt and wiped his palms on his thighs.

Toby's stare bored into him. "You gonna tell me what the hell's going on now?"

"I don't know what's going on."

"The hell you don't."

"I don't." Marco glanced at the wall that abutted the

waiting room, right about where Paige would be sitting. He
paced in the other direction. "All I've got are a couple of
names—Lewie Kinsale and Tomas Oberas. Maybe you
could check them out for me?"

"Done. Anything else?"

"There is one more thing." Now was as good a time as
any to bring up the only other way Toby might be able to
help him. If it came to that. Turning to face his friend, he
rubbed a hand down his face, grimacing. His whiskers
rasped against his palm.

He could see from Toby's expression that his friend already suspected he wasn't going to like what Marco had to
say.

That was all right; Marco didn't much like it, either.

"I have a plan," he started tiredly. Now all he had to
do was convince Toby to go along with it. As his friend
Toby would want to help. But murder was a lot to ask—
even of a friend.

Marco set Paige on the back of the ATV he'd borrowed
from Toby. Toby's wife, Jala, and their little girl—the toddler who had wanted to pet Bravo—waved goodbye.
Chuckling despite his desperate circumstances, Marco
waved back. He'd climbed into the driver's seat when
Jala's older boy pounded up to him, breathlessly holding
out a gnarled maple branch.

"What'ya got there, Micah?" he asked.

The boy blinked his blue eyes seriously. "It's...for
you."

Marco took the broken branch and turned it over in his
hands, studying the foot-long branch, about five inches in
diameter, and the various appendages sprouting from it.

"What do you see?" the boy asked.

"I'm not sure." Marco glanced at Paige, saw her watching the exchange curiously, then turned back to the boy.
"What do *you* see?"

Micah squished up his face. "An…animal maybe?"

"Maybe," Marco said.

The kid looked at Bravo. "A dog?"

"Maybe," Marco said again. He turned the branch over one last time and narrowed his eyes, lowering his voice. "Or a grizzly bear."

Micah squealed in delight. Marco turned the branch so that a particularly long, thin branch angled up. "Or a giraffe."

"*Or*…maybe not an animal at all?" The boy looked up at Marco through a forest of dark lashes. "Maybe an airplane?"

Marco caught the note of hopefulness in Micah's voice. "Hmm. Maybe it is an airplane, after all. We'll see." The boy smiled. "You run on home now."

Micah skipped off toward his mother, and Marco tucked the branch into a compartment behind the seat. He managed to avoid Paige's gaze, wishing he could avoid the inevitable questions as easily.

No such luck.

"What was that about?"

"Just a game." He shrugged. "See what's inside a piece of wood. You know, kind of like looking for shapes in the clouds."

She narrowed her eyes, but he couldn't tell if it was because she didn't believe his answer or because he'd climbed onto the four-wheeler.

"I don't think I'm going to like this," she announced, staring down at the all-terrain vehicle as if it was some giant, man-eating insect.

Reaching behind him, he pulled her arms around his waist. "Relax. All you have to do is hold on to me."

"I know." She squirmed farther back on the seat. "That's why I'm not going to like it."

An oath burst from his mouth, but he loosened his grip on her. "Well, you can walk if you'd rather, but I wouldn't advise it. Even with two good legs a body could get lost in those woods and never be found.''

Paige retorted promptly, ''Is that what you plan on doing with my body when you decide you don't need a hostage anymore?''

No oath would do justice to what he felt at that moment. He hoped she didn't feel the shudder that ripped through him as his mind painted the image of her lying dead among last year's leaves.

''There are a lot of things I'd like to do with your body, sweetheart,'' he said, ''but dumping it in the woods isn't one of them.''

Not another word passed between them for the first few miles. Marco kept the ATV in low gear, partly so Bravo could keep up and partly because he was enjoying the feel of her wrapped around him too much to hurry.

Despite her protests, she'd melted against him. She was exhausted; he could feel it. Her hands circled low on his hips. Her chin rested against his shoulder blade and every now and then he felt the brush of her hair across the sensitive place on the back of his neck.

He told himself sex was the only reason he couldn't stop thinking about her. He'd been six long months without. Being in forced proximity with Paige without respite from the memories and the craving was enough to drive any red-blooded male crazy, and he was definitely red-blooded.

And definitely male.

Each time she shifted, pressing her chest a little closer to his back, he was acutely reminded of that fact.

After a while, he started to wonder if she'd fallen asleep. That must be it. She was probably snuggling against him instinctively, drawn to his warmth. The hard little nipples scraping his back were surely a reaction to the cold, not to him.

''The doctor called you Walks-in-Moonlight.'' Paige

broke the quiet. Her voice sounded dreamy, almost asleep. Almost, but not quite.

He wondered what she'd been thinking about back there, so quiet all this time. Wondered if her thoughts had drifted the same direction as his.

Probably not, he decided wryly. Paige hadn't wanted him before he'd gone to prison. She surely didn't want him now, despite the messages her body was sending his.

"Is that some kind of Indian name?" she finished.

"No." He forced his thoughts back to neutral ground. "It was a warning."

She waited in silence for him to explain.

"Moonlight. Pale face. Get it?"

She shifted restlessly, heightening his sensitivity everywhere she touched him. "I get it."

"He only calls me that when I'm in trouble. Like a mother who only uses her kid's middle name when she's got him by the ear."

He felt Paige sigh against his back.

"How did you come to be so friendly with them?" she asked.

"You mean me being a white man and all?"

"I mean you being from New York City and them in Oklahoma."

He pondered the question a minute, deciding how much he could tell her, then wondered why he hesitated, how he'd become so adept at keeping secrets that he didn't know how to answer a simple question anymore.

Maybe it wouldn't hurt to give her something of himself, something of the truth, to make up for all the deception.

"I didn't always live in New York." He paused. It had been a long time since those years after he'd left his home state—a wilderness of busy streets and skyscrapers—for the wilderness of Oklahoma. "I moved here with my dad when I was teenager."

"That's a tough age to make new friends."

"It wasn't so bad." He shrugged, delaying getting to the bad part another second or two. "I had my dad."

"Your mom?" she asked. He could hear the hesitancy in her voice.

"Not in the picture," he said simply.

"I'm sorry."

"Don't be. My dad was all I needed."

"What made him move out here?"

"He didn't want to die in the city."

Marco felt Paige tense behind him. He took a breath, pushing away dark memories and gathering the strength to tell the whole story. "When I was ten, he was diagnosed with Lou Gehrig's disease. By the time I was fourteen, his medical insurance ran out, and we moved out here. In spite of what he said, I think he just didn't want me to live in the city. I was…a little out of control there. I'd already gotten into some trouble."

"Imagine that," she said dryly.

He looked over his shoulder, caught the humor in her eye that said she was trying to make this easier for him, and continued. "Dad had always been fascinated with Western stuff. You know, cowboys and cattle ranches. We didn't have any family or anyone to help out so we sold what little we had and headed toward Texas. This is as far as we got. Without the medical care, he went downhill pretty fast. He was stuck in a wheelchair by then and he just sort of…withered."

Her palm softened, splayed against his diaphragm. It felt as though his heart dropped to rest beneath her touch. He tried to focus on the story.

"We lived in a trailer house on a gravel road outside town, and he liked to sit on the front porch, in the sun. By the time I'd get home from school, he'd be covered with dust from that damn road. I'd take him inside and clean him up. It used to make me so mad because he'd complain about me making a fuss over him, but he couldn't do it himself. And then…''

"What?" she asked after a moment.

"Then he lost his ability to talk, and I'd have given anything to hear him complain again. Anything would have been better than having him just sitting there, staring at me while I bathed him and fed him.''

"It must be hard to watch someone you love hurt like that.''

"Yeah, well, I didn't have to watch him long.'' Bitterness crept into his words despite his attempts to prevent it.

"How long?"

The pity in her voice told him she already knew… Damn it, he didn't want her pity. He wasn't sure why he was telling her all this. He hadn't talked about it in years.

"He hung on just long enough to get me through school. I figure he knew I'd never finish without him.''

"I'm sorry.''

"Don't be,'' he said. "It was what he wanted.''

"What do you mean?''

"About a month after graduation, I came home one day and he pushed some papers at me across his bed tray. Before it'd even sunk in that he was showing me his life insurance—a hundred thousand dollars' worth—he shoved a note toward me. He must have had the lady from social services that came around once in a while write it out for him. It said, 'Go to college. Make me proud.'''

"You sound angry.''

"College.'' He couldn't keep the disgust from his voice. "I wanted to stay home and take care of him. College could have waited.''

She was quiet a moment, and then she said softly, "Maybe he couldn't.''

"He could've,'' Marco said, harsher than he should have. This was an old hurt. It shouldn't feel so raw. "He willed himself to die so he wouldn't hold me back.''

"And you hate him for that?"

Her accusation hit him unexpectedly, like a blind-side tackle. "No, I don't hate him," he answered too quickly. "But—"

"But you are angry."

He opened his mouth to protest, but caught himself before he lied. "I guess I always thought he quit when he could have kept fighting."

Marco supposed he *was* angry. Leave it to Paige to call him on it. Not much got by her, and not much daunted her. She had some presence of mind, rigging that truck to trip him up. Not to mention setting out for help alone, in the dark.

Thank God it had been the Caddo who had found her.

Marco's throat tightened at the memory of her on her knees, and no one offering to help her. No one except him, the last person whose help she would accept. There had been resignation in her eyes, but no defeat. No surrender.

God, she was stubborn.

She'd called a truce for now, but as soon as she'd had a little sleep she would have a new strategy all mapped out; he would bet on it. She never gave up, never gave in. She never accepted less than perfection from anyone—including herself. It was one of the things he admired about her. One of the things that had drawn him to her even though he knew better than to get involved with someone he was investigating. He sure didn't need to be thinking about getting involved with her again. Lord knows he tried not to think about it. But every vow he made to keep his distance turned out to be an empty promise.

Forget the marijuana he'd stolen; he had no use for it. She was his drug, his addiction. And if she snuggled any closer against his back as she nodded off to sleep, this ride was going to throw him seriously off the wagon.

He laughed harshly to himself. As if he hadn't fallen already.... Only two things in this world had a chance in hell of keeping him away from Paige: jail and death.

And jail had already failed.

Chapter 7

The sound of running water woke Paige the next morning. It was raining.

Stifling a moan as she stretched, she sat up. Yesterday's one-legged jaunt through the hills of Oklahoma had cost her. She was stiff in places she hadn't known existed before today.

"Coffee?" Marco asked. He was sitting by the hearth with a fire crackling behind him and Bravo curled up at his feet. Every few seconds the flames hissed as a raindrop made its way down the smokestack and evaporated on the blazing logs.

She nodded, and he poured her a mug from the pot on the hearth as she swung her legs over the side of the bed and wrapped the blanket around her shoulders.

The mug felt blessedly warm in her hands. Not that it was cold in the cabin, with the fire, but there was a dampness in the air that permeated the rough log walls to settle deep in her bones.

When they'd arrived yesterday, she'd thought the place

was primitive. But then she hadn't looked too closely. She'd been too tired. She'd drifted off to sleep almost as soon as Marco carried her through the door. Judging by the rumpled pallet of blankets on a second cot braced in front of that same door, Marco hadn't been far behind her in dreamland.

Taking a closer look now, Paige adjusted her perception from primitive to rough but homey. Antique fishing gear hung on log walls that had obviously been carefully hand-crafted. The floor was plank, but had been sanded smooth. A thick hooked rug brightened the center of the room, and gingham curtains framed a large, paned window on the west wall.

Under other circumstances, she would have considered the place a dream come true—remote, rustic, romantic. She would never have wanted to leave. Under other circumstances.

"It's a lot prettier in the summer," Marco said without looking up. He had a knife in his hands and was concentrating on shaving a sliver of wood from a pole resting across his legs. He stopped carving long enough to gesture at the winter-gray lake outside and the sky above it. "And in spring, when the Indian paintbrush turns the meadow orange, and in fall, when the leaves are changing color."

She hobbled to the window and looked out through the great driving sheets of rain, trying to see the land as he described it. "I imagine it is."

"Just our luck, being stuck up here the one time of year it's ugly."

She lifted her fingers to the glass and looked outside with her mind's eye. She imagined the jutting pyres of rock, the sweep of the plain, the crystalline depths of the lake as they must look with the sun glistening from them. "It's not so bad," she said.

Looking down, she noticed that someone had carved initials into the windowsill. She traced them with her finger.

T.R. in the left corner, and M.A. in the right. "You own this place?"

"No, it's on Caddo land." He shaved another knob off the staff in his hands. "But I built it. Me and a friend, a couple summers in high school."

She limped around the room to the fireplace. A carving on the mantel drew her attention. She picked it up, admiring the handiwork.

"It's not done," he said. Was that a note of shyness in his voice? Insecurity about his art?

She turned the model over in her hands, recognizing it as the broken branch the boy, Micah, had given Marco yesterday. "It's wonderful," she told him honestly.

He'd carved an old-fashioned biplane, mostly just roughed out so far, but amazingly detailed in the parts that were finished, from the gentle convex wings to the thread-thin struts.

"I thought I'd make the propeller from a separate piece and fix it on with a rod so it would really spin."

"I'm sure he'll love it."

Marco shrugged as if it hardly mattered, but she suspected it mattered a lot. "Micah wanted a plane."

Paige jumped at the chance to get information. This was a different Marco Angelosi she was seeing this morning, she realized. Not the cop, or the convict, but the man. The man she'd glimpsed yesterday on the ATV as he told her about his father. The man she needed to know more about if she hoped to convince him to give himself up. "You're close to him."

Marco hesitated. "His dad is an old friend."

"This friend have a name?"

The hesitation was longer this time. She could see his mind working, processing options. "It's really better if you don't know too much about the people here."

A surge of anger made her lash out when she should

have been working toward peace. "You should have thought of that before you involved them."

He tightened his grip on the staff he held. "You're the one who involved them. If you hadn't gone on your little hike, they would never have seen you."

"I asked them for help and they refused. That makes them accessories to kidnapping."

The knife slipped in his hand. Blood bubbled up where the blade had nicked his index finger. He held the finger in his mouth a second, sucking, then pressed his thumb over the cut. "Only if you make an issue of it," he said. "No one's going to know they had anything to do with this unless you tell them."

"You're asking me to forget they committed a crime?"

"These are good people, Paige. Don't condemn them for standing by a friend."

"Fine," she countered. "Surrender yourself to me right now and I'll leave them out of my report."

"I can't do that."

"Hmmph. I guess this friendship thing only works one way, huh?"

He threw aside the pole he'd been carving and loomed over her. "Dammit, Paige, don't use them against me."

"You're not leaving me any choice. Give me the gun and the keys to the ATV."

"I can't do that."

"Why not?" She realized she was yelling.

"Because if I go back to prison I'm dead," he boomed. Her heart stuttered. "Wh-what?"

He sank back to his stool and dropped his head into his hands. "Did it ever occur to you that maybe I didn't run away from that wreck because I wanted to, but because I had to?"

Blood drained from Paige's head, leaving her dizzy. All of her indignation, all of her outrage sifted through her fingers like a handful of sand. *Marco could have died.* A thousand questions reeled through her mind, but only one came to her lips. "The prisoner you were fighting with— Oberas? You think he was trying to kill you?"

Marco didn't confirm or deny. Paige stalked away, showing him her back, barely containing a scream of frustration. How could he drop a bombshell like that and then clam up?

But as his silence stretched on, and the implications of what he'd said sank in, she went back and bent to one knee at his side. Gently she rested her fingers on his thigh. Even with that light contact, electricity arced between them.

"Oh, Marco," she said, "what's really happening here?"

He snatched up the pole he'd been working on. "I've already told you more than you need to know."

The color that spotted his cheeks and the jerky way he sheared the next chunk of wood from the staff were a pretty solid indication that she'd hit a nerve. They were also a pretty solid indication that she wouldn't get any more out of him.

She retreated to her cot and lay down to watch the rainfall, sipping her coffee and turning the new information over in her mind. He could be lying about someone trying to kill him. His story could just be one more trick to get her to cooperate. To manipulate her into being a good little hostage.

But something in the dark intensity of his eyes and the pent-up frustration in his voice when he'd said it made her believe it. Made her believe him.

She rolled her face into the pillow. Oh, she didn't want to start believing in him. She wanted to think of him as an escaped con. A fugitive.

Not as a man.

Especially not as a man who bounced babies on his shoulders and carved wooden airplanes for little boys.

He could hurt her—not just physically, but emotionally. He'd already proved that.

She'd wanted him to open up to her today, and he had, but she was no closer to solving the riddle that was Marco Angelosi than she had been six months ago. She would keep trying to learn what she could, but she wouldn't make judgments on what she heard. It wasn't her place to try. Truth and lies would be sorted out by a court.

All she had to do was get him there.

After a time had passed and the beat of rain on the roof had washed some of the tension from the air, she hobbled back to the fire for a refill from the coffeepot. Stopping next to Marco, Paige looked down at the staff he was carving. "What do you see in that one?" she asked, trying to keep her voice light. "A two-by-four?"

A touch of slow humor tugged up one corner of his mouth. "I see me not having to carry you outside to the, ah, facilities in that storm."

He propped one end of the rod up on the floor. The upright end was Y-shaped.

"A crutch?"

He nodded. She studied it dubiously, thinking twice about the appeal of remote, rustic and romantic. "If you had to kidnap me, couldn't you at least have picked someplace a little more comfortable to hide out?"

"We've got the fire, plenty of blankets to curl up in and the rain to listen to." Marco lashed a layer of sheepskin that looked suspiciously like the collar of his coat around the Y of the branch. "What else could we ask for?"

"Indoor plumbing?"

He grinned. "Sorry. I guess we're roughing it."

Great, Paige thought. Just her, Marco and a roomful of secrets in a cozy little hideaway in the middle of a monsoon.

Roughing it didn't begin to describe the experience.

* * *

After two days of storms, the clouds finally evaporated into a clear blue sky and the rain stopped. When Marco opened the door, the brilliance of the sun singed his eyes. But when he stepped over the threshold, his boot sank four inches into the sodden earth.

Sighing, he pulled his foot back. Paige leaned on him from behind, peering over his shoulder.

"I wouldn't try it unless you're dying," he said.

"I'm dying." She pushed past him, hardly limping. In another day or so she wouldn't even need her crutch. The swelling in her ankle had gone down nicely, probably because their forced confinement encouraged her to stay off of it. "At least my bladder is. I'm going for it before the next deluge."

He suspected her bladder wasn't dying as much as she had a bad case of cabin fever. They both did, after two days locked together in a grueling battle of wills.

The pattern had been consistent. Paige asked an innocent question. Trying to keep the peace, Marco answered. Encouraged by her success, Paige asked a slightly more probing question. Marco hedged. Madder than hell, Paige zapped him with a question meant to strike a nerve, and it did.

They argued until one of them stalked off, sulking, and then a few hours later, they started the game over again.

Thank God for sunshine.

He almost smiled as Paige took her first tentative step off the porch, slipped, gasped and planted her crutch into the ground just in time to regain her balance. She hobbled more carefully for five or six more yards. Halfway to the edge of the clearing, she struggled to lift her good foot. With a great sucking noise and a good bit of effort, her foot came free of the muck, but her shoe did not.

She stood there leaning on her crutch and her bad leg, holding her pink-socked foot in the air and cursing a blue streak.

Crossing his arms over his chest, Marco chuckled to himself and bit back the urge to say, "I told you so."

Paige propped her crutch to the side for balance and leaned over to wrench her shoe from the mud. She pulled and grunted and dug in the mud up to her elbows, without luck.

He supposed he should go and help her, but he was enjoying the sight of her pretty little mud-splattered behind pointed his way while she heaved and tugged at the shoe.

Finally she dragged the shoe free. Unfortunately, the sudden loss of resistance sent her spiraling onto her backside with a splash.

Marco laughed out loud.

Coated head to toe in red-brown sludge, she glowered up at him. "You think this is funny?" She reached up to push her hair out of her face and left a trail of the sludge across her cheek.

Marco laughed harder. "Yes."

She scooped up a handful of the slime and chucked it his way. He ducked, and the missile splattered harmlessly on the wall behind him.

Muttering something to herself, Paige stuck her crutch out to the side for support and levered herself up. Her face twisted in pain as her good leg collapsed beneath her.

Marco's laughter died. "What?"

Paige clasped her lower leg. "I think I twisted my ankle."

He eyed her warily.

"Great. Just great," she said between grimaces. "I get one leg fixed and wreck the other." She grasped her crutch and struggled to stand again, the pain lines on her face deepening as she glanced sideways at him.

Marco reached her side before she'd made it halfway up. In a flash, she gripped his wrist and delivered a leg chop to the back of his knee, felling him in the muck beside her.

Even if he'd seen it coming, he wouldn't have been able to do anything about it.

Groaning in defeat, he flopped his arms out to the sides, slimy wet clay already soaking through his shirt to his back.

Paige swung her body over his chest, straddling him and laughing. She dipped her hand into the muck, plopped a sloppy mud ball in the center of his chest, then streaked her coated fingers over his cheeks and forehead.

He sucked in a breath. "What are you doing?"

"War paint, Tonto."

She gazed down at him, and her smile slowly flattened to an uncertain expression.

Marco's chest rose and fell against her thighs like a bellows. The intimate friction sent his heart rate soaring, his blood chugging like a freight train in his veins.

Their gazes locked and the scent in the air changed, became heavier, headier. Marco watched in awe as her pupils dilated, her nostrils subtly flared.

Taking her fine-boned hand in his coarse one, he swirled her index finger in the mud beside them, then raised it to her forehead, drawing it down from the little peak at the center of her hairline, over the bridge of her nose, across her lips and stopping with a little dot, like the point of an exclamation mark, on her chin.

"What are you doing?" From her breathlessness, he guessed he wasn't the only one having a hard time dragging enough oxygen into his lungs.

He pulled on her hand, urging her body down until she hovered over him, her lips inches from his.

"Peace paint, Lone Ranger," he explained.

Her brow wrinkled, a little furrow cracking in the mud streak already drying on her forehead. Gold-flecked confusion swirled in her eyes. With one hand, he still clasped hers. With the other, he reached up and cupped his fingers around the back of her neck. She didn't close the distance between them, but she didn't widen it, either.

Could she really want him to kiss her after everything that had happened, everything he'd done?

Her eyelids fluttered and a tremor rippled down her back. Yeah, she wanted him. She just didn't want to want him.

Ever so slowly, giving her plenty of time to change her mind, he lifted his head off the slippery ground. The want, the need, the have-to-have that he'd held in check so tightly the last few days strained at its tether. He opened his mouth. Just a touch, that's all he wanted. A taste.

Like hell.

He let his head fall back into the mud. One taste of her would never be enough.

He let go of her hand and clenched a fistful of mud at his side to keep from pushing himself up to her, pulling her down to him.

"It's a nice day," he said, hoping he'd didn't sound like a man calling on every bit of control he could muster to keep himself from flipping her onto her back and having his way with her, mud or no mud. "How about we get cleaned up and go for a ride?"

Another clear day passed. An afternoon ride on the ATV became their routine. The fresh air improved both their attitudes, as far as Paige could see, and they didn't have to talk much over the roar of the engine.

Which left entirely too much time to think.

Paige didn't know what was happening to her, or why. She knew better than to trust Marco Angelosi. She'd always known better. Yet it was hard to condemn a man who'd shown her nothing but concern.

He'd doctored her wounds. Made sure she ate even if it was only canned goods from the cabin's amply stocked pantry. Kept the cabin warm enough to suit her, even if it meant chopping wood in the rain. Without complaint, put up with Bravo prowling the cabin, though the dog's presence clearly made him uncomfortable.

He'd even brought along the book she'd been reading, and when she shunned it because she was confused about him, afraid of the feelings for him their forced proximity dredged up, he sat by the fireplace and read aloud to her. He'd restored peace in the cabin, lulled her to sleep two nights in a row that way.

Even their afternoon journeys into the Oklahoma countryside confused her. Their companionable meandering made it too easy to forget he was wanted, forget she was his prisoner.

They wandered along dry creek beds and skirted the edges of thick stands of trees. If he ever followed a trail, Paige couldn't see it. Every so often the terrain would break enough to allow a glimpse of grasslands, flowing into the distance. They were brown now, but in the summer she imagined they'd look like wide, emerald rivers.

She smiled. It wasn't hard to imagine the Caddo people of old, riding horseback over this same ground, following the herds of buffalo that had once grazed on that grass.

A sound like the rustle of leaves in a thousand trees grew stronger as they picked their way up a rocky incline.

"What is that?" she asked, needlessly as it turned out, since at that moment they crested the rise and she could see the water, tumbling and frothing below.

"The Washita River. The edge of Caddo land."

He rolled the throttle backward and drove onto a trail that merged with a road. A few feet ahead, the road entered an old iron trestle bridge spanning the river gorge. A two-lane highway ran along the edge of the gorge on the far side of the bridge.

Marco pointed back to the Caddo side, to a valley where a small cluster of buildings stood out like blisters in the grasslands. "That's the Caddo settlement there."

She could just make out the little doctor's office she'd visited.

"Look," she said, pointing to a triangle of boulders that

formed a wading pool along the riverbank. Three boys, twelve or thirteen years old, lay on their stomachs on one of the boulders, dangling over the edge and laughing and splashing each other. One of the boys scooted close enough to the edge to dunk his head underwater, hold it there several long seconds and then lift his face, whooping and screeching.

Thinking of the stream where she and Marco washed up each morning and night, she didn't blame him for howling. "What are they doing? That water is freezing."

"They're Caddo boys," Marco said, as if that explained everything.

She frowned. The boys had turned, and were sitting up with their feet in the water, kicking up a storm.

"It's sort of a tradition."

"I don't see how risking pneumonia could be something people would want to pass from generation to generation." This looked like foolish child's play. Nothing more.

"In the old days, the Caddo would bathe their young in cold water. They believed it toughened them up. Then when they were older, the boys would swim in cold water to prove their courage. Their manhood."

"Hmmph. Manhood." She gestured toward the boys, who were now retreating back to shore, arms crossed over their chests and their young shoulders shaking. "All this proves is that the onslaught of testosterone that comes with puberty addles Caddo brains the same way it does every other male of the species."

Marco's chest quivered in what might have been a suppressed laugh. "Maybe," he said. "Maybe not." He swung his right leg over the seat of the ATV and stood beside her.

"Is that how you came to be such a good swimmer?" She lifted her eyebrows. "Did you swim with the Caddo boys?"

"Maybe."

"Maybe not," she finished for him. "Why? Did you need toughening up?"

As he leaned over the ATV, his left hand on the seat in front of Paige and his right hand draped behind her, the bright humor in Marco's eyes fell dim. He stared past her as if he could see across the red hills, across time.

"Sometimes when the school bus came by to pick me up, the other kids would laugh and point. Make faces at my dad, sitting out there on his porch." He shook his head. "He never said anything, but I know he saw them. It used to make me so mad...."

Paige's heart turned to clay. "Kids can be cruel, especially when they're faced with things they don't understand. Things that frighten them. Thank goodness most of them grow out of it."

"Yeah, well, I couldn't wait that long. I picked a few fights with boys older and bigger than me, got knocked around pretty good and picked a few more."

"Caddo boys?"

"No. They pretty much kept to themselves. These were just good ol' Oklahoma farm kids."

"So you did need toughening up."

"The first year we were here, I got the tar knocked out of me pretty regularly."

"And after that?"

"After that I noticed that the Caddo boys could spit farther, run faster and hit harder than anyone else in town. Even the school bullies didn't mess with them."

Marco looked up at Paige, the shadows on his face clearing and a slow grin taking their place. "I decided I wanted to be just like them."

"So naturally you made a nuisance of yourself until they let you hang around."

"Naturally."

It wasn't so different from what he'd done with her. He'd wanted her, and he'd gone after her—moved in and didn't take no for an answer. He'd charmed her, beguiled her and bedded her, and somehow in the process, she'd lost everything to him—her mind, heart and soul.

He picked her up now, cradling her in his arms the way he always did, even though she was perfectly capable of walking. But this time something coiled deep and tight inside her at his touch.

Their gazes caught, hung on each other. At the bridge rail, he lowered her slowly, letting her body slide down his. Sparks jumped between them at every point of contact.

"Paige." The single, dragged-out syllable was an oath, a prayer and a plea all in one. He pulled her to him, crushing her against the hard wall of his chest. His jaw nuzzled the top of her head. "You're killing me. You know that. Don't you?"

If so, they were going to die together, because he was killing her, too.

He held her still against him. His face was expressionless, but his heart ricocheted wildly against her fingertips. Her own pulse leaped in answer.

She turned her face up to his. "You did it, didn't you?"

"What?"

"Swam in the river in winter. Made yourself tough."

As he stared down at her, his carefully bland expression transformed. Unfolded, revealing layer upon layer of emotion in the span of a second. Wonder. Worry. Sorrow. Respect.

The complexity of what he was feeling astounded her. The depth of those feelings astonished her.

Her nerves tingled. Her mind raced. This was the Marco she knew existed but hadn't been able to reach. The Marco with the capacity to love and laugh, hate and cry. The Marco who had seduced her.

Seduced her still.

He lowered his mouth to hers. The first brush of his lips was safe, chaste. For a moment, she thought that was the end of it, and an irrational disappointment pooled in her blood like lead. But Marco wasn't through.

"Not tough enough," he murmured in her ear. "Not nearly tough enough."

Then he captured her mouth under his, and lead turned to quicksilver in her veins.

Chapter 8

Marco held Paige hostage with lips and tongue and teeth, nipping and sucking, taking and giving, committing the crime and then begging for clemency.

She surrendered to his possession. Welcomed his invasion. Returned his advances with a conviction that impugned her victim status and raised her to full-fledged accomplice.

He trapped one of her legs between his, slid his hands down to cup her backside, lifted her and crushed her against his solid arousal. When he lifted his thigh, stroking between her legs, her will slipped away, replaced by his demands.

She sagged against the intimate friction. His strong hand closed over her breast and she gasped, arching into his touch. Her body seemed more his than her own. There was no beginning and no end to the feel of him closed around her. No one had ever had such power, such control over her.

Too much power. Too much control.

''No.'' A moan tearing from her throat, she pushed at his chest. ''No.''

Marco's back went rigid as a tent pole. His shoulders tensed. He reached for the pistol tucked behind his back. It took a moment, while she untangled her limbs from his and gathered the reins on her runaway pulse, to realize that his reaction wasn't entirely due to her rejection.

The sucking sound of soggy hoofbeats warned of an intruder approaching from behind him. Recognizing the little figure perched bareback on the fat pony waddling down the trail, Paige clamped down on Marco's wrist before he could raise the gun.

His nostrils flared, his eyes widened, but after a long breath, he pushed the gun back into his jeans. She squeezed his hand before letting go, recognizing the trust he'd just put in her. Despite the lack of trust she'd just shown in him.

He turned to see who was coming, and she felt him unwind as he recognized the boy. ''What're you doing way out here, Micah?''

''Lookin' for you.'' Micah pulled his pony to a stop in front of them, eyeing them suspiciously. Paige's cheeks warmed, wondering how much he'd seen. ''What're you doin' out here?''

''Just, uh…'' Marco shuffled his feet, glancing at Paige. His cheeks looked a bit flushed, too. ''How did you find us?''

Luckily for them, the boy didn't seem to notice the sudden change in topic. He pointed at the deep ruts their ATV had left in the mud and rolled his eyes. ''You left a trail any kid could follow.''

''Mmm,'' Marco said. ''So we did.'' He stepped forward and took hold of the pony's reins. ''How come you're looking for me?''

''There's a meeting at the schoolhouse. You're supposed to come.'' He looked over to Paige. ''You, too.''

"What kind of meeting?"

"I don't know," Micah said. "Grandpa just said tell you to come."

Warning bells clamored in Paige's mind. She sensed the same alarm in Marco.

Had they been found?

"Was anyone else there?" he asked. "Any white men?"

Micah shook his head, looking confused. "Just Grandpa. He said you both should come."

"All right." Marco pulled the pony's head up from where it was tearing Bermuda grass, roots and all, from the soft ground and grinding it side to side in its teeth. "You ride back and tell him we'll be there soon."

He gave Micah a squeeze and pushed the boy gently away. "You be careful in this mud, now. Stay off the steep trails and keep that pony to a trot."

"Yessir." Micah headed his pony back the way he'd come, his little legs flapping to keep the animal up to speed.

"What do you think?" Paige asked when Micah was out of earshot.

Marco shrugged. "I don't know."

"Do you think someone's found you?"

He spun around. "I don't know, all right? I don't know any more than you do."

She reached up to rest her hand on his shoulder. "Don't go."

He faced her. "What?"

"Don't do it like this. You don't know who is waiting for you out there. Let me take you in. We can go to a town somewhere, with a courthouse. We'll find a judge to take you back into custody peacefully."

"I'm not going back into custody, peacefully or otherwise." He stalked back to the ATV. "There's no one out there. My friends wouldn't set me up. And the police sure as hell wouldn't use an eight-year-old boy to lure me in."

"You don't know that. You don't know what's going

on.'' To her mortification, Paige's eyes were hot and full. She gathered her control. "If the police have found you, they'll have a SWAT team waiting. One wrong move and they'll kill you."

He was quiet a moment, as if he'd made peace with everything that had happened. Everything that might yet happen. "Then at least you won't have to worry about me kissing you anymore, will you?"

A sweat breaking on her palms, Paige peered around Marco's broad shoulders. They'd stopped on the crest of a grassy ridge. Below them, a valley carved a wide swathe from the red rock hills. On its floor the Caddo made their home.

Kids on bikes pedaled one direction down the main road, while a pair of unleashed dogs raced the other way. Like wagons around a campfire, pickup trucks circled a large building near the edge of town. She assumed this was the school.

A dozen or so men and women moved purposefully from the trucks to the building, or clustered around picnic tables out front. Micah's pony was tethered to a maple tree nearby, munching happily on the few dead leaves clinging to winter boughs.

Marco put his hand behind him as if to guide her off the ATV. "Stay here. I'll check it out."

He was letting her off the hook, she realized. Giving her a chance to stay out of whatever happened down there.

She wasn't having it. If he was going in, she was going with him. If things got crazy, maybe she could talk some sense into one side or the other. If not, at least with her clinging to his back, no one was going to take potshots at him. "No way."

"I don't want you down there."

"First you won't let me go and now you won't take me

with you. And they say women can't make up their minds.''

"You're putting yourself in the line of fire. You could get hurt."

She fixed him with a pointed stare. "Then at least you wouldn't have to worry about kissing me anymore, would you?"

The expletive he blurted expressed her sentiments exactly. For a moment she thought he'd throw her bodily off the four-wheeler, but he turned resolutely and started down the slope. "What the hell," he grumbled. "There's nobody down there, anyway."

Paige wondered if it was a breach of her duty as a police officer to hope that there was not. She wasn't quite sure what was happening between her and Marco, but she knew it was getting harder and harder for him to push her away—not only physically, but from the truth, and the truth was all she was after. The truth, and maybe justice. With a little more time, she was sure she could convince him to turn himself in. She wouldn't let herself examine the implications of the pain that thought caused.

Many of the people gathered around the school waved as she and Marco rode in. Others smiled and went back to their tasks, carrying tools and sheets of wood and tarpaper, or serving up food at the tables.

Marco pulled up beside the old doctor. "Doc, Micah said you needed me."

So the doctor was Micah's grandfather.

"I do." The old man chuckled in a voice well used through the years. "At least, I need your strong back." He motioned toward the school building. "The rain damaged our classrooms. We must repair them."

Marco sighed, the titanium-hard muscles in his back softening to, oh, tempered steel. "Doc, I'd like to help, but—''

"You would not deny our children an education, would you, Walks-in-Moonlight?"

Marco shifted on the ATV seat. "No sir."

"Good. Then get to work. I will escort your...guest."

The hand the old man offered Paige was much weathered and curled like a crow's foot. Trying not to lean on him too much lest she break him, she accepted his support as she climbed off the ATV and limped to one of the tables brimming with stew and cornbread and coffee.

After he'd parked the ATV near the pickups, Marco brushed her shoulder as he leaned over to pick up a foam cup. "You can bet the keys are in the ignition of at least one of those trucks over there, if you want to make your getaway while I'm working."

Was he hoping she'd leave? Maybe this morning's kiss had scared him as much as it had scared her.

"And by the time I got back with the cops, you'd be long gone."

His patented expressionless expression met her accusing look.

"Forget it, Angelosi." She took the foam cup he offered and poured coffee for herself. "This isn't over until I've got you in my handcuffs."

A lecherous grin scrolled across his face. "Now *that* thought is almost enough to make me give myself up."

Leaving her spitting and sputtering hot coffee, Marco sauntered toward the school.

The day passed in relative calm. Paige admired the co-operation and spirit of the workers. The sense of community here was strong, as if they were all part of one big, extended family. A family that included Marco.

It was strange, seeing him elbow to elbow with the Caddo, sharing a thermos of coffee or holding a board while another pounded nails. In Port Kingston, he'd had a reputation as a loner. Here, he was anything but.

Every now and again she caught him looking at her from the roof, where he was nailing shingles. Every now and again he grinned, catching her looking at him over the rim of her cup. On one of the latter occasions, she glanced quickly away and found herself face-to-face with the woman who had told her the tribe had no quarrel with Marco.

Paige sucked back reflexively, and the woman smiled.

"I don't bite."

"I—I'm sorry. You startled me."

The woman glanced up at the roof where Marco had been. "Your attention was elsewhere."

Paige felt a faint flush creep up her neck. Fissures of laughter crisscrossed the old woman's face. But even marked by the years, the woman had a timeless beauty. Her silver hair was thick and straight and piled into a bun on her head. Her bronze cheeks were high and her jaw finely sculpted. Three tiny silver feathers dangled from each delicate earlobe. And her eyes were bright, intense and...blue. Like Micah's.

"You remember me?" the woman asked.

"Yes. You're the one who wouldn't—" She broke off.

"Wouldn't help you?" The woman sat on the bench next to Paige and poured herself a cup of coffee. "If I wanted to help you now, what would you have me do?"

"Why would you?"

"Perhaps because I can't help him." She nodded toward the rooftop. "Not as much as I would like."

"And you think I can?"

"I do." Steam spiraled off the woman's cup as she blew on her coffee. "I'm Kia."

Not knowing what else to do, Paige held out her hand. "Paige Burkett."

"Yes." Kia shook her hand and looked up to the rooftop where Marco had been. Paige resisted the urge to turn and see if he was still there. "Don't worry. He's still watching."

Paige pulled back her hand. "Probably to make sure I don't run off."

Kia's blue eyes sparkled. "And is that why you were watching him? To make sure he didn't run off?"

Paige couldn't say why she had been watching Marco. The kiss on the bridge had confused her. Her reaction to it had terrified her. She didn't want to be his pawn, moved from square to square with a flick of his wrist. A kiss.

"I don't think there's much danger of that," she said. "He hasn't let me out of his sight in three days."

The humor in Kia's eyes said she didn't doubt it.

Paige picked at the wooden table. "Did you know Marco before...before he went to jail?"

"I've known Marco many years."

"What was he like as a boy?"

"Quiet. Always thinking, watching, but..." she smiled, as if reliving fond memories "...holding everything inside here." Kia clutched a fist to the center of her chest. Then she asked, "What is he like as a man?"

Paige glanced up, surprised.

Kia shrugged. "He does not visit as often as he should."

"He's the same, I guess. Never telling anyone what he's feeling."

"Perhaps words aren't required for you to know what he feels."

She felt Kia's hands on her shoulders, turning her.

"Look there," Kia ordered.

Paige looked up to see Marco on the roof, silhouetted by the sun dipping low in the afternoon sky. His head was tipped back, his eyes closed.

"Close your eyes. Lift your face." Paige complied, not knowing why. "What do you feel?"

"The breeze. The sun."

"No, what do you feel *inside?* In your heart?"

Paige thought of Marco, standing on top of that roof and staring across the copper landscape, just as he'd stood on the bridge earlier. Filling himself with a sight that was as life-sustaining as filling his lungs with oxygen.

She choked back a rise of emotion. It wasn't hard to imagine what a man whose only view of the landscape for the past six months had been through chain link fence and razor wire would be feeling at a moment like this.

"Freedom," she whispered. "It feels like freedom."

"Do you need words to understand this?"

"No, but—" Paige snapped her eyes open and twisted out of Kia's grip. "He gave up his right to freedom six months ago."

"Yes. Now why?"

"I don't know."

"Then ask him."

"I have. He won't tell me."

"Then ask again. But this time, listen for the answer not in his words, but in his heart."

Before Paige could make sense of Kia's advice, little Micah ran over. Their identical blue eyes shined as they shared a hug.

"Howdy, Miss Paige," he panted once he'd been released from the hug. Then he took Kia's hand and tugged. "Meema, come see my fort I built."

Paige put the deeper questions aside. "Micah is your...grandson?"

"Yes."

"Then the doctor is your husband?"

"For fifty years."

"Meema, come see," Micah complained in his childish voice.

Kia cupped the boy's head, silencing his pleas. "In a moment, sweetie."

"Marco told me he and Micah's dad are friends."

"Did he also tell you that without him, Micah would never have been born?"

Paige angled her head inquisitively.

"My son and a group of boys were...being boys. Drag

racing pickups. There was an accident. The truck caught fire.'' Kia's eyes became glossy.

Micah smiled. He'd obviously heard this story many times. ''Uncle Marco was the youngest and scrawniest one there, but it was him that ran to the truck and pulled my dad out before he got burned up.''

Kia laid her hand over Paige's. The woman's skin felt thin as tissue. ''Now you understand why the tribe has no quarrel with Marco.''

At a loss for words, Paige nodded.

Micah dragged Kia away from the table, then stopped and ran back to Paige. ''If you want my dad to tell you the story again, he went that way.'' The boy pointed a stubby finger at a building down the street. ''With Uncle Marco.''

Paige found Marco in the doctor's office, just as Micah had said. Standing in an examination room down the hall from the doorway where he'd disappeared, she peeped around the corner. Marco paced across an office. She couldn't see the other man; she could only hear him.

''You're hot and getting hotter, man,'' a deep voice said.

''Thanks for the news flash.''

''That was just a little reminder.'' Something slapped on a tabletop—a book or newspaper, maybe. ''Here's the news flash.''

A few moments of silence followed, then Marco said, ''Damn!'' and threw a crumpled wad of newsprint right at her. At least it seemed to be right at her, although she was sure he didn't know she was there. Still, he scared three years off her life.

''You need a plan, brother.''

''I told you my plan.''

Deep Voice snorted derisively. ''As plans go, I don't think much of that one.''

''It's a worst-case scenario.''

''What's your best-case scenario?''

''I'm still working on that one.''

"You'd better work fast. It's no secret you lived in this area for a time. There are men in Johnson City looking for you already. They haven't come out to Caddo land yet, but they will, sooner or later."

"What kind of men?"

"Don't know. Plainclothes. Feds, maybe."

"You're sure they're cops?"

"Can't be positive. Not without walking up and saying howdy, and I'd rather not draw that kind of attention to myself, but they act like cops. Dress like cops."

Marco muttered an oath and paced back to where she could see him.

"You're worried they might be private talent?"

Marco nodded, rubbing the back of his neck.

"Nat Turkson's talent, by any chance?"

The name brought chill bumps to Paige's flesh. Nat Turkson was the biggest crime boss on the Texas Coast. He was into everything: drugs, prostitution, stolen goods. Anything he could buy for one price and sell for a greater amount. If Marco was tangled up with him...

Marco's full attention bore down on his friend. "What've you got?"

"The name you gave me, Kinsale? He works for the Turk."

"Great. Just great."

"So what does the Turk want with you?"

"I wish I knew." Marco sounded tired. Defeated. The echo of footsteps told her he was pacing again. He stopped by the door and looked over his shoulder. "Thanks for the help."

"Help, hell. I still don't even know what kind of trouble you're in."

"You saw the paper. What kind of trouble am I not in?"

"I don't mean the public version. I want to know what started all this. The stuff you're keeping bottled up inside."

"I don't know what you're talking about."

"And elephants fly."

"Obviously you've never seen Dumbo."

"You're still not letting me help you."

"I told you how you can help me, if it comes to that."

"What about this woman of yours?"

"I can handle her," Marco said, then sighed. "She'll... cooperate."

"You're going to hurt her, man," Deep Voice muttered.

"It won't be the first time." Marco stopped on his way out the door. His head bowed. "She's tougher than she looks. She'll get over it."

Paige's heart went cold. She sucked back against the wall as Marco walked out. His words echoed in her mind. Deafening her. Deadening her.

Pausing only long enough to make sure the other man wasn't looking and to grab the discarded newspaper from the floor, she pounded outside on numb feet.

Hours after they'd returned from the Caddo settlement, Marco poked at the embers in the fire with a stick while he watched Paige make her preparations for bed. She dipped out a cup of clean water from the pail warming on the hearth and scrubbed her face, then another to brush her teeth. When she'd finished, she poured the few drops left around the edge of the flames, where it sizzled and hissed, the only sound in the cabin.

And then she combed her hair. She closed her eyes as the silken strands fell effortlessly through the teeth of the comb and kissed her neck, only to be lifted and combed again.

An urge to comb that golden hair for her swept over Marco, its current as strong as the river that had carved the valley where this lodge stood. He wanted to feel her silken locks slide between his fingers. He wanted to kiss her neck like they did.

Which was why he stayed as far away from her as he

could in the tight confines of the cabin. More than physical distance lay between them tonight, though. She'd been quiet on the way home, offering no clue to what she'd been thinking.

He wondered if she'd been thinking, as he had, that their relationship had shifted today. They were no longer mere kidnapper and victim, cop and criminal. Once again they'd become man and woman.

He couldn't get her out of his mind. It was crazy, his obsession for her. He didn't have time for it. Toby could distract the men in town for a day, two at best, but then Marco would have to move. Do something. He should be figuring a way out of this mess, not digging himself in deeper by fantasizing about what couldn't be.

But sweet Jesus, the way she'd melted against him on that bridge... The way she'd looked at him while he'd worked on the schoolhouse roof...

Maybe all this fresh air had him feeling feisty. Maybe knowing that the chances of him coming out of his present situation alive were slim gave him little reason to worry about tomorrow and every reason to make the most of tonight.

She stood, walked to the cot and laid out the oversize sweatshirt she wore to bed. Even the way she walked turned him on. Her stride was compact, efficient. Like she always had somewhere to go. Always knew her purpose.

He loved that about her, that she was always so sure of herself. Always knew what she wanted.

Today, at least for a time, she'd wanted him.

As he wanted her.

He was behind her when she stopped at the end of the bed, his hands on hers when she crossed them over her body and took hold of the hem of her thermal shirt.

"Don't," he said simply. "Not tonight. If you do, I don't know if I can stay away from you."

She turned in his arms and his body's inevitable response

frightened him with its force. The tightening. The surge of blood. The aching fullness.

He wasn't the only one affected. Paige's breathing deepened. Her pupils dilated. Her hardened nipples scraped his chest when she leaned against him ever so slightly. She cupped her hand over the juncture of his thighs, her thin fingers exploring his hardness, and he thought he would explode in her palm.

"You want to make love to me tonight, Marco?"

"Yes."

"Why?"

"I don't know." He cursed himself a thousand times a fool for getting this close to her. Sweat beaded his temple. The fire in the hearth was no match for the furnace inside him. He burned for her.

"Sure you do." She raised her hand under his shirt and scraped her thumb across his flat nipple, and he hissed. "Tell me."

He swallowed hard, closed his eyes, but that only heightened the feel of her touching him. "Because you're beautiful," he said. "Desirable."

"Is that all?" Paige scraped her fingernail across the metal teeth of his zipper and his heart nearly stopped. He was going to have to take control of this situation soon. Very, very soon, or...

"Because I can't get you out of my head." His hands found the hollow of her waist and held on tight. "Haven't been able to for months."

"What else?" she breathed against his neck. Her hair fell like silk over his shoulder as she angled her head to access his ear.

"Because I want to give you something...something good to make up for the rest of this whole miserable experience." His hands moved up, finding the underslope of her breasts. "It—it was good between us."

Her tongue curled in the hollow of his throat. "Very

good," she agreed, her soft breath cool on the skin she'd moistened. Her fingers popped the button on his jeans and dipped inside, but stopped just short of touching him. "Is that really why?"

Yes. No. It wasn't just sex. It wasn't just feeling good for a few beautiful minutes. It was *her*. He wanted her— all of her, body and mind. But he couldn't tell her that. Words were beyond him. Everything was beyond him except the feel of her small hand so close. Tantalizing. Teasing.

"Or is this just your way of *handling* me. Of making sure I'll *cooperate*." Her tone of voice changed. Sharpened to a fine point. Dazed, he opened his eyes. She greeted him with a feral gleam. "So that you can manipulate me. Use me."

"No."

"Is that why you really brought me here, so I could be the patsy in whatever scheme you're cooking up?"

"No."

"How could you not, with this hanging over you?"

Paige reached into her back pocket. When she withdrew her hand, she held a familiar sheet of newspaper—the front page of yesterday's *Oklahomian*.

His eyes drifted closed on a groan. The blood surging through his veins calmed in the blink of an eye, a storm blown quickly out to sea. He didn't have to see the newspaper's headline to know what it said: Prison Van Wreck No Accident.

As if he didn't already know what it said, she read aloud. "Stakes in the manhunt for escapees Marco Angelosi and Tomas Oberas, also suspected of aggravated kidnapping of a police officer, rose today when investigators confirmed reports that the prison van wreck that set them on the loose was not an accident. Department spokespersons say the van's tires were spiked with a device similar to that used by police to disable suspect vehicles in pursuit situations.

What at first appeared to be an accident was, in reality, a premeditated jailbreak. Police also confirmed that the death of a guard and the van's driver would now—"

"—now be treated as a murder. The hunt for Angelosi, Oberas and their accomplices will be escalated nation-wide," Marco finished from memory. Reading the story once had been enough to permanently brand the words in his mind.

"You lied to me, Marco."

"I never lied to you."

"You didn't tell me that the van wreck wasn't an accident." Hot rage stained her cheeks. A single tear slipped over one eyelid and coursed across the crimson. The sight of it made the back of his throat burn.

"If you planned it... My God, Marco, killing a prison employee in an escape attempt, even if the death was un-intentional, is a *capital* crime."

"So I read."

She shook her head slowly, looking shell-shocked. "Then tell me why! Say something. Anything. Defend yourself!"

The soul-deep hurt in her eyes tore the truth right out of him, but he wouldn't give it all to her. Some things she would have to figure out for herself. "I already told you why."

He watched her think, saw her desperately searching for the answer among half-truths and ambiguity. "You said Oberas tried to kill you."

"I said *someone* tried to kill me."

"Are you saying the van wreck wasn't an escape at-tempt?"

"I'm saying it was a murder attempt."

"By who? Why? Tell me."

The truth died on his lips as he realized he'd told her too much already. As he remembered why he couldn't tell her more.

He could defend himself—at least he could try. But then who would defend her?

One by one he shut off every emotion. Clamped down on every feeling he had for her. Only then did he trust himself to answer her challenge.

"I can't," he said.

She whirled away from him. Her shoulders shook and he thought maybe she didn't want him to see her cry.

"Then there's nothing else I can do here."

A warning shiver buzzed up his spine. "What are you saying?"

Wiping her face with her sleeve, she kept her back to him. "I'm saying I'm leaving. Right now."

Chapter 9

"It's eighteen miles to town. And that's if you don't get lost."

"Then I won't get lost."

"It'll take you all night. And then some."

"Then I'll be back to civilization in time for lunch."

"It's dark out there."

"I'm not afraid of the big, bad wolf."

Except maybe the big, bad wolf standing in front of the door, Paige added silently. She watched him out of the corner of her eye as she gathered her belongings in a blanket and slung the bundle over her shoulder hobo style.

"You can't go," he said.

Paige didn't bother to be surreptitious when she looked at Marco this time, taking in his tall frame, top to bottom. He had his back propped against the door, a not-so-subtle warning that she'd have to go through him to get out. The arms folded across his chest added that going through him wouldn't be easy.

Nothing about him ever was.

"You're not leaving."

His voice was as deadpan as his expression, but Paige had a feeling there was emotion there somewhere, tightly coiled, deep, deep inside him. Stark, violent emotion.

Her stomach did a slow roll. "You can't stop me."

He lifted his dark brows a fraction.

"You won't stop me," she corrected, lifting her chin.

"No?"

Turning away, she busied herself putting on her coat and shoes. When she straightened up from tying her laces, Marco wasn't at the door anymore. He stood right in front of her, looming over her, so close that she could count the dense lashes that framed his eyes. The firelight playing over his face added to the sensual, dark angel look.

The crack of a log on the fire sounded like a cannon shot in the silence of the room. Even Bravo had stopped whining, as if holding his breath to see what happened next. Then Paige realized she was the one holding her breath, and exhaled forcefully. "I'm not afraid of you. You're not going to hurt me." Bravo brushed her thigh as if to remind her he was there. "Or my dog."

"If you believe that," Marco said, "why haven't you left before now?"

Paige swallowed a tremulous sigh. She'd been wondering the same thing herself. Surely she could have escaped. She was a cop. She had a duty. Justice to serve.

But she was also a woman, and she felt womanly things, whether she wanted to or not. She needed more than justice. She needed the truth.

About him and about herself.

"I—I wanted…"

She wanted to believe that he wasn't guilty. Despite all the proof to the contrary, she wanted—desperately wanted—to believe he hadn't used her. That he wasn't using her still.

She wanted the impossible.

Yet if Marco had done the things the newspaper accused him of, she'd know it, wouldn't she? She'd feel it.

Foolish thought, for a cop. Dangerous thought.

When she didn't continue, he lifted her hand, tangled his fingers in hers. Not restraining, but inviting. He stared at her until she felt the connection between them form. Grow.

"You want me to stop you," he said.

A thousand wants and don't-wants reeled through Paige's mind along with the regrets and the might-have-beens and the questions. Always so many questions.

Kia had said Paige would find her answers not in Marco's words, but in his heart. As far as Paige could see, Marco's heart was a cold and desolate place. Devoid of life, much less answers.

She pulled her hand away, and the pain was like no other she'd felt before. Like severing a limb. "No."

Marco took a step back. The muscles of his jaw quivered with tension and restraint. "Then go. Run away while I'm still willing to let you."

Paige felt as if her feet were sunk in concrete.

"Go," he boomed, and reached behind him to pull the cabin door open. "Now!"

She took one step past him. Two. Three. She called Bravo and hurried through the door. At first her gait was slow and heavy. When she reached the tree line, she quickened to a jog, then did as he bid, and ran. She ran as far and as fast as she could from the silent cabin behind her, and the man inside.

Nearly an hour passed before Paige stopped to catch her breath. Bravo automatically sat at her side. She leaned against a barren silver maple tree, seared down the middle from a lightning strike, and let the stillness of the woods close in on her. Leafless limbs rattled overhead like old dead bones, but there was no breeze to speak of. No physical storm this night.

The maelstrom was inside her.

Her nerves buzzed, in tune to every sight in the silver moonlight, every sound in the dark, every scent. Her heart thudded painfully, both lightened by a freedom she hadn't felt in days and heavy at leaving.

Especially leaving without knowing why.

Why ruin a career, a life, for five lousy kilos of marijuana? Why use her to do it?

Maybe he'd needed the money, but she didn't think so. Revenge could have made him take the drugs. Simple anger that she'd rejected him. Or maybe his reasons had been much more sinister. His rage much deeper.

Maybe he'd planned on blaming the missing evidence on her.

It made sense. As an investigator sent in to target a corrupt cop, he would have the means and the opportunity.

But then why the rest of it? Why the escape? Why the story about someone trying to kill him? Why kidnap her?

Perhaps he'd just plain lost it. Like an avalanche, once his mind started to slide, it picked up speed and force—theft, jailbreak, kidnapping, murder.

Perhaps he hadn't intended to use her at all, rather she was simply the vibration that caused the first chunk of ice to slip.

She shuddered as she looked into the dark woods behind her. Why had he let her go? Surely he knew she'd be back for him.

She had set this disaster in motion; now she would be the one to bring it to an end.

Calling Bravo to her side, she set out again, more slowly this time. More carefully. Regret weighted her footsteps, but she felt centered. Marco had said it was eighteen miles to town. Even with ankle throbbing, she would be there by morning.

An hour later, climbing a narrow trail along the face of a bluff that crumbled beneath her tennis shoes with each misstep, she wasn't so sure. With her back plastered to the red-rock wall, she looked up to the top of the ridge. Only ten or twelve more feet to go. Ten or twelve steep, treacherous feet.

She turned her eyes the other direction. To head back down would double that distance. Plus she'd have to skirt around the bluff, adding miles to her journey. She'd have to climb eventually to reach the top of the plateau and find the river, the bridge and the road to civilization she'd seen on her rides with Marco. There was no guarantee she'd find an easier way to the top. Better to stick it out on this trail and get the hard part over with.

She looked at Bravo, who was also leaning against the rock. "What do you think, boy?"

The dog's un-answering eyes reminded her of Marco for a moment. Inspired to keep going, she slid her foot forward another step, her back and palms tight against the rock behind her. A spray of pebbles clattered down the slope. Palms sweating and heart pounding, she moved again anyway.

Four feet from the top, the narrow ledge disintegrated beneath her right foot. Paige gasped. Buckled. Prayed. Clutched at the wall behind her as if she could pierce the rock with her scraped and ragged fingers.

Righting herself before she pitched into the abyss of darkness, Paige fought for a steady breath. Her heart lurched so hard in her chest, she was afraid the pounding might shake loose what was left of the trail beneath her feet.

Gradually gathering her wits, she checked on Bravo behind her. "You okay, B.?"

A three-foot gap in the shelf they'd been using as a trail stretched between her and her dog. He whined and stepped toward her.

"No. No, stay." She freed one hand from her death grip on the rocks to give him the "stay" signal. He could jump the distance easily enough. But the trail on her side wasn't wide enough, or stable enough, for him to land. "Stay, boy."

Frantically she racked her mind for a way to get him across to her, or for her to get back to him. But there was no way. He couldn't go up; she couldn't get down.

Her only option was to leave him in a long stay, climb to the top of the plateau, circle around to the bottom of the trail and call him down.

A moan welled up inside her. She closed her eyes and let her head fall back to the rock behind her. First of all, that meant leaving her dog. Her partner. Second, it meant she had to get to the top of this cliff. Third, she'd lose hours working her way back to the bottom of the trail, only to end up right where she'd started.

But she had no choice. She wouldn't leave Bravo behind.

Opening her eyes, she scanned the remainder of the trail in front of her. Four feet. Maybe only three. She could make it.

Bravo whined behind her. His tail thumped against the rock face, sending pebbles swishing down the slope.

Paige tore her attention away from the rock to reassure him. "Stay, Bravo. Stay."

He sat, though she didn't know how on the narrow trail. He shifted his front paws restlessly.

"No, B. Stay still."

He stood and barked. Then barked again before she could order him to stop. His tail thumped the cliff side and he took an anxious step forward, then back, then forward again.

Paige forced herself to take another step up the trail. Maybe if she got out of his sight...

Behind her, she heard him scratch at the ground, then grow quiet.

Her body electrified with the sudden knowledge of what

he was doing. She turned, the "stay" command already half out of her mouth, but it was too late.

Bravo had backed away from the missing span of trail. He took one powerful stride for momentum, then leaped. Moonlight glinted off shiny black-and-tan fur and determined whiskey eyes as his body stretched, reached for her. His teeth were bared, his ears laid back with effort.

For Paige, the filaments in the thread of time snapped in horrifyingly rapid succession. Bravo kicking his haunches out behind him, one final thrust toward his goal. His front paws hitting the ledge. Him hunching up, bringing his hind paws forward to grab on.

The trail disintegrating beneath him as it took his weight.

A short, high, puppy yelp as he realized he wasn't going to make it.

Falling.

The flat thud of dog on rock.

Darkness below her, and quiet.

She covered her mouth with her fist to silence the shriek that had torn out of her. Dangerously close to tumbling over the edge of the precipice herself, she peered into the abyss. "Bravo?" Her teeth pierced the skin on her knuckles.

"Oh God, Bravo."

Paige's scream sliced through Marco like a whetted blade. He'd been following her trail since she left, hanging back just enough that she—or her dog—wouldn't detect him taking shortcuts to get ahead of her. But as the echo of her cry died, so did all his concern for stealth. He broke into a run, headed toward the origin of the sound. Thorns tore at his jeans, cut his knuckles as he pushed away the scrub. Oblivious, he ran harder. Moved faster. Nothing would slow him down; nothing would stop him.

He broke from the hedge of bushes and immature trees so suddenly that he nearly tumbled over the cliff. His breath clouding the air, he stopped, head swiveling, listening. "Paige?"

He couldn't hear anything except the pounding of his heart.

"Paige! Answer me, dammit!"

This time a choked cry rose from the darkness at the edge of the plateau. In an instant, he was on his belly, looking down at her precarious position on a ledge, just out of arm's reach.

"Jesus, Paige."

The moon whitewashed her pale complexion, giving her an ethereal air. But when she glanced up, her eyes, usually bright gold, were huge, dark voids in that quixotic face.

Marco recognized shock when he saw it.

"Listen to me, Paige," he said, trying to make his voice a beacon of calm, of reason in whatever tumult had carried her away. "You're okay, you hear me? Just give me your hand and I'll pull you up."

He stretched down to her, but she made no move to reach up.

"Come on. Just stretch your hand out."

Still she stared out over the horizon as if she could see something other than a field of stars on a black canvas.

"Paige!" he snapped.

Her shoulders jerked. Some measure of recognition—and of hate—flashed across her expression. He didn't care. He'd take hate over the twilight zone anyday.

"Reach up to me," he ordered. Ever so tentatively, she complied. When he had a firm grip on her wrist, he heaved her up. She dug for purchase with her toes. Debris clattered down the slope beneath her. With her free hand she pushed on a stable rock, and then she was beside him on the ground at the top of the plateau.

Awash in a sea of relief, he cupped the back of her head and pulled her close, holding every inch of her against him and inhaling her scent, her essence. Baby shampoo.

"Are you all right?" The question groaned and shuddered, heavy with fear.

Her body shook against his and she burrowed closer.

"Paige?"

She curled her fingers in his jacket.

"Sweetheart, what happened? Are you okay?"

Dazed, glassy eyes raised to his, then she turned her head toward the abyss. "Bravo," was the only explanation she offered.

"Oh, Christ, Paige. I'm sorry." He wiped a smudge from her cheek, and a tear with it. "I never meant for this to happen. Never."

Her pliant body turned to stone in his grasp. Eyes burning like enemy campfires, she pulled away from him. "What did you mean then?" she asked. "What were you thinking when you brought Bravo and me to the middle of nowhere and held us here?"

Her blow couldn't have better aimed. He'd been asking himself what he'd been thinking the whole time he'd been following her. How had he ever believed that bringing her here could end any way but tragically?

"Still no answers, Marco?"

"None you'd care to hear."

"None you'd care to share, you mean."

He shrugged, determinedly careless as the claws of guilt shredded him inside. "That, too."

She got to her feet and he followed suit, to find her standing only inches away. Close enough that he could hear the angry rattle in her breath. With her fists, she lashed out, pounding him once on the shoulders. "Damn you. Damn you, damn you, damn you!"

He didn't bother to defend himself. He just stood, watching her fury, the flare of her nostrils, the pyres of grief and rage in her eyes. Let her beat him. He deserved that, and more.

The flutter of her fists was anemic, anyway. After a moment, she didn't look like she had the strength left to stand, let alone fight. Still she arched her back, and he thought he was in for one solid kick in the shins—or a couple of feet higher—when a sound from below stopped her.

She cocked her head and he could see her holding her breath, utterly still. Marco held his breath, too.

The sound rose up again, thin as a ghost—a whine so faint it sounded more like pained breathing than a cry.

Paige ran to the edge of the cliff. She dropped to her belly on the rim of the plateau and reached down into the darkness. "Bravo?" The opposing notes of hope and helplessness in her voice tore at what was left of Marco's self-respect.

He stepped up beside her, jamming his fists into his pockets to keep from holding her back when she inched closer to the dropoff. He figured she'd had enough of his interference in her life.

"Where is he?" he asked, trying to see where she was looking.

"I don't know."

Lying on his belly like a snake next to her, he focused on the jumble of rocks and brush far below. He couldn't see anything. Another whine drifted up, stronger this time. Marco tracked the sound. Bravo wasn't at the bottom of the cliff. "There!"

He pointed to a rock shelf about halfway down, where Bravo's fur melded with the light and shadows of the ledge. One paw scratched weakly at the dirt.

Paige swung her legs over the edge of the rock wall.

"Whoa, wait a minute!" He clamped a hand on her shoulder. "What are you doing?"

She brushed his hand away. "I'm going after my dog."

"You're nuts. That's a near vertical climb. Those rocks are loose. You'll start a slide."

"I have to get to Bravo." She slid her rump toward the edge.

His jaw tightened and he grabbed her arm. "You don't know what you're doing."

"I'm going down. That's all I need to know."

"What are you going to do when you get there? He weighs nearly as much as you do. You can't lift him."

Bravo's whine deepened to a low, forlorn howl.

"I can't just leave him."

Marco didn't know which was worse, listening to the dog's lonely dirge or looking into the agony of her eyes. Either way, his fate was sealed.

"I'll get him," he said, slinging his legs over the side of the cliff.

Her mouth fell open. "Y-you're nuts. That's a near vertical climb a-and those rocks are loose," she protested, repeating his own argument suspiciously.

"Like you said, you can't just leave him. And I can't just leave you."

Without waiting for her reaction, he lowered himself a few inches down the rock face. She grabbed his arm. "Are you sure you know what you're doing?"

He grinned, suddenly more confident than he probably should have been, given the circumstances. "I'm going down. What's to know?"

She didn't smile at the replay of her nonsensical logic.

"I climbed all over these hills when I was a teenager. I can do this." Gently he pulled his arm from her grasp.

She scowled. "Be careful."

"Watch out," he whispered, "or I might think you're worried about me."

She angled her chin up in a defiant slant, but he wasn't buying it. Little as he deserved it, he had her concern. "I'm worried about my dog," she said.

"Then stop yapping and let me go get him."

Her frown deepened as she watched him slide over the edge.

The climb proved more treacherous than he'd expected.

Twice he lost his handhold. Each time, mingled with the skitter of pebbles down the slope and the tattoo of his heart, he heard Paige gasp. Funny how one little puff of air could give a man reason to keep going, but it did.

However unbelievable, she still cared what happened to him, after all he'd done. She worried—and not just about the dog.

Despite the chill in the air, by the time he reached Bravo, sweat stuck Marco's shirt to his back. With his feet stable on the rock shelf, he took a moment to rest, sucking in a cleansing breath. He'd made it.

"Is he all right?" Paige cried.

Quickly he checked the dog. His fear set aside for the moment—Bravo wasn't in any shape to hurt him—Marco skimmed his hands up and down the animal's sturdy legs, over his rib cage and around his muzzle. "I don't feel anything broken," he reported.

"What about blood? Is he bleeding from the nose or ears?"

Marco gently probed around Bravo's skull. "I don't think so."

The yelling roused the animal some. Bravo struggled to get to his feet, failed and settled for raising up on his front legs in a sitting position.

"He can't get up, though. Looks like one of his back legs is hurt. He's not going to be able to walk." As if it mattered. Unless the dog could walk straight up, he wasn't going anywhere. "Throw me your jacket."

He shed his own coat, already formulating his moment of inspiration into a workable plan. He knotted the two jackets together, rolled the dog onto them and strapped the whole bundle on his back, using the sleeves.

Bravo didn't take well to the sling. He wiggled and whined. Marco hoped the dog didn't have strength to put up a more substantial fight—the wet nose on the side of his neck meant the mutt's fangs were too close to his jugular for peace of mind.

"What are you doing?" Paige called.

"Just getting cozy," Marco responded, gritting his teeth and easing Bravo's muzzle away from his neck.

One look up at the vertical cliff above him was enough to convince him he wasn't going that way. Not with ninety pounds of squirming German shepherd strapped to his back.

"I'm going to have to take him down," he yelled to Paige. "Follow the edge of the plateau to the south. It levels out about a mile from here. I'll meet you there."

"Be careful," she called back, and made his day.

Suddenly he was Superman. He would carry a dog, move a mountain, jump the moon, if he had to, for her.

"How's he doing?" Marco poured two mugs of steaming coffee from the iron pot over the fire. Paige sat on the floor with Bravo stretched out beside her on a blanket, his big head in her lap. Behind her, a fire crackled, throwing light into the corners of the room left shadowy by the clouds that had moved in that morning. Marco rolled his stiff shoulder, trying to loosen the kinks. It had taken them until well past dawn to get back to the cabin, and Marco had carried the dog most of it.

"Better, I think," Paige answered.

"Do we need to get him to a vet?"

She looked up at him, one fine brow arched. "That would be a little risky for you, don't you think?"

"If we need to, we'll find a way."

She turned to her dog, nudged a knuckle behind his ear and stroked her hand down the length of his side. Bravo's skin twitched once, then he sighed, boneless under her touch.

Funny, boneless wasn't quite the reaction Paige's touch created in Marco's body. Still, he wouldn't mind giving it a try, except he doubted he could pry her away from her dog.

His hands tightened around the cups he held. Geez, he'd really lost it now. Jealous of a dog.

"No," she said. "You were right. Nothing's broken, and he doesn't seem to have any internal injuries. His stifle is probably just sprained. Torn tendons at worst. He'll be okay."

"Good."

Marco stood over her, watching as she raised her hand and stroked the dog again. Bravo's eyes rolled back as if he could die from the pleasure. Such simple creatures, dogs, Marco thought. Throw them a few scraps and scratch behind their ears and they'll give up their lives for you.

Kind of like him.

Paige turned somber eyes up at him. "Is it?"

"Is it what?"

"Good."

"Of course it is."

"Why?" she asked. "You don't even like Bravo, but you risked your life to save him."

While she petted Bravo with one hand, with the other she reached up for the mug Marco held out. She had changed her damp sweater for Marco's sweatshirt when they'd made it back to the cabin. The sleeves drooped over her hands.

He squatted beside her, set both mugs on the floor and cuffed the fleecy fabric back on her wrist, then handed her one of the coffees. She looked pensive, and he wondered which way her mind was turning now.

"Do you think I did it to manipulate you?" he asked, trying not to sound bitter. "So I could use you, like before?"

"Did you, Marco?" Her eyes were huge, the same color gold as the flames flickering behind her. "Use me before?"

His heart hammered. "What do you think?"

"I'm not sure."

Without breaking eye contact, he took her mug, set it on the stone hearth next to his and stretched out beside her. He needed the warmth of the fireplace as much as she did. He'd almost lost her last night. Not to any masked men, but to his own uncontrollable need for her. He'd driven her into the darkness.

Now he felt a need to bring her back into the light.

Bending over her, he grazed her lips with his, tasting, remembering, and conjuring the memory in her. Memory of a time when she'd trusted him. With her body, if not her heart.

He raised his head to look at her sad, beautiful face. Then slowly, giving her time to push him away, he lowered his mouth toward hers again.

"Maybe this will help you figure it out."

Chapter 10

When Marco's mouth first touched Paige's, he felt her shudder, but she didn't pull away. He kept his touch light, caressing her like a butterfly whose tender wings were easily crushed. Her lips slowly softened under his touch, warmed like kneaded clay, and he moved the kiss along her jaw, his tongue lapping at the sensitive zones as it passed, teasing, taunting. His touch dared her to respond to him, dared her not to.

At last she moaned against his neck. She rested her fingertips on his cheek. For a moment he wasn't sure if she was going to pull him closer or push him away. In the end, she did neither. She just touched, as if mapping his contours. His soul.

Without stopping to doubt or to question, he pressed her back to the blanket on the floor and rolled his upper body over her. His mouth found hers again, this time pressing hard against her, his tongue slipping into her when she gasped, sweeping through her, tasting her, possessing her, urging her to pull him deeper, possess him.

Sliding his hand beneath the hem of her sweatshirt, he reached for her breast. She arched into his touch, trembling and wriggling, pressing herself into his palm. He could have her if he wanted her, and he did want her. Painfully so.

But at what cost, to him and to her?

He had her surrender. But bending her to his will wasn't enough, wouldn't satisfy him. He wanted her to give herself to him freely, without coercion. He wanted her to want him as badly as he wanted her—not out of lust, but love.

The last thing he deserved was her love.

Even as her sharp nipple prodded his palm and her teeth tugged on his lower lip, he wrestled with his conscience.

Paige let out a frustrated mewl and slipped a slender leg between his. Her thigh pressed blessedly against his arousal.

He closed his eyes. He should never have started this. He should back away, run away, as far and as fast as he could. But he couldn't move. Couldn't think. He could only feel. Feel the friction of her calf against his, her peach-soft cheek skimming across the ridged column of his throat.

He was lost and he knew it. He had to touch her the way she was touching him. Just once.

He moved his hand down her stomach, across her navel. Inside the elastic band of her sweatpants he caressed her intimately, shaking with the effort of holding back. Going slow. He touched inside her folds. Felt her shake, too, and groaned.

He'd lost his mind. Didn't care.

He eased two fingers inside her, felt her try to hold them there as he withdrew, bringing her moisture back with him. She was slippery and hot, and she arched into his hand as he lifted her higher, watching her climb the slope of ecstasy. She squeezed her eyes shut, strained to touch him the way he was touching her, but he shifted out of her reach.

"Shh. This is just for you. Just for you."

Her head thrashed from side to side, but her body wriggled closer as he rotated his thumb over her and thrust deeper with his fingers.

Opening her eyes again, she locked her leg over his hips. Her mouth fell open and her eyes became glazed. This was the way he needed to see her. Not angry, not frowning, or crying in grief, but lost in the passion. Lost in him.

He leaned close to her ear. "You're almost there, aren't you?" he whispered.

Gulping, she nodded.

"Just let go."

She shook her head. A puff of air and a whimper brushed his jaw. "No. With you."

He kept up his slow stroking. "Not this time."

"But I want you."

"You can have me. Just not that way. Not now."

He curled his fingers and watched her face until he found just the right spot. "It's not like this with anyone else, is it?"

She shook her head again.

"It never will be." He pressed his thumb down hard over her. "Not for either of us," he added, but the words were lost in her cries.

She came off the floor, rising into him as if levitated by a master magician. Waves of contractions rippled through her, shaking her, shaking them both from head to heel. He wrapped his arms around her as if, should she break apart, he would absorb the jagged shards into himself.

Gradually the spasms faded. The high color drained from her cheeks until her skin glowed like polished ivory. Marco rolled to his back, pulling her on top of him.

Flattening her palm over the crazy thrum of his heart, she lay silent a moment. Her lips moved slightly as if she were mentally counting the beats, or listening to music only she could hear.

When she opened her eyes, he steeled himself for the questions he was bound to see there. Instead, her eyes were clear. Content. Almost awed.

"Listen for his answer not in his words," she whispered, "but in his heart."

"What?"

"Something Kia said." She turned lips still swollen from his kisses up to him. "My God. You didn't do it," she said. "You didn't do any of it."

He rolled away from her. "You're the one who found the drugs on me."

She turned with him, curling up by his side. "But you never said why you took them. And you haven't confessed to anything else. Not directly."

As casually as he could manage, as if every part of his being, spiritual and physical, wasn't about to explode, he got to his feet. "How much more evidence do you need?"

She sat, propped up on her hands behind her. "What just happened was evidence enough for me. A cold-blooded killer, even a thief, doesn't feel what you were just feeling. Doesn't make me feel that way."

"You're confusing lust with decency, darlin'."

"Then why did you stop?"

Not able to come up with an answer to that, and not trusting himself to stay in the room with her a second longer, Marco stalked out of the cabin onto the porch, where the chill air eased the fever inside him.

Getting intimate with Paige again was a mistake. Making love to her would be a big mistake. She'd already come too close to the truth. What was all that stuff about listening to his heart, anyway?

Whatever it was, it was dangerous. His plan—the plan that would keep them both safe—depended on Paige believing he was desperate. Believing she was his hostage.

He couldn't jeopardize that.

As he sat down on the steps to watch the sun set, the

irony of his situation didn't escape him. The woman he wanted more than life had just told him she wanted him, too.

And because she had, he couldn't touch her again.

Sometimes life just wasn't fair.

The clip-clop of hooves woke Paige the next morning. Opening one eye to the garishly golden light streaming in the window, she admonished herself silently and threw the covers back. She hadn't meant to sleep so late, but she guessed she'd needed the rest. Yesterday had been a draining day, both emotionally and physically. Today didn't promise to be much easier.

She and Marco needed to talk.

At least she did. Marco had never been big on talking. Everything he needed to tell her he could express better with his body, he'd said that magical night in her apartment. And he'd been right. He hadn't spoken much when he'd first come in, but once the lights went out, he'd discoursed volumes in the dark.

Today, though, he was going to have to express himself the conventional way. With words. Sentences. Explanations.

He couldn't deny what he felt any longer. Couldn't deny that this kidnapping of his wasn't exactly what it seemed.

She wouldn't let him deny it.

She'd ignored the little voice in her head that questioned Marco's guilt long enough. Maybe six months too long. Had she accepted him as a dirty cop because it was convenient for her? Because she assumed all men were out to use her and she was looking to prove herself right? She wasn't sure she could live with herself if her jaded view of men and relationships had somehow kept her from seeing the truth about Marco, but she was sure of one thing. She knew she couldn't live with herself if she didn't find out for sure.

With one arm raised to shield her eyes from the brightness, Paige stepped out onto the porch. Marco sat on the steps, watching the sunrise. More than watching. In profile, he seemed to be savoring the slow spread of morning the way a man lost in the desert would savor the last drop of water from his canteen.

As if he knew he would never see another.

The hoofbeats she'd heard picked up speed. Her eyes better adjusted to the light, Paige spotted Micah riding toward them, boy and pony flouncing pell-mell down the trail leading to the cabin. At the edge of the clearing, the boy slid to the ground and looped his reins over an oak limb. He smiled, white teeth stark against skin as flawless as the bottom of a bronze kettle, and dashed toward Marco. With a whoop, he threw himself the last three feet into Marco's open arms.

Marco squeezed the boy tight, rocking him side to side.

Paige felt like she had a walnut lodged in her throat. Out of nowhere the image of Marco hugging a son of his own appeared in her mind. He was so wonderful with Micah. He would make a terrific father. She wondered if he'd ever get a chance, now. Life as a fugitive didn't lend itself to raising a family.

Micah giggled. Marco tightened his grip, holding on until the little boy in his arms wriggled in earnest. "Uncle Marco, you're squashing me!"

Looking reluctant to end the embrace, Marco set the boy back and plucked at the child's nose. "That's 'cuz you're so squashable."

"Aw." Micah wrinkled his nose. "I'm not squashable." He stuck out his arm and flexed his tiny biceps. "Feel my muscles!"

Marco's hand circled the boy's whole arm, but he tested the muscle seriously. "You're right. No squashing there. What's your mother been feeding you?"

Micah tilted his head sideways. "Chicken mostly. With green beans and peas and stuff."

Marco laughed. The sound was so foreign to Paige, she realized she hadn't heard it often. "You sure she's not feeding you spinach?"

"No way! But on Saturdays sometimes we get macaroni and cheese."

"Mac and cheese is your secret, huh? I'll have to remember that next time I need to bulk up."

He pulled Micah into another hug. A moment of raw sentimentality flashed across his face. As if he sensed Marco's need, the little boy wrapped twiggy arms around Marco's neck and held on. The walnut in Paige's throat suddenly felt more like a grapefruit.

After a minute, the boy pulled his head out of the crook of Marco's neck and looked up. "Hey, Aunt Paige."

Marco turned. Stubble darkened his jaw and shadows haunted his eyes. "Aunt Paige? When did that happen?"

She crammed her hands into the pockets of her parka. She couldn't quite say when she'd become a part of the community here, but she couldn't deny that this primitive landscape felt like home, and its people felt like family. Pushing away the thought that her place here was no more than an illusion—an illusion that must end soon—and the rush of emotion that came with it, she cleared her throat, smiled at Micah and ignored Marco's question. "Hello, Micah. What are you doing here so early?"

"My dad sent me."

Was it her imagination, or did Marco stiffen at the boy's words? He shifted uncomfortably. Leaning to one side, he picked up the carving he'd been working on.

The boy's eyes widened until they nearly swallowed his face. "There *was* an airplane in that old branch!" He hopped up and down next to Marco.

"Yep," Marco said.

"I knew it. I knew it."

Marco sent the propeller spinning with a flick of his finger and handed the carving to Micah. "What do you think?" The hint of anxiety buried behind Marco's dark eyes as he waited for Micah's answer made Paige's heart clutch.

The boy's response was a roar as he held the airplane as high overhead as his arms would reach and then swooped it toward his feet. He ran off, dive-bombing imaginary enemies, then climbing and doing loop-the-loops.

There was nothing buried in Marco's smile but joy.

Halfway across the yard, Micah turned. "Oh, Uncle Marco, my dad said he hopes you'll come by soon, 'cuz there's some people coming 'round that are anxious to meet you."

Marco's smile froze a split second, just enough to be noticeable. Then the look of guarded indifference she'd come to know so well fell over his features again.

Micah zoomed off with his biplane, flying high all the way to his pony. As the animal trotted away in its rolling gait, Micah on its back, holding the reins in one hand and cruising the biplane alongside with the other, Paige laughed. "I think he likes his new toy."

Marco sank against the porch rail, his cool demeanor frozen in place. "Ah, he probably wanted a space shuttle or something."

Instead, he had carved the delicate double-winged model—so intricate, so unique.

"I think you could have carved him a wooden block and he would have loved it, just because it was from you."

Marco picked at an imaginary piece of lint on his jeans. "Little boys are like that. They get...attached."

"Hero worship."

He smiled wryly. "Some hero he picked."

Unable to think of a response that wouldn't start a fight, she let the comment go. "You must have stayed up all night working on it."

"Couldn't sleep."

"Me neither," she lied. She sat beside him. Their hips were almost touching, but an awkward silence created a vacuum between them. Even Bravo felt it. The dog's tail swished nervously against the plank flooring. She couldn't put her finger on it, but she sensed something had changed in Marco since yesterday. Something important. For a moment she wondered if he was feeling morning-after jitters. But then, she was the only one having a "morning after," so that couldn't be it. There had to be something bothering him, though. His emotional reaction to Micah, and the speed with which it had died, worried her. She opened her mouth to ask what was wrong, but Marco growled at her first.

"You should get some shoes on," he said, eyeing the bare toes she held curled up off the cold porch. "Your feet are going to freeze."

She wiggled her toes. "I'm fine. I think it's going to be warmer today."

His sigh made her smile. She could practically hear him mentally cursing her stubborn pride. He leaned toward her, grabbed her ankles and swung her legs into his lap. His lean, strong, warm fingers wrapped themselves around her little feet.

Then he started to massage. He moved his hands in a sad, slow rhythm, gradually easing the tension from her. Before long, her bones felt soft as clay and her blood thick as honey. Of the ways he had of doing that to her, this one was her favorite.

Almost her favorite, she amended when she thought back to yesterday in front of the fireplace.

Oblivious to her thoughts, Marco applied himself to his task. Was he purposely distracting her from serious conversation? If this was another escape-and-evade tactic...

It was working.

He kneaded her left ankle, singling out and melting each

small bone in the joint. One more minute and she could have fallen back to sleep.

Instead she tilted her head and took a deep, focusing breath. "I think we have a problem."

He chuckled. "Just one?" His heavy fingers slid along the sole of her right foot and bit deep into the instep.

She flexed the foot against him. The honey in her veins turned to liquid gold and spiraled toward her core. "This one is the root of all the others."

"So what is it?"

"I think we have…feelings for each other."

What had been a chuckle before now exploded into a humorless laugh. "Oh, yeah. Don't we just look like the perfect couple?"

She forced her lazy eyes to open and let her gaze pour over him. Reluctantly she bypassed the open jacket, the chest beneath that stretched the seams of his crumpled shirt, the narrow waist banded by a plain, black leather belt, and the muscular thighs. Finally her gaze landed on her own feet, which were still in his lap, and the big hands holding them securely. Possessively.

Yes, they looked exactly like the perfect couple.

His cheeks turned ruddy. He shoved her feet away. Her soles landed on the steps with a thud.

"I'm holding you prisoner, remember?" he said.

"Some job you're doing, letting me walk away the other night."

"I was right behind you."

"Watching over me, not stopping me."

"If that's what you think."

He lurched to his feet, shoving his fingers deep into his front pockets. The denim of his jeans only molded closer to his shape.

Regretfully, she drew her gaze up. She knew from the irony in his eyes that he'd caught her staring. He pulled his hands from his pockets and clomped off the porch.

"Where are you going?" she asked.

"To chop wood."

To chop wood. After everything that had happened between them, was still happening, he was going to go chop wood as if he hadn't a care in the world. *Not in this life.*

She wasn't letting him off that easily.

She hurried after him, her steps jerky partly because she was mad, and partly because the rocky path hurt her bare soles.

"You still want me," she announced to his back when she caught up.

He stopped, turned, crossed his arms over his chest and raked her with his gaze, but it was a cold evaluation. "What's not to want?"

For a moment, anger stole her power of speech. When he started to walk away, she moved around in front of him. He barely stopped in time to avoid bowling her over.

She found her voice in a rush. "Then why are you running away?"

He fixed a glare on her. She'd been wrong about his assessment being cold, she realized. There was heat there, fierce heat, but deep, deep inside him, like the fire at the heart of a volcano.

"Because," he said, his words snaking out like a lava trail, "maybe I want you too much."

Marco had a knee-high pile of split logs beside him before he realized he wasn't alone. Damn, why did she have to be such a stubborn woman? And why did he find it so appealing?

Figuring there were no answers to questions like that, he hefted the ax over his shoulder and pulled it down in the graceful arc he'd perfected through years of practice in this very spot.

"What do you mean, you want me too much?"

His perfect swing wobbled and he hit the log off center.

A splinter of wood ricocheted off his left thigh. The bulk of the log rolled onto his right foot.

Hopping in pain, he dropped the ax. "Ow, hellfire and damn—"

Paige's giggle cut off the rest of his expletive. He didn't need to make himself look like any more of a fool in front of her than he already had. Without so much as acknowledging her presence, he leaned over and assessed the damage to his leg.

He'd live, although he was lucky he hadn't lopped off a foot. "Don't you know better than to come up behind somebody when they're swinging an ax?"

"You knew I was there."

He didn't bother to deny that.

"Now what did you mean about wanting me too much?"

Buying time to figure out how to avoid this discussion, he balanced the fallen log back on the stump he'd been using as a chopping block and picked up the ax. The problem was, he still hadn't figured out a way to avoid the subject. "Nothing. Just forget I said anything, all right?"

"Oh, no. You're not getting out of it that easy."

Marco focused on the center ring of the log before him and cracked the blade down. Two perfect halves—minus the splinter that had separated on his first attempt—fell to either side. He added both to the woodpile behind him and placed another log on the stump.

"Marco!" Paige complained as he lifted the ax.

He applied all of his attention to that center ring. No distractions this time.

Just as he was about to drive the ax down, Paige propped her pale, slender foot, still bare, on the stump.

He nearly threw his back out jerking his swing to the side and burying the blade harmlessly into the red Oklahoma clay. "Jesus, Paige!" he exclaimed.

"Have I got your attention now?" she asked, smiling innocently.

He scowled at her, holding his breath until he could feel his pulse in his temples and knew his heart was still beating.

It was—quadruple time.

Paige studied him like he was a specimen under glass, a new species. "You're afraid."

"I damn near cut your foot off."

"Not of that. Of us."

"There is no us," he said, his voice booming despite his efforts to stay calm, detached. The only thing detached about him around Paige was his common sense. He shouldn't even bring up the old anger seething inside him. He should just let it drop, but he'd suppressed it too long. The memory of that morning in her kitchen welled up inside him. "That's the way you wanted it, remember? You're the one who said it was over."

Paige gave a start. "Is that what this is all about? Your bruised ego?"

"No," he said too quickly, and cursed himself for it.

"Then what is it?" She waited for a response he couldn't give her.

When he lifted his ax again, she kicked the woodpile, clucking in disgust. This time she was the one hopping around yelling, "Owww." She clamped her fingers over her bare toes. "Dammit, Marco. For once why can't you just tell me how you feel?"

"Because I don't like how I feel. I don't want to feel this way."

He took a step back, but she materialized in front of him again, as if by magic, before he could escape. She snagged his wrist in the circle of her fingers. His pulse leaped under her touch. He could have broken her grip. He had the strength. He just didn't have the will.

"I was afraid, too," she said, nearly whispering. "That's why I told you not to call. The power of this thing between us terrified me."

She ducked her head. "It still does."

Slowly he straightened. Her words weighed on him like stone collar. She'd been afraid of him? *Paige?*

"Why?" he asked, though he wasn't sure he wanted to know.

"I was afraid of what it would cost me. I was afraid there would be so much *you* in my life that there wouldn't be any more *me.*"

He shook his head. "I don't understand."

"I've worked hard to take control of my life, Marco. I was afraid you'd take that away from me."

Which was exactly what he had done, he realized. Taken away her choice. He hadn't asked her opinion about anything that had happened. He'd made his decisions alone, and she'd been forced to live with them. He hadn't given her even a modicum of control over her own destiny.

"I wouldn't have taken anything you didn't want to give," he said, hoping it was true.

"That's the problem," she said. "I would have given you anything. Everything."

As she had last night. She didn't have to say it aloud; they were both thinking it.

A breeze chilled the sweat on the back of his neck. "What do you want me to say?" he asked.

Her eyes pleaded with him. "Say that you feel this connection between us, too. That it means something, whether we want it to or not."

Nothing would have made him happier than to be able to stand there and tell her she was wrong. But he couldn't, because she was right.

"I feel it." His throat closed around the words.

An indefinable look of wonderment and sadness and...oh, God, he couldn't think it...*love* swept across her fine features. "Then why are you fighting it?" she asked.

"Because it's impossible."

"Nothing is impossible." When he didn't respond, she

shook her head slowly, as if caught in a dream. "I never took you for a quitter, Marco."

She was right about that, too. It wasn't like him to give up without a fight. Yet the morning after they'd made love he'd let her push him away without a word. Without a fight.

Maybe she hadn't been the only one afraid of what had happened—what might have happened—between them.

Why else would he let himself be railroaded into an eight-by-four-foot cell the next morning with hardly a whimper? He would have stayed there, too, if they'd left him alone. But caging him like an animal hadn't been enough for them.

They wanted him dead.

Paige was better off—safer—without him. Once she forgot about him, she'd probably marry an accountant and have half a dozen beautiful, brainy kids.

The thought made him growl.

It took a supreme force of will, but he picked up his anger, his indignation and his shame and held them before him like sword and shield. "There's a difference between quitting and knowing when you're beat," he said.

"What does that mean?"

"It means you win." He freed his wrist from her grasp with more violence than was necessary. Then he straightened his shoulders and raised his face to the sun, knowing it might be a long time before he saw it again. If he ever saw it again.

"It's time to give you back control of your life," he finished flatly, dying a little inside already. "Time to let you go."

Chapter 11

Stunned, Paige hesitated a moment before following the crunch of Marco's footsteps back toward the cabin. A few gray clouds had formed in the sky. The air smelled like rain. She hoped it held off until the other storm—the one between her and Marco—had passed.

At the edge of the clearing, she drew up short, sucking in a breath. A flash of something reddish-brown that didn't belong appeared briefly at the tree line, then was gone. Marco appeared suddenly at her side and wrapped his arm around her elbow. He must have seen it, too, because he urged her silently back into the woods.

"What is it?" she whispered, eyes wide.

"Shh."

Motioning for her to stay put, Marco darted through the trees in a crouch. Ignoring his warning, Paige followed. A moment later, the flash of color that had drawn their attention stepped into the open.

No assassin. No masked men with guns.

Micah's pony happily chewed a clump of weeds just beyond the trees.

"Micah?" Marco called, frowning. When no one answered, he called a little louder, a little more urgently. "Where are you?"

Paige moved close beside him. When her hand touched his arm, she felt fear-hard muscles. "What's going on?"

"I don't know," he answered. "Looks like his pony came back alone."

The blood drained from Paige's face. Oh Lord, if Micah had been hurt...

"Get your shoes," Marco said, each word sounding like it had been expelled by force. "We've got to find him."

For the next half hour, Bravo hobbled along bravely in front of Marco while Paige rolled slowly along behind them in the four-wheeler. The dog's nose moved from hoofprint to hoofprint, backtracking the pony's path to the cabin. At a slight dip in the terrain, he stumbled, but picked himself up and moved on to the next sign.

Marco glanced back at Paige, his eyes pained. "Are you sure he can do this?"

Pushing away the ache she felt at seeing Bravo, her partner and her friend, in pain, she tried to evaluate the dog's gait objectively. He was putting weight on his bad leg. Taking full strides, moving quickly, intently, even as he limped. It was as if the shepherd knew a boy's life depended on him. "He's okay," she assured Marco.

Stopping as Bravo took a sudden tack to the west, Marco cursed the pony. Paige couldn't blame him for the display of temper. Micah's mount hadn't taken a straight course back to the cabin. His path zigged and zagged from half-eaten bushes with a few scraggly leaves hanging on them, to a patch of winter-deadened grass, to a sprig of hardy weeds.

"Damn glutton," Marco said, fingering the chewed limb

of a sapling as he waited for Bravo to find the scent again. "How are we supposed to follow a trail like this?"

"Bravo will find him." She pumped all the confidence she could muster into her voice.

Marco watched the dog limp ahead another stride. A muscle ticked in Marco's jaw, a visible sign of how close to the edge of control he was. She touched his arm, felt the rock hard muscle bunched beneath his sleeve. "We'll find him," she said again, squeezing gently.

He nodded, his breath evening out. "Damn straight we will."

Bravo circled the edge of the rocky patch. Paige couldn't see any signs that the pony had passed here, but Bravo's senses were much keener than any human's. She trusted his nose.

A minute later, Marco dropped to his knees, tracing a hoofprint with his fingertips. "Over here."

Paige climbed off the ATV and knelt next to him. She pointed to the U-shaped indentations in a stretch of clay between the rocks. The spacing was just about right for the stride of a fourteen-hand pony. "It can't be much farther," she said. Her heart pounded as she scanned the area.

"Micah?" Marco yelled, but no one answered.

"Micah?" she called in turn.

Before the echo had faded, they heard a whimper. Then a sniffle. Then they were on their feet and running.

Rounding an outcropping of rocks, Paige saw him first. Her heart ballooned at the sight of the little mass of misery huddled against a boulder, his arms folded across his middle and his knees drawn up, shoulders rounded and head bowed.

Marco zipped past her and fell to his knees beside the boy. "Are you all right? Micah?"

Micah raised his little head. Tears weighted down his lashes and left wide tracks over his chubby cheeks.

Looking as if he was scared to death of what he might

find, Marco was already prodding and probing the child, examining arms and legs and fingers. "Are you hurt? Micah, say something. Talk to me, please!"

He had hold of the boy's left elbow, examining a scrape that looked no worse than anything a boy might suffer in a typical day's outing. But Micah's voice told of pain far greater.

"It's broke," he whined. "I broke it."

Marco paled. "Your arm?"

"No." The boy unfolded his hands. The model airplane lay crunched in his grip, the propeller sheared off and one wing hanging lopsided. "My plane you made for me. I broke it when I fell."

He scuffed a heel in the dirt and bit his quivering lip, fresh tears spilling out of his eyes. "Dumb old pony. Bucked me off and made me break it."

Marco sagged against the rock and pulled Micah to his chest, cradling him like fine glassware. "It's okay. I'll fix your plane. I'll fix it. I promise."

"Can you?" Micah asked.

"Sure I can."

Micah smiled unevenly and planted a teary kiss on Marco's jaw. "You can fix *anything*," he said, his voice filled with childish awe.

"You bet."

Tears sprang from Paige's eyes as Marco smoothed his cheek over the boy's hair and rocked him slowly, fiercely. This side of Marco was a sight to behold. So different from the powerful, seductive side of him that had frightened her six months ago. Frightened her still.

This was the side that wanted to make love to her to give her pleasure to make up for the pain he'd caused. The side that blew on her scrapes to keep the antiseptic from stinging. The side that stayed up all night to carve airplanes for little boys.

This was the side that made her feel safe, when safe was the last thing she should feel.

And that was dangerous.

Bravo padded up to Marco. Marco looked up, for once not flinching as the dog came near. Bravo sat and thumped his tail on the ground.

Tentatively Marco reached out and stroked his hand over the crown of Bravo's head. Then a smile kicked up one corner of his mouth and he rubbed the dog's ears a little more roughly.

"Thanks, Bravo," he said, his voice raspy. "Thanks a lot."

It was a tight fit for all three of them on the four-wheeler, and they had to go slowly, both because Marco was afraid of jostling Micah and so that Bravo could keep up. Paige's stomach was rumbling as they rolled down the last hill toward the Caddo settlement. It was almost lunchtime.

They stopped in front of the doctor's office and Doc himself stepped out, wiping his hands on a blue towel. Marco swung himself off the four-wheeler and reached for Micah.

"Aw, I can walk, Uncle Marco."

"Yeah, but I want to carry you so I can tickle you."

He feathered his fingers across the boy's sides, and Micah exploded into a fit of giggles.

"Micah took a little fall," Marco said, looking up at the doctor, some of his humor fading. "He says he's okay, but I thought you'd better check him out."

"Yes, yes. Inside." The doctor held the clinic door wide.

Micah stared adoringly up at his "uncle" as Marco carried him inside. What was it people said about children and dogs being the best judges of character?

Micah's faith was unswerving. He had no doubts about Marco's dependability, his character. Even Bravo had accepted Marco as master far more quickly than he should have, given his training.

That left only her.

Her doubts. Her fears. Her insecurities.

Oh, she didn't believe he would hurt her now. She knew he wasn't a killer, despite what the newspaper had said. She wasn't even sure she believed he had stolen the drugs six months ago, despite the fact that she'd caught him with the marijuana herself.

There was more to his story. Something he was holding back. But when she tried to talk to him, to pry his secrets out of him, it was like trying to lift an apple from the bottom of a deep barrel. She could smell the fruit. Hear it rolling around in the dark. Skim the tips of her fingers over the smooth peel.

But he wouldn't let her close enough to grab on.

A pang that wasn't hunger darted through her middle. Whatever secrets Marco was keeping, he still didn't trust her enough to share them.

Marco realized he hadn't drawn a steady breath since the moment Micah's pony had stepped into the clearing riderless. As soon as Doc had pronounced the boy fit and popped a sucker in his mouth, Marco had ducked out back to collect himself. Leaning against the wall, he tilted his head back and tried to will away the shakiness that fear had deposited in his limbs. He was still working on it when he heard footsteps.

Toby.

His old friend clapped him on the back, his face serious. "Thank you."

"For what?"

"Finding my son. Bringing him here."

"It was my fault he was hurt."

"No. I sent him to you. And he's fine. On his way home with his mother fussing over him."

"This time," Marco said roughly.

"There won't be a next time."

''No, there won't.'' Marco kicked away from the wall and paced down the alley. ''I was on my way to see you, anyway. It's time, Toby. Time to do it.''

''No.''

''I can't put any of you in danger any longer.''

''Let us decide that.''

''Micah could have been killed today.''

Toby's stance hardened. ''It was just a fall. He's fallen before. He'll fall again. It's part of learning to ride.''

''What if it hadn't been a fall? What if it had been Kinsale or his buddies, grabbing him? Using him to get to me?''

''It wasn't.''

Marco stepped back and turned, shaking off the rage, the helplessness he'd felt when he thought Micah had fallen victim to the men who were after him. ''It's time,'' he said again, more firmly.

''I told you, I don't know if I can do it.''

''You have to do it. You're the only one I trust to do it right.''

Toby sighed, his head hung low, and Marco knew his friend wouldn't let him down.

''It's time to end this,'' he said quietly. ''But I want to make sure you and your people aren't implicated for aiding and abetting. Call the Feds. You have to be the one to turn me in.''

''Where are we going?'' Paige asked, gripping the door handle of the old pickup truck that had mysteriously appeared in front of Doc's clinic, keys inside, just before Marco had pronounced them ready to go. He said he'd borrowed it for Bravo's sake. The dog couldn't ride on the ATV, and Marco didn't want him to have to walk home on that bad leg.

But Paige knew her way around Caddo land well enough

by now to know this wasn't the way back to the cabin. And that made her nervous. She repeated her question.

"Into town," he answered.

"Why?"

He flicked a gaze to her side of the truck, then away. "I told you, I'm letting you go."

"You're just going to drop me off?"

"Something like that."

"And then what? You're going to run again?"

His silence told her all she needed to know.

"You can't run forever, Marco."

"You can when the alternative is the electric chair."

Too much blood drained from her head. She was dizzy. Nauseated. "Texas doesn't use the electric chair anymore."

He took one hand off the wheel and waved carelessly. "Lethal injection. Whatever."

"Marco, you're scaring me."

Both his hands were back on the wheel in a grip so tight that all ten fingertips blanched white. His lips were clamped so tightly together they'd turned gray.

"Now you're scared." He laughed harshly. "Not when you were shot or kidnapped—no, you were a trooper then. But now that I'm telling you it's over and you're safe, you're scared."

"I'm scared for you, you jerk." She rolled her head back, her face crumpling. "God, it's happening again."

"What's happening?"

She could've screamed, she was so frustrated. "Whatever happened last summer. Whatever I did that made you steal those drugs."

Marco slammed the truck into Park. Paige braced herself with a hand on the dashboard. By the time she looked up, Marco had already hurled himself around the hood of the truck and was opening her door. They'd reached the bridge that marked the end of the Caddo Nation.

And apparently, the end of the line.

"Out," he ordered.

"Here?"

"Yes, here."

They stood face-to-face on the iron trestle bridge, near the spot where he had kissed her so recently. It seemed like a lifetime ago. Bravo sat up in the driver's seat of the truck, nose pressed to the window, watching them.

Sixty feet below, white water swirled and stirred. The warmer days must have started the spring thaw. The river ran full and fast, frothing against boulders sprinkled in its path. The earth had a voice all its own here, and it was powerful. Paige drew from its strength for a few moments, then turned to Marco.

"What are we doing?"

"Nothing that you did—or did not do—caused this."

"Then what did?"

"I did," he said, pointing his finger at his own chest. "I had choices. For better or worse, I made them."

"You want me to believe this is all for five kilos of marijuana?"

"Believe what you want, but know this—I did what I did—all of it—for me. It wasn't about you."

"It certainly seems to have *become* about me."

"I'm the one who's responsible for everything that is happening."

"Exactly what *is* happening, Marco?"

He jerked his chin to the side. "I don't want you blaming yourself for this. It's crazy that you'd even think you could be at fault. Forget it, all right? Forget me."

"I can help you. We can fight—"

"No!" He grabbed her by the shoulders. "Whatever happens, you stay out of it. You were my hostage, nothing more."

"It didn't feel that way the other night."

He let her go, scrubbed the back of his neck with his

palm. "That was a mistake. I shouldn't have taken advantage of you like that."

Her voice rose an octave. "Taken advantage of me?"

"You'd been through a lot. You were worried about Bravo."

"I was perfectly aware of everything that was happening to me. *Everything.*" Her cheeks flushed. He shuffled uncomfortably, and she knew she wasn't the only one remembering her coming apart in his arms, pushing herself into his touch.

"Fine," he said tightly. "You handle that however you want. Put it in your report if that makes you happy. But no matter what happens to me from here on out—do you hear me?—*no matter what happens,* I don't want any help from you. Just leave me alone. Is that clear?"

The words knocked the breath from her. After the way he'd held her, caressed her, could he really toss her aside so casually?

Apparently he could.

"You couldn't be much clearer," she choked out. Her eyes stung and her chest began to shake. Refusing to succumb to the almost overwhelming urge to reach for him, to plead with him, she raised her head. "So I guess this is goodbye."

He shuffled his feet, his jaw set hard as the boulders that held fast against the raging current below.

Her lungs burned, unable to pull in another breath. She held out her hand. "Goodbye, then."

He stared at her hand as if it belonged to an alien.

"We may not get another chance alone," she explained, feeling foolish, but needing to touch him one more time, to feel his warmth, the life in him.

His face twisted—the first fissure in his iron self-control. From there, cracks splintered in every direction. The breath whooshed out of him as if he'd been kicked by a mule. "Aw, hell."

All pretense of restraint shattered as he pulled her into his arms and crushed her against him, swaying, squeezing too tightly, coursing his hands across her back too hard.

She stood stiffly in his embrace, alternating between wanting to sag against him and wanting to tear away with every heartbeat. She'd known before Marco came into her life that love could hurt. She just hadn't known how much.

Comparing what she'd felt when her previous relationship had ended three years ago with what she was feeling now was like comparing a paper cut to open-heart surgery. Open-heart surgery without anesthetic, she amended.

The shudder that passed through Marco's hard body said that he hurt, too, but she needed to hear the words. "Do you love me at all, Marco? Even a little bit?"

He ground his cheek against her crown. "I'm trying to show you how much."

She lifted her head from his shoulder so she could see his face. He looked tired. Worn. How had he described his father? Withered…

That was how Marco looked. Withered.

"By sacrificing yourself?"

"In the only way I know how."

Something broke loose inside her and was swept away on a current of pure, sweet emotion. She raised her arms jerkily, feeling as if she'd been encased in glass, which was now shattering. "No, don't do this. Whatever you're planning, don't do it."

She sagged against him, holding him as tightly as he was holding her, reveling in the solidity of his chest under her cheek, the breadth of his strong back under her hands. She felt her way up his back, fingering her way inside the fleecy lining of his jacket, seeking warmth.

She was cold. So cold.

And he was—

Cold, too. No heated skin seeping warmth through the cotton of his shirt. No smooth muscles rippling beneath her touch. She raised her head to look in his eyes, confused by what she felt. Before she could form a question, Marco pushed her roughly away. She followed his gaze to the far end of the bridge.

A black sedan nosed onto the end of the bridge.

"It's too late."

The sedan stopped. Both front doors opened.

"Who are they?" she asked.

He shoved her away from him. "Get in the pickup."

She plastered herself to his side. "No. What's going on?"

Two men got out of the car and paced slowly toward them, their hands close to their hips. Paige knew that position. It was one a man used when he wanted to be able to get to his gun in a hurry.

She twisted Marco's shirt in her fingers. "Cops?"

"Feds," he answered. "Get in the truck with Bravo and get your head down. Hold his down, too."

"No."

At her refusal, he spun her around in his arms, pinning her back to his chest as if using her as a human shield. Then he glanced over his shoulder to the Caddo end of the bridge again.

Paige's head whirled with the sudden turn of events. Marco wouldn't use her like this. He was protecting her—wasn't he?

The men in suits pulled their guns and ducked behind the doors of their car. "Give it up, Angelosi," one of them yelled. "You got nowhere to run."

She turned her head in time to see Marco's gaze flick to the Caddo end of the bridge again. A man in a khaki shirt, jeans and a cowboy hat stepped out of a crack in the rocks and stood with his feet braced, a rifle leveled at them. "Tribal Police, Angelosi. Let the woman go and get on the ground!"

''Marco, please,'' she begged. ''Give up before someone gets hurt. I'll stay in front of you. They won't shoot.''

He took another step toward the bridge rail, pulling her along. She could feel his heart thundering against her back. He checked both ends of the bridge once, twice.

One of his hands let go of her. She puffed out half a breath in relief, then cut it short. He was reaching behind him. The pistol. No. Marco wouldn't shoot at cops. He wouldn't.

But they didn't know that.

She twisted, pulling with all her might to break his grasp, and reaching for his gun hand.

It was too late. He shoved hard, sending her tumbling to the ground. As she fell, each moment ticked off a more horrifying sight.

Bravo howling, clawing at the window of the truck as if he could dig his way out.

Marco stumbling backward as he released her. Pulling the pistol from his waist. Swinging it toward the cop on the rocks.

A shot from the rifle, its echo roaring down the river canyon like an avalanche. Marco jerking backward from the impact of a bullet. Firing a return round, gone wild, as he stumbled. More shots, from the Feds' end of the bridge this time, and Marco flung backward twice more. Harder.

Toward the rail of the bridge, and over.

Falling. Twisting, tumbling and disappearing into the white waves of the thrashing river.

Paige's thoughts tumbled and crashed in her head like the current below. Horror at what she'd seen beat against denial of the truth. The bits of truth she'd learned about Marco over the last few days—about his father, Micah and the Caddo people, the fact that he still wanted her, always had—swirled with her unanswered questions, dragging her under, drowning her in a raging current of loss, of grief.

She still had so much to learn about him. She couldn't let him go yet.

Her palms and knees raw and bleeding where she'd scraped them as she fell, Paige crawled to the edge of the trestle, desperate for a sight of him. Frantically she searched the teeming river.

Downstream she caught a glimpse of a jean-clad leg. A sleeve, and his hand, tossed limply with the current, not swimming, not clinging to passing rocks.

A moment later, there was nothing left to see at all.

Chapter 12

"**W**hat was your relationship with Marco Angelosi before you were abducted?"

Numbly Paige's mind registered people moving around her in the police station, the countless cups of steaming coffee thrust into her hands, the sunlight slanting across her back through the window behind her. But her body heard nothing, saw nothing, felt nothing. Nothing except the pressure growing inside her like steam in a teakettle.

The recording, checking, correcting and rechecking of her statement was a torture to be endured. The endless questions of the FBI agents an exercise in restraint. Hers was wearing thin.

"None of your business." She rubbed her temples. "Are you charging me or not, Agents?"

"And after?"

"I was trying to bring him in."

Perkins, the older of the two agents, gray-haired and wearing a charcoal-striped dress shirt that looked like it had never seen the underside of an iron, snickered. "Is that what you call what you were doing on the bridge when we arrived? Trying to bring him in?"

"Yes."

The other agent, younger, owlish-looking in his round eyeglasses with black rims, slid his hip off the corner of the table where he'd been leaning. His leather soles squeaked on the tile floor. "Must be some new restraint technique they teach down in Texas, Perk," he said. "The lip-lock hold."

"Are you charging me or not?"

"Let's see…we've got aiding and abetting a fugitive and obstruction of justice so far. And if we link you to the prison van wreck that set him loose—" Perkins planted both fists on the opposite side of the table and leaned across until they were face-to-face. "That would make you an accomplice to murder, wouldn't it?"

The need to get out of the stuffy interview room pulsed inside Paige like a living creature. She needed fresh air. Breathing room. Space to think about whether or not she was making the biggest mistake of her life.

She drew a shaky breath. It was too late. She'd already made her statement. She had to stick to it.

"You've got nothing to link me to the escape," she said flatly, scraping her chair back and heading for the door.

Agent Perkins stopped her with a hold on her upper arm as she passed by. "Yet."

The younger agent leered at her. "Don't try to out-cop us, lady. We're FBI."

"Can I go or not?"

Perkins made a production of letting go of her arm. "Just don't be going far."

"I'll be in the first motel I can find on the highway later tonight, then at my home in Port Kingston tomorrow evening." She stopped in the doorway, presenting them her back. "I'm sure you'll be able to find me. After all, you're *FBI*."

On her way out, her sneakers slapped a rapid rhythm against the worn gray linoleum of the police department. If running wouldn't have stripped away the very last of her dignity, she'd have made a mad dash for the front door.

Five more steps and she'd be able to breathe again. Four. Three. She bumped her knee on an end table, sending a stack of dog-eared magazines flopping to the floor. She grabbed for the swaying lamp, and saved it from toppling as well. Murmuring an apology to no one in particular, she hurried on.

"Ma'am?" someone called from behind her. "Ms.—Officer Burkett?"

Casting a longing look at the sun setting over the street outside, she turned. A desk clerk held up a phone receiver. "Call for you."

Hope surged in Paige, making her fingers and toes tingle with the first sign of life she'd felt in hours. The sensation faded just as quickly.

She'd seen Marco shot twice, knocked from a bridge and swept away in a rushing river current. He certainly wasn't calling her at the police station.

The young clerk smiled. "Been trying to get through for hours. Says he's your brother."

She grabbed the phone. "Matt?"

"You okay?" The mixture of relief, love and worry in her older brother's voice dredged up a little life inside her.

"I'm fine." She wasn't, but she wouldn't tell him that. Matt had enough problems of his own.

"You don't sound okay."

She heard a blurred voice, like a loudspeaker, in the background and decided to try one of Marco's techniques and change the topic. "Where are you?"

"The airport. I've been trying to get a flight out all afternoon, but there's a snowstorm up in the Midwest and over the Rockies. It's got the airlines all backed up here."

"You—you're coming here?"

"Of course I'm coming there. The family's been worried sick." She was pretty sure it wasn't frustration, but a much deeper emotion that made him have to stop and clear his throat before he continued. Paige's family was small, just her brother and her grandfather since her parents had died when she was a girl, but their love was as big as any extended clan. "I'm coming to get you."

"Thanks, but that's not necessary."

"I'm already on my way. As soon as I can get a flight."

"I've already booked a flight home for myself, tomorrow, and I think the time alone will do me good, you know? Give me a chance to clear my head."

"Great," he said with dangerous levity. "You clear your head. I'll sit beside you and watch."

"Matt—"

"I'm not arguing about this, Paige. I'll be there in a few hours. Tomorrow morning at the latest."

She knew that mule-headed tone in her brother's voice. She played her final card. One she hated to use, knowing it would hurt him. But also knowing it was the only card that would win the hand.

"Matt, I know you've been through some tough times lately, and there were days when the family crowded you, when all you wanted was to be left alone, right?"

"Paige—"

"Like when everyone was milling around your house, and all the guys from the department and their wives kept bringing food, and you tried so hard to be a good host, but you ended up putting your hand through that plate-glass window?"

"Paige—"

"And I let you borrow my car—even though you bled all over it—and drive yourself to the emergency room for stitches, because you said you needed the time alone, right?"

She heard his resigned sigh on the other end of the phone. "Right."

"And I stood up for you with the family and smoothed it over with Grandpa when everyone thought someone should go with you, right?"

His sigh was louder, more unhappy, this time. "Right."

"Well, I'm the one who needs the time alone right now. I know you love me and want to protect me, but you, more than anyone else, have to understand how I feel."

A long silence spanned the distance between them. "That's playing damned dirty, Paige," Matt finally said.

She closed her eyes, hearing in his voice his wounds reopening. He'd been through so much, her brother, with the loss of his son to leukemia and his wife leaving him. "I'm sorry," she said, and she meant it.

"You're coming straight home tomorrow?"

"Straight home. As soon as I can check Bravo out of the vet clinic where they're boarding him."

"You'll call when you get here?"

"The second I land."

"I'm going to have a heck of a time explaining this to Grandpa."

"You'll do fine."

"If you're late, I'm sending out the National Guard."

She smiled into the phone. "I'll be on time."

And she would. She hung up the phone. Tomorrow she'd be home. But that still left her the night. One night to find the truth. And hopefully to find herself in the process, since she seemed to have lost herself somewhere on this journey.

The person she used to be never would have taken this chance. Put her career, her freedom on the line. She wouldn't have withheld information—even this tiny scrap of information, no matter how irrelevant it might prove to be—from the FBI. Paige hardly recognized this shell of a human she'd become, driving a hastily rented car along winding country roads like a woman possessed, clinging to an improbable—nearly impossible—hope without knowing where she was going, how to prove or disprove her belief.

She knew only that she had to try.

Halfway across the bridge to the Caddo Nation, she pulled her car to one side and shut off the engine. For a long while she stood at the bridge rail, listening to the tumbling current and watching the play of white water beneath her.

The water reflected so much light that the night looked almost like day. Paige sat on the bridge, huddled against a trestle for a windbreak, waiting. One by one the lights of the Caddo houses across the plain winked out. And still she waited.

Cold settled in with the weary ache that had already invaded her bones. Numbness deadened her fingers and toes. And still she waited.

An hour passed, then another and another. Snowflakes began to fall. Ice crystals mingled with tears, weighing down her lashes.

And still she waited.

When the settlement was nearly dark even though the night was bright, she pulled her stiff body to her feet, got in her car and drove toward the one remaining light—a tiny glow coming from a narrow back window on the main street.

The doctor's office.

The lock on the door to the clapboard clinic jimmied easily enough. As she crept inside, a floorboard squeaked beneath her foot. She stopped, her heart pounding, and listened, but heard nothing other than her own rapid breath.

Gathering her courage, she stepped forward again, easing each foot down more gently this time. At the end of the hallway ahead, a sliver of light shone through a door ajar.

Focused only on the light, she passed the darkened doorways of the examining rooms without care. From one of them an iron forearm lashed across her neck as she passed. Another heavy arm clamped across her chest.

Her heart slammed against the restraint once, then a joy as intense as any she'd ever felt filled her. She twisted in her captor's grasp. Faced her former lover.

"Marco," she whispered, breathless from shock and more as she traced the line of his clean-shaven jaw with her fingers.

His chest was naked, damp, as was his hair. She must have caught him just out of the shower. His jeans were unsnapped and riding low on his lean hips, as if he'd thrown them on hurriedly. His feet were bare.

She let her hand fall to a drop of water caught in the mat of curls on his chest and traced her finger downward, watching the moisture disappear behind her touch, as if seared away by the heat she felt rising inside him, heat that threatened to incinerate them both.

"Marco," she repeated, finding no more breath than she'd found before.

"Jesus, Paige." He groaned. "Can't you even let me die in peace?"

Marco closed his eyes as her hand skimmed leisurely over his skin. He didn't have to see to know that her fingers were trailing softly down his sternum and across his rib cage. A thousand tiny nerves sparked beneath his skin in the wake of her touch. He swallowed hard, steeling himself against the sensations building inside him. Against life.

He didn't want to feel her touch. Didn't want to feel anything. He was a dead man, but every time she laid her hands on him, his cold corpse warmed another degree. And another.

Her fingertips moved to the side, stopping directly over ribs bruised by three bullets. "You're not dead, Marco."

"You felt the Kevlar under my shirt. On the bridge, when you hugged me."

"Yes."

"Then you knew all along."

"No. It happened so fast. I—I didn't realize it was a bulletproof vest until later. Even then I wasn't sure. Even when I saw the Tribal Police officer up close, I still—"

"Toby? What—?"

"His eyes. They're blue." A smile flitted across her lips and then was gone. "Just like his mother's. And his son's."

Marco swallowed hard. "Micah."

She nodded. Her words started to spill out in a wild rush. "I figured out that he was the boy you saved from the burning truck and the friend who built the cabin with you. He wouldn't have shot—not for real, but I still wasn't sure you were alive. The FBI agents fired, too, and even if the bullets didn't kill you, it was such a long fall, and the water was so cold and fast—"

She choked and her hands gripped his shoulders as if he was slipping away again and she could stop it, if she could just hold on tight enough.

"Shh, shh." He pried her hands away, holding her wrists.

She looked up at him, her eyes huge and limpid in the moonlight. He realized she was shaking. Shaking and cold and breathing too fast. Too shallow.

"Oh, God, Marco. I was so scared."

Scared for him? After all he'd done? She should have been cursing his damned soul. Instead she'd been scared. Was still scared, if the frantic pulse pounding beneath the grip he had on her wrist was any measure.

With a groan, he pulled her against him. "Shh."

Brushing his hands up and down her back to calm her, he bent his head next to her ear and opened his mouth to soothe her with words, to reassure her. But before he could, she turned her head and covered his lips with hers.

It was she who did the soothing, the reassuring, the restoring. She breathed life into his empty lungs, dredged a pulse from his still heart. With a nip and a caress and one bold thrust of her tongue, she made him face the future he'd turned his back on. The possibilities.

She made him remember the man Marco Angelosi once wanted to be. Still wanted to be, against all the odds.

"What do you want from me?" he whispered against her throat.

"Make love to me, Marco." Her words were low and sincere. Warm against his temple. "Please."

Dead or alive, he couldn't turn his back on that. He ran his hands down the length of her back to her buttocks and scooped her against him, letting her feel his length, his desire.

Breathing hard, she arched her head back, exposing the milky column of her throat. He bit her there, pulling the skin between his teeth and sucking. Marking her. Branding her as his own. He'd been a fool to think he could ever let her go. She was his, just as surely as he was hers.

He lifted her and she locked her legs around his waist. Carrying her, he staggered forward, looking for somewhere...anywhere. She ground herself against him, and nerves he thought long dormant exploded to life, their rebirth almost painfully pleasurable. The onslaught of sensation was so intense it was dizzying.

He staggered, peddled backward to regain his balance, bumped into an examination table and turned, grateful. The table's paper covering crinkled as he set her on it. She kissed him, breaking away only to let him slide the sweatshirt over her head and toss it to the floor. A moment later her bra joined the puddle of fleece at his feet.

He stepped between her thighs, and she looped her arms around his neck, rejoining her lips to his. When he reached out to hold her breasts, his hands trembled like those of a raw teenager. He could hardly contain the need expanding inside him. Her nipples puckered instantly at his touch, and he had to have them—*had to have them*—in his mouth.

With her arms still draped around his neck, he placed his palms flat on either side of her and walked them back, one hand at a time. She hung from his neck, letting him lower her slowly until she lay across the table beneath him, her legs dangling off the end.

Then he straightened. As if sensing what he wanted, what he needed, she let go of his neck and let him look.

At last he could see her, all of her. The snow-reflected light filtering in through the windows made her skin glow like a new moon, highlighted the tiny blue veins just below the surface, like polished marble. He let his eyes travel over her, mapping each rise and cranny he intended to traverse, absorbing her perfection.

Just looking at her was humbling. Funny, she was the one exposed, but he felt vulnerable. He was beaten, battered and bruised. Scarred inside and out.

And she was flawless.

He'd given her everything, including his life. At least his life as Marco Angelosi. But it wasn't enough.

It would never be enough.

She wanted his soul, too.

And he was ready to give it to her.

Slowly he bent over her and touched her with his mouth. He laved the under slope of her breast with the broad surface of his tongue, then flicked just the tip over her nipple.

Each texture was like a new landscape. He explored the rugged and the smooth with his lips and teeth, like a traveler explores new vistas, marveling at each new discovery, recording in his mind every detail, in case he should never return.

She moaned in response and then her hands traced the length of him through the denim of his jeans, igniting him in the process. He turned his cheek against her and rubbed. Her chest was wet from him, warm and slick, just like he knew she would be inside. He touched her intimately, through her jeans, and knew he was right.

She pushed against his hand, and the heat of her sent his arousal up another level. His chest heaved as if the air in the room had suddenly grown thin. Prickly fingers of perspiration peppered the back of his neck.

His hands fumbled with hers as she reached for his zipper at the same time he reached for the snap of her pants. She let him win, and he shucked her jeans off, tossing them on the floor with the rest of her clothes.

She tugged his open jeans down his hips, freeing him, then lay back. "Come inside me. Now."

He thought his knees would buckle before he could get there. The roughness of his entry testified to the intensity of his desire. Almost mindlessly he pushed her thighs wider apart, planted his feet on the floor, lifted her buttocks and drove himself home.

For a moment the night seemed to stand still. Only their harsh breaths, gasping, broke the quiet. Marco closed his eyes, struggling for control.

"I'm sorry," he said. He'd heard her stunned cry. He'd taken her too suddenly. Too hard.

"It's okay."

"No."

She reached a hand out to stroke his hip. Grimacing, he squeezed his eyes tighter. She was going to kill him yet.

He was too close to the edge. He'd almost lost himself on that first hard thrust, before she'd even fully accepted him, before he'd had a chance to give her anything but pain.

But she felt so good, and it had been so long for him.

Her hand paused in its petting. "Are you going to just stand there all night?"

The question wrung a desperate laugh out of him. "Give me a second, okay?"

"Is something wrong?"

"No. It's just been awhile."

She gave him a second, but no more. "It's been awhile for me, too. And I'm tired of waiting on you."

He had a feeling she was talking about more than sex, but his brain wasn't getting nearly enough blood to puzzle out her meaning at the moment.

Paige lifted herself closer to him. Reflexively he arched, pushing deeper inside her.

He opened his eyes. She smiled—both a victory cry and a challenge. How could he not love a woman with spirit like that?

Rallying himself, he straightened his back, rising and pulling his upper body away from her. Their lower bodies still joined, she grabbed at his shoulders, following him up, but he caught her hands, flashing her a smile of his own, one that he hoped communicated everything he felt. Everything he had planned.

Slowly he pushed her shoulders back, locking his knees to brace himself against her weight. Catching on, she locked her own legs around him and arched her back, lifting herself from the table until nearly all of her weight was supported on his hips.

He pulled her up a few inches, his arms cording with the effort, and lowered her again, thrusting his pelvis forward in time with her fall. Her head tipped back and her mouth opened. The angle and her weight deepened his penetration. He'd never been so much a part of her.

He did it again and this time she helped, arching and clamping her legs tighter. He felt himself being pulled up a long rise as he lifted her, let her fall, lifted her again, faster.

The air grew thin. His blood rushed hot and thick in his veins. His heartbeat pounded in his ears. He might be dead, but he'd never felt more alive. She'd done this. Resurrected him.

And now they were both about to die the sweetest death.

Paige cried out, and this time when he lifted her close

she wouldn't let go, clutching at his shoulders and burying her face in his neck. Her body rippled and flexed, liquid in his arms, then tightened, every muscle clenched in a spasm that shook her to the core. Shook him.

He held her until the spasms passed, then lowered her back to the table. She gazed up at him weakly, dazedly, her pupils huge in the moonlight.

"Kiss me," he ordered, leaning close.

She stroked her lips across his, then thrust her tongue inside.

Marco found the strength for one more thrust, two before he reached the top of that rise he'd been climbing, only to find it wasn't a rise at all, no rounded slope to ease his trip back down. It was a cliff. Sheer and deep.

He tottered for a moment at the precipice, savoring the taste of her in his mouth, the feel of her heart beating against his, her moist heat clasping him in the last throes of her orgasm.

Then for the second time that day, he found himself falling.

Toppling end over end in free space. Land and sky and water spinning by too quickly to distinguish one from the other. Flailing. The bottom rushing up at him. Him roaring Paige's name.

At least this time, the landing didn't hurt so much.

He opened his eyes to find himself pillowed on top of her, her hands in his hair, his forehead on her breast.

With great effort, he lifted his head.

She smiled at him.

Groaning, he collapsed on her again.

The chuckle that rattled her chest shook him back to his senses, at least partway. He stood on rubbery legs, pulling her to her feet with him.

"Are you okay?" she asked, still brushing his hair with her fingers.

"Sure," he said against her temple. "Okay. Fine. Great."

Except that he had very nearly died today. Twice.

She stroked his back solemnly. "Then will you tell me the truth just one time?" she asked softly. "Tell me just one thing?"

"What?" He could almost feel the shutters battening down inside him. He didn't want to answer questions. But he didn't want to fight, either.

Damn her, it was her fault his defenses were down like this. Sex with her cut him deep. She made him vulnerable. Laid him open. That's partly what scared him about her—about them. When they were like this, all she had to do was look and she'd see everything inside him.

He just wasn't sure she'd like what she saw.

Mentally, he tried to place some distance between them—not an easy thing to do, since physically, they were still part of one another—while he waited for her question.

She pulled her lower lip between her teeth, then soothed it with her tongue before she spoke. "Please tell me I didn't just make love to a murderer."

Chapter 13

Marco's stomach did a barrel roll. He didn't want to answer Paige, but he had put that quaver in her voice, that chink in her confidence. It was up to him to fix it. He'd already taken too much from her tonight. He couldn't live with himself if he took her self-respect, too.

"I thought you'd already decided I wasn't a murderer," he said.

The fire their lovemaking had lit in her eyes flamed out. Damn, she must have thought he was evading the question again.

She was probably right. Some habits were hard to break.

She twisted away from him, breaking the physical connection as surely as he'd broken their bond of trust.

A moment ago he'd been soaring. Her wings had lifted him higher than he'd ever been, made him a better person than he'd ever dreamed of being. Now with one slip of the tongue, he was nothing but a callous jackass with his pants around his ankles and his foot in his mouth.

Quickly he pulled up his jeans and fastened the zipper.

Curse all the years he'd spent working undercover, anyway. He wished he'd never learned to skirt the truth so easily.

Paige slid off the table, stepping into her pants sans underwear and then reaching for her sweatshirt. Once she'd tugged it over her head, she reached under the examination table for one shoe. He held the other out to her and she snatched it from his hand. Before she could step away, he took her by the arms and brought her close. Probably too close, but what the hell, the damage was already done.

"You wouldn't have let me touch you if you thought I was responsible for that guard's death."

"I need to hear you say it."

The words stalled in his throat. He wanted to tell her—he'd wanted to tell her for a long time. But the truth would change everything between them, and not necessarily for the better. If he hadn't just made love to her, if she hadn't given herself to him with an openness and an honesty that made his heart ache, he might have been able to come up with some evasion, contrive some half-truth to sustain his deception. Only he had made love to her, for better or worse. She'd held nothing back, hidden nothing. She deserved no less from him.

"I didn't kill anyone," he finally admitted.

He thought she'd be pleased. For a moment she was still, silent. When she moved, he thought maybe she was going to hug him. He tried a tentative smile on her, but she wasn't having any of it. Her gaze hardened.

So did her fist when she jabbed it in his rib cage.

He doubled over. "Ow, Paige, my ribs…"

"Are they sore?"

"I got shot," he gasped. "Vest or no vest, you know that hurts."

"Good." She poked him again.

He backed up, holding his hand out to defend himself as she followed. "What is wrong with you?"

She stopped in front of him. Usually she'd have to tilt

her head back to look him in the eye, but now they stood nose-to-nose. His six-inch height advantage shrunk considerably with him hunched over, clutching his middle.

"What is wrong with *me?*" she asked, enunciating as if speaking to a slow learner. "What is wrong with *you,* letting someone shoot you? What if he hadn't hit the vest?"

"Toby doesn't miss. He's a marksman. Hell, he's the one who taught *me* to shoot."

"The FBI agents fired, too." She edged a fraction closer.

"Damn Feds." He grimaced, backing up. He hadn't counted on the FBI agents firing. Not after Toby hit him with the rifle. "Guess they never heard of the word *overkill.*"

"You jumped off a sixty-foot bridge."

"I knew it was survivable. I'd seen some of the Caddo boys do it when I was a kid."

"Into freezing cold water running like a class-five rapids?"

"Well…" No. The Caddo boys had jumped in the summer, but he wasn't about to admit it. Luckily for him, she was running out of steam. She looked worn out. A bud of pleasure sprung up inside him as he imagined it was the thought of what could have happened to him that sapped her strength.

"You are completely insane," she said, but the venom was gone from her voice.

"Yeah." He grinned tentatively.

"Are—are your ribs really hurt?"

"Just bruised."

She reached out and touched his head; he tried not to wince.

"What happened here?" Her fingertip danced lightly over the five stitches Doc had put in.

"There's rocks in that river," he said seriously.

She outlined a scrape across his shoulder. "And here?"

"It wasn't as deep as I might have liked where I landed."

"You could have been killed for real." She lifted her face to him, and her skin glowed like pearls in the moonlight. "You could have drowned."

"Nah. Toby had some friends downstream in boats, waiting to fish me out." He crossed his arms over his chest and rubbed the sole of one foot against the denim covering his other calf. The sweat from their lovemaking was beginning to chill, and the tile floor was cold. "Despite what you think, I don't have a death wish."

"Quite the contrary, I'd say. You've gone to a lot of trouble to avoid the death penalty. What I don't understand is why. Why not make your stand in court instead of on some damn bridge?"

She turned away from him. He reached out and tucked in the tags sticking up at the collar of her sweatshirt, hoping she couldn't feel his hand shake. This was it, he knew instinctively. Time for total disclosure. He'd gone too far to hold back now.

"Because my life wasn't the only one on the line," he said.

She whirled around. "What? Who else—?"

She plopped into the little wooden chair behind her, shaking her head as if admonishing herself for not seeing the truth sooner. "Me? You did all this for me?"

He couldn't speak, waiting for her reaction. Could hardly breathe. How had his whole life come down to this one moment? This one answer? A single syllable either way— yes or no.

He took a deep breath, feeling as if he was about to plunge off another bridge. And this time, there was no one waiting downstream to fish him out.

"Yes," he said.

"It goes all the way back to the warehouse, doesn't it?" she said in a rush.

She took a step toward him, but he stopped her at arm's length, holding her by the shoulders. He needed to get this out while he still could, and he couldn't do it with her in his arms. "It's a little more complicated than that."

"Someone threatened me to get to you. They forced you to steal the drugs."

He hated to crush the hope he'd heard in her voice. But she needed the truth now. The whole truth. "I took the marijuana of my own free will," he said, and waited for her gaze to come back to his. When it did he held it tight. "But the stuff I took didn't come from the warehouse, Paige."

"Then where?"

He doubted she even realized she was shaking her head.

"It came from your car."

Paige took the coffee Marco offered. They'd moved their discussion to the doctor's paneled office. It was easier to think amid the clutter of physician's references, insurance paperwork and Native American artwork than it was in the examination room, amidst the scents and the echoes of their lovemaking. Somewhere along the way Marco had found a plaid flannel shirt and some socks. His shoes were still drying, he'd said.

She sat at the doctor's desk, a pile of wood shavings in the garbage can next to her, and Micah's biplane, fully restored, on the blotter in front of her.

That explained how he'd spent his day. There was something surreal about a man who would fake his death, risk dying for real and then calmly whittle a child's toy. But he'd promised to fix it. She should have known by that alone that he wasn't dead.

Marco wouldn't go back on a promise.

He poured himself a cup of coffee, freshly brewed in the pot behind Doc's desk, turned a wooden chair around backward and straddled it, balancing his mug on the seat back.

"You think *I* tried to steal the drugs?" she asked. She wrapped both hands around her mug for warmth.

"No." He looked far too calm. How could he be so blasé about all this? Maybe because he'd had six months longer to deal with it than she had.

"But you found the marijuana in my car."

"A setup."

"You think someone wanted to get rid of me?"

"Actually—" he took a noisy slurp of coffee "—I think someone wanted to get rid of *me*."

"By planting drugs in *my* car? How exactly is that supposed to get rid of you?"

"By giving me exactly what I was looking for."

Her forehead wrinkled as she worked the puzzle with the few pieces she held. "And you were looking for a dirty cop, right?"

He sipped and nodded. "There had been too many of those no-account little busts. Some of the honchos thought maybe you and your dog were hitting on throwaways to placate the brass, then letting the big shipments go by." He sat back. "It wouldn't be the first time some druggie had paid off a cop—canine or otherwise—to look the other way."

"I would never—"

"I know. I had figured that out long before we…" He waved his hand in the air. "But I got a tip that morning that I could catch you in the act if I showed up at the Battan Industries warehouse. It was just too easy. Too pat. That's why I took the weed out of your car. I knew you were being set up because of me, my assignment."

The implications of what he was saying rippled out in ever-greater circles like the splash of a stone in a pond.

"And then I caught you with the marijuana," she said. "But why didn't tell anyone? Why didn't you defend yourself?"

"Because my only defense would have put the blame on you. And I couldn't do that."

Emotion welled up inside Paige at the conviction in his voice. No one had ever put so much on the line for her. Nor had anyone left her so little choice over the direction of her own life.

"You could have at least told me," she said.

He hesitated. Old pain flickered across his face. "After the way we'd left it just a few hours before, can you honestly say you would have listened to me?"

Her breath caught as if she'd been slapped. Slowly she recovered her composure, setting her coffee on the desk before her. "I'm a cop. I would have listened."

He expelled a heavy breath. "All right. I should have told you. But you caught me carrying the drugs before I had a chance, and then the whole world just went to hell."

"You could have told *someone*." She shook her head, realizing there had to be more than poor timing behind his silence. "You were angry. Your pride got in the way."

He stood, paced in front of the doctor's desk. "Hell yes, I was angry. I thought what we had was worth more than just one night. And yes, my pride was hurt. But I wasn't hurt or angry enough to let you take a fall because of me. Because of my job."

"I could have defended myself. I didn't do anything wrong, and we have a legal system that protects the innocent."

He stopped pacing, dragged his hand choppily through his short hair, and she knew there was more.

"I got a note. While I was in the lockup before the bail hearing."

"What kind of note?" She had a bad feeling she already knew.

He met her gaze steadily, and the dark intensity in his eyes made her stomach quiver.

"The kind that said you were dead if I didn't keep my mouth shut."

She gasped. He walked to her chair, slid one warm hand beneath the hair on the back of her neck and kneaded her knotted muscles.

"So I kept my mouth shut," he said. "But it wasn't enough. Oberas picked that fight with me for a reason, Paige. I'm sure of it. I'd never even spoken to him before that day. Someone paid him to start trouble just to get me on the van at that particular time. There's no other explanation. Then they wrecked the van to get me. They wanted to be sure I *never* talked."

"But you got away. They came after you, but I found you before they did in the woods that night, so they shot me. And you took me with you...to protect me?"

"They would have come after you."

"And still you didn't tell me."

"I didn't think you'd believe the truth, then," he said. "I'd done too good a job selling you on the lies."

"You faked your death so they wouldn't have any reason to come after me..."

"It was the only way I could think of to keep you safe."

"...like some kind of martyr." Incredulity ballooned inside her. "Saint Marco, patron saint of foolish cops and witless women."

His hand went still on her neck. "No."

She scraped her chair back from the table. "I've got news for you, *Santo Marco.* I don't need your kind of religion." Before she could get out of the office, he blocked the door.

"Believe me," he said darkly, planting his arm across the door frame and preventing her escape. "Religion was the last thing on my mind."

"What was on your mind then?"

He cocked his head toward the examination room.

Heat flaring in her cheeks, she plunked both palms flat

on his chest and shoved. Her effort didn't budge him, but he stepped out of the way on his own.

"I think you need to have that bump on your head re-examined, Angelosi," she called out, tromping down the hall. "If you think killing yourself is a workable technique for getting me in the sack."

She picked her jacket off the back of her chair and headed for the front of the clinic. He slipped around in front of her at the end of the hall. She stopped just short of running into him.

His white teeth fairly glowed in the darkness. "Seemed pretty workable tonight," he said in his best bedroom voice.

Her palm didn't have any trouble finding his cheek. She just aimed for those smiling teeth. A solid crack reverberated through the darkness. Her palm stung like crazy.

He stood stock-still, as if she'd never touched him. "I didn't want you involved."

"Well, I am involved, aren't I? Way involved."

"Amen to that, brother," a male voice drawled from the doorway. Both Paige's and Marco's heads snapped toward the figure stepping out of the shadows, his blue eyes luminescent in the moonlight.

The tension seeped out of Marco. "What are you doing here, Toby?"

"I brought your ride." He threw a set of keys to Marco.

"The old Camaro?"

Toby nodded. "Used to belong to my cousin's uncle's brother-in-law. Been sitting out on his property since he passed away four months ago. No one will miss it." One corner of his mouth crooked up. "But you're going to have to bring this one back. Cops impounded the truck. We keep giving you vehicles and we're going to be running a little low on transportation around here."

"You got a way home?" Marco asked, ignoring the jibe.

"Pulled my cycle over on a trailer behind the Camaro."

"Good." He tucked the keys in his pocket. "Now what did you mean, 'Amen'?"

Toby shuffled forward, taking his time. "Feds think she's involved." He looked from Marco to Paige and back, open curiosity in his scrutiny. "They saw her on the bridge looking a little, ah, compromised, before the shooting started."

Marco rolled his head back. "That true?"

Paige supposed the question was meant for her. "That they saw me looking *compromised?* How would I know?"

"That they're hassling you about being involved."

"They don't have anything on me. Other than what they saw," she added belatedly. "But they think I helped you get out of Rowan State Park." She ducked her head a moment, then continued. "And that I might be the one who tagged the prison van."

A string of oaths as blue as Elvis's suede shoes hazed the room. When he was through, Marco glared at her. "Why didn't you tell me?"

"You didn't ask."

"Would you have told me if I had?"

"Probably not." She raised her chin in the air. "You have your secrets. I have mine."

He stalked forward. *"Paige..."*

Toby stepped between them, pressing the point of a single finger into Marco's chest. "Hey, brother. This isn't the time."

Marco stopped. He fidgeted a moment. Shuffled his feet. Paige couldn't help but smile at the male surrender ritual.

"So what the hell do we do now?" he asked.

She lowered Toby's arm and moved past him to stand in front of Marco. "Now we quit keeping secrets, and start working together."

Paige dreaded the thought of another goodbye. Toby had gone outside to unload his motorcycle. Marco stood awkwardly inside the rear entryway of Doc's clinic, hands shoved in his pockets. Paige propped herself against the wall across from him with her arms folded over her breasts.

"Let's not leave it like this," he said.

"How would you like to leave it?" The words sounded surprisingly calm, given the war raging inside her.

He stepped in front of her, so close she could feel the heat emanating from him. So close she didn't trust herself not to reach out and touch him.

"I don't want to leave at all." His dark eyes bored into her. "I never did."

That stung. She didn't need him to remind her that she'd been the one to send him away six months ago. If not for her cold words in the kitchen that morning, this whole scenario might have unfolded very differently.

She ducked around him, pacing the length of the room. When she reached the wall and turned around, she found him standing with his head hung, the tanned nape of his neck stretched taught as he stared at the floor.

"I thought you'd be…happy once you knew the truth," he murmured.

She bit her lip, not sure how to answer when, in this case, the truth was both bitter and sweet. "I am happy you're not a crooked cop, or worse. But happy that you lied to me? No."

"I never lied to you."

"You purposely misled me. It's the same thing."

"Not in this case."

"You used me, Marco. I know you think you had good reason, but you used me just the same. You played your little mind games and led me around, throwing me little crumbs of information now and then to suit your purpose."

"It wasn't like that. I was trying to protect you."

Her heart shrank at the wounded look in his eyes. She must sound like a shrew. The man had saved her career, maybe saved her life, and all she could do was find fault.

How could she make him understand, when she wasn't sure she understood herself?

"Did it ever occur to you that I can protect myself?"

His silence told her all she needed to know.

"Of course not," she said. She fumbled with her coat, her fingers suddenly too shaky manipulate the zipper. "I'm just a woman. A canine cop. No match for the great Angelosi."

Marco watched her silently as she yanked on the zipper tab, but the ends weren't lined up right. It wouldn't pull. She yanked harder.

"Never mind that I'm an adult. That I have a mind of my own. Never mind that everything you did, you did to suit yourself. That you never considered what might suit me."

He closed his hands over hers on the troublesome zipper. "Stop."

"Never mind that it was *me* someone tried to frame."

"Stop," he said more firmly, pulling her hands away from the confounded jacket before she tore it.

"Never mind that I'm a cop, same as you. Just feel free to manipulate me as you choose. Use me anytime."

He dropped her hands, took hold of the lapels of the jacket and pulled her close. "I'm sorry."

"Never mind that—"

"I said I'm sorry, dammit. I should have told you."

His warm breath, faintly scented by coffee, fanned over her cheek. His dark eyes burned through her. His head dipped close to hers. She wanted to run but she was trapped in the cocoon of the jacket he held snugly around her. Trapped by his big body. By his tender lips.

It was a kiss of restraint. Just a brush of his mouth over hers. But it drew the anger out of her like poultice drew poison. When it was over, he rested his forehead on hers.

"I never meant to hurt you."

"Then why…?" She meant to say more, but stumbled over the words.

"Because I was falling in love with you."

She jerked back, and he let her slip away. Her thoughts reeled dizzily. Before she could slow her mind enough to formulate a response, the clinic door opened and Toby poked his head inside. Marco's friend did have impeccable timing.

Toby looked curiously from Marco to Paige and back. "You two about ready?"

"Yeah," Marco answered, never taking his eyes off her.

"Here, take this." Toby handed Marco a black ski jacket. "The truck's all set. Kia sent a thermos of her succotash and there's some cash for you under the front seat. Once you're gone, I'll follow Paige back to her motel on my motorcycle."

No one answered. Shaking his head, Toby withdrew. Marco slid on the jacket and started after his friend.

Paige pulled him back with a hand on his arm. "We need to talk about this."

He looked to the door. "There's no time."

He was right, she knew. But if Marco had his way, she feared there would never be time. "You're going after the Turk, aren't you?"

"He's the only one who knows what this is really about."

"He's also trying to kill you."

"If all he wanted was to kill me, he could have done it without going to all the trouble to bust me out of jail. I think he wants something from me first."

"What?"

Marco rubbed his forehead. "If I knew that, I would have already given it to him, sweetheart."

Paige frowned. She knew Marco well enough to realize he wouldn't give scum like the Turk anything for his own benefit. There he went, protecting her again. "Promise me you won't do anything crazy until we've had that talk."

"Paige—"

"Promise me!"

He shifted from foot to foot, then sighed. "Where?"

"My place."

"It's risky."

Though she did her best to contain it, a wan smile spread slowly across her face. "Like jumping off a bridge."

"They may be watching you."

"What would they be expecting to see? They think you're dead."

"They haven't got a body."

"They'll be busy looking for it. That will buy us time."

"Not much."

"Then we'd better make the most of what we have."

Almost of its own accord, her hand raised to the bruise on his jaw. Her fingertips skimmed the discolored skin. His eyes darkened, but not from pain, she didn't think. As if he could inhale her touch, he drew a slow, deep breath. When he blew the air back out, he nodded.

She reached for the doorknob before he could change his mind. "I'll leave the door unlocked, so you can get in quickly without being seen. And Marco..." She glanced back over her shoulder, searching for a lighter way to part. They both had enough to heavy thoughts to weigh on their minds. "Try to find yourself another shirt before then."

"What's wrong with this one?"

"Didn't anyone ever tell you?" Barely managing a wobbly grin, she gazed pointedly at the checked flannel. "Dead men don't wear plaid."

Chapter 14

Paige's grandfather clock chimed ten bells as she battened down her apartment for the night. Less than twenty-four hours had passed since she'd left Marco in Oklahoma, but already the doubts had crept in. He'd said he would come. But it was late already, and there'd been no sign of him. Maybe he'd been here while she was still at her grandfather's house being stuffed with roast beef and russet potatoes as if she hadn't eaten in weeks, and insisting over and over that she was fine. Maybe he'd left when he'd found she wasn't home.

Or maybe he'd gone after the Turk alone.

Pushing the thought away, she put Bravo in his kennel with a bowl of food and fresh water, then padded back through the kitchen, stopping long enough to pour herself a glass of wine. Normally the dog slept in the bedroom with her, but if Marco did come tonight, she didn't want him walking into a darkened room and surprising the dog.

Or the dog surprising him. He'd come a long way in

overcoming his fear of Bravo. She didn't want to undo the progress.

She checked once more that the door was unlocked, then headed to her room to change for bed. In her lingerie drawer, her fingers closed on a peach silk gown. Lacy and expensive, the slinky material flowed through her fingers like liquid gold.

Sadly, she set the silk aside. Her body tingled with anticipation at seeing Marco, but tonight wasn't about seduction. Tonight was about the truth, and understanding. Until they sorted out fact and fiction, right and wrong, love and hate would continue to twirl in her mind like multicolored pinwheels.

Marco had manipulated her, kept the truth from her. He'd also said he was falling in love with her. And the sacrifices he'd made for her both awed and enraged her.

Real love wasn't based on sacrifice. Sacrifices were easy. She should know; she'd made plenty in her previous relationship. And when the man she'd made all those sacrifices for left her for a woman who could give him even more—more money, more prestige—it had almost been a relief. She'd realized she'd never really loved him. She'd simply been living up to an ideal. An unrealistic image of what love was supposed to be like.

Just as Marco was trying to live up to the image of his father.

Her long winter nightgown whispering around her ankles, Paige fluffed the pillows on her bed and pulled back the spread. Snuggled beneath the covers, she waited. At first she tried not to think about Marco or the craggy emotion in his voice when he'd proclaimed that he was falling in love with her, but her attempts at forgetting quickly proved fruitless. He existed in more than just her mind. He was a part of her every cell, every fiber.

She could feel him out there somewhere, in the darkness. Feel his heart beating. His blood moving. Closing her eyes, she gave up trying to banish the sensations and concentrated on exploring them instead. The notion was silly, but she kept thinking that if she concentrated hard enough, maybe he would feel her, too.

Marco couldn't get Paige's face out of his mind. The fog had settled back in at Port Kingston, and it was like she was out there somewhere, just out of sight in the mist. Just out of reach.

Damn her, he could be halfway to California by now. Halfway to a chance to start over with a new name, build some sort of life for himself. So why was he slouched behind the wheel of an ancient Camaro in a cold, dark alley in Port Kingston instead?

Because he'd promised he would come, that's why.

And because he loved her.

To him, love and sacrifice were one and the same. His father had taught him that. Marco hadn't understood the lesson at first. He'd been too angry, had carried too much guilt over his father's death. Not until he'd met Paige had he truly understood what drove a man to give up everything—gladly—for the one he loved.

But Paige didn't want his sacrifice. Didn't want anything he had to give. She'd made that clear enough.

But her body—the way she responded when he touched her—and the yearning in her eyes said something else.

The thought warmed him from the inside out. Whistling a low tune, he started the car and headed east, toward Paige's.

Paige woke to the sound of growling from Bravo's kennel. She lurched upright in bed, automatically fingering her hair into some sort of order. Marco!

Bravo growled again, more vehemently. Paige's hand went still. This wasn't right. Bravo didn't growl at Marco anymore.

Hackles raised on the back of her neck. She whipped the covers back and lunged for the top drawer of her dresser as she heard footsteps in the hall.

She got her hand around her gun and was fumbling for the clip when a dark figure came into the room, followed by another. The first man's backhand sent her spinning. She dropped the gun. Rolling to the floor, she reached for it, but his booted foot came down on her wrist, pinning her with crushing weight.

"Where is it?" the man asked. The Turk. She's seen his photo, heard his name taken in vain around the station often enough. The other man she now recognized as Tomas Oberas, the prisoner who had escaped from the prison van with Marco.

"Where is what?"

He backhanded her again. Paige tasted blood.

"Next time I won't be so gentle. Where is it?"

She pressed the palm of her free hand to the corner of her mouth. It came away wet and smeared red. "I don't know what you're talking about."

"We want what Angelosi took. It's all over the papers. You and him were in it together. You've been helping him."

"I don't know what you're talking about!" she repeated.

The Turk tipped her head toward him with the muzzle of his gun. "Tell me where my Magic is."

Magic? He thought Marco had his drugs? But Marco hadn't said—

The Turk raised his hand again.

She flinched, expecting a blow that never came. "I don't know, exactly."

The Turk pressed his pistol into the hollow beneath her jaw.

"It's hidden," she ad-libbed quickly. "I don't know exactly where, but I can find it."

"Hidden where?"

"At the warehouse."

"We searched the warehouse. We didn't find nothing."

Slowly she angled her chin away from the gun. "You searched with human eyes. But Bravo's nose is a thousand times sharper. He can find things you can't."

Oberas grinned sickeningly at the Turk, grabbed her clothes off the back of the chair and shoved them at her. "Let's go."

Clutching the clothes to her chest, she rolled to her feet, reaching out to the table beside the bed for support and knocked her wineglass over in the process. Automatically she grabbed the box of tissues beside the lamp and began blotting at the mess on the carpet.

"Leave it!" the Turk ordered.

Biting her lip, she swiped at the stain twice more, this time with more thought. She rubbed the red liquid in rather than dabbing it out. She finished the crude message—BI for Battan Industries—just as Oberas rounded the end of the bed.

She stood quickly, hiding the message on the floor with her feet. "S-sorry." She shrugged. "Habit."

"Get dressed and get the dog."

She did both, hurrying. Glancing at the clock, she saw it was almost midnight. If she moved slower, she might have been able to keep them there until Marco showed up, but she didn't want him walking into this situation unawares. It was best if they were gone before he arrived.

She just hoped that he *did* arrive. And that he wasn't too late.

Icy fingers of fear clawed at Marco's back as he pounded down the stairs outside Paige's apartment three at a time.

Gone. She was gone.

Sweet Jesus, he should have known she'd be a target. Every radio station between here and Oklahoma had been

blasting reports of her involvement in his escape. He had
to get to her.

Running for the Camaro, he hit the sidewalk at the bottom of the stairs hard, and came to a bone-wrenching stop
as a hand bunched in his T-shirt. A second fist, big and
hard as a ham hock, slammed into his face. His head
snapped backward. Fireworks exploded before his eyes.
The man holding him let go of his shirt, and Marco reeled
backward. Sensing his assailant following him, Marco
poised for another blow. Automatically his hands came up
to protect his head. Another hit like that first one would
finish him. And if he was finished, so was Paige.

The blood in his eyes clouded Marco's vision. Close
quarters battle, where his opponent couldn't put his full
weight behind those meaty fists, was his only hope. Roaring
like a bear, he lowered his head and charged.

His tackle sent both him and his attacker spinning off
the porch. The man grunted as Marco's weight crushed his
shoulder into the ground at the bottom of the porch steps,
but he rolled again when he hit the front walk, flipping
Marco over him.

Damn, Marco thought, lying on his back in the driveway.
He didn't have time for this. He had to get to Paige.

The other man groaned and Marco opened his eyes. His
attacker loomed over him, hauling him to his feet by the
shoulders of his jacket. With a start, Marco recognized the
angry face.

"Matt!"

Matt Burkett let go of Marco's jacket and clipped him
in the jaw. Marco toppled backward, probed the crevice in
his split lip with his tongue and tasted blood.

"You're supposed to be dead, Angelosi."

"I can...explain."

"You've got a lot of nerve showing up here."

"I didn't come here to hurt her."

Matt made a feral noise, half howl, half growl. "I know

why you came here, you bastard. I work deep nights in this section. You think I don't cruise by my little sister's place—"

Marco cocked his head, never taking his eyes off Matt. "You knew about us?"

"What I don't know is why. Why would she risk everything for you?"

Wiping a drop of blood from his mouth with the back of his hand, Marco smiled weakly. "Maybe because she loves me."

Head down, Matt bellowed like a bull and rushed him. The moment before impact Marco turned sideways. He hooked Matt's arm and twisted as he passed, flipping the bigger man to his back.

Hands on his knees, Marco stood over Matt, panting "Listen to me. Paige needs—"

Matt's leg whipped him, bringing him to the ground. Marco rolled, but Matt crushed his knee into Marco's groin before he could stand. For several seconds, the world stopped. Sight, sound, movement, there was nothing. Nothing but pain.

When the world jolted into full motion again, Marco was bent over the still-warm hood of a vehicle. A cold metal bracelet pinched his left wrist. "Matt, no."

"Shut up before I change my mind about arresting you and just kill you right here." The second handcuff closed over his right wrist, tight enough to cut off circulation.

He managed to turn his head far enough to see Matt over his shoulder. "Paige is in trouble. She left a message. Inside."

Matt pulled Marco's head back by the hair and glanced toward the dark apartment. "What kind of trouble?"

"The Turk's got her. Or some of his goons. They're at the Battan Imports warehouse. We've got to go get her."

"The only place you're going is to jail."

"But Paige—"

"I'll call in the emergency response team."

"You'll put her in the middle of a war."

"They're trained for hostage situations."

"And you're the best negotiator in Texas, but that's still no guarantee she'll walk out alive," Marco said, forcing himself to think rationally. "It doesn't have to go down like that. We can make a trade."

"A trade for what?"

"For what the Turk really wants," he said. "Me."

Oberas pushed Paige through the warehouse door. She caught her balance and murmured to Bravo in German, ordering him to search. She hated to make him work again on his sore stifle, but if she ever needed her partner, it was now. Bravo was her only weapon, her only hope if Marco didn't show soon.

"Get lookin', lady," Oberas growled.

"What exactly am I looking for?"

The Turk's eyes closed to white slits in a tanning-bed complexion. "I thought you said you knew—"

"I mean how much? How big is the stash?"

Oberas chuckled, spinning his gun around his finger by the trigger guard. "How big is the stash? About one pot's worth, that's how big."

"A pot?"

"The pott-er-y. The pretty little vase the marijuana was in." He smiled. "It's pure Magic, darlin'."

At last she understood. The marijuana had been a misdirection. Something to throw the dogs off. Even if the canines had hit on the vases again after they'd been taken into evidence, the cops would have assumed it was only because they still had the scent of marijuana on them.

Those pots must have weighed eight or ten pounds. Ground up and diluted by a measure of fifty, that much Magic could easily be worth a million dollars or more.

And how many lives?

The Turk turned serious. He checked his watch. "Get to work. You've got twenty minutes."

Twenty minutes. Twenty minutes for Marco to catch up to her. Twenty minutes to live.

Twenty minutes later, Paige squirmed under the Turk's heavy stare. She'd stalled as long as she could. Searched the warehouse inside and out, but found nothing.

Oh Marco, where are you?

"Now what are we gonna do with her?" Oberas said.

"Get rid of her," the Turk replied impatiently.

Oberas's callused hand reached out. Paige stiffened, and flinched even though she'd resolved not to. She'd go out with dignity, at least.

"I wouldn't touch her if I were you." Paige's heart leaped at the sound of the deep, male voice. Not Marco, as she'd expected, but Matt! Matt had come for her. "Not unless you want to lose that hand," her brother warned.

Oberas and the Turk looked toward the shadows on the warehouse floor. Paige strained to see. Not one, but two men stepped from the darkness. Matt in back, and in front of him...

"Marco!" she cried. She started to her feet, but Oberas pushed her back into the chair. Matt lifted his gun in warning. Paige hardly followed the action. Her eyes were riveted on Marco.

Something was wrong. His back was straight and proud, but his gaze spilled onto the floor and his arms were behind him like...like a prisoner in handcuffs.

"Marco?" she called again, her voice deflated. When Marco raised his head, her stomach turned. His lip was split in two places. One eye was swelling and a new bruise marked his cheek.

She turned a dagger-filled glare on her brother. "Matt, you don't understand—"

"Easy, Punk," he said, calling her by her childhood nickname. "I'm gonna get you out of here."

Just as she was about to tongue-lash her brother for what he'd done to Marco, she caught the warning in both men's eyes.

The Turk had moved behind her. "Just how do you think you're going to do that, Sergeant Burkett?" he asked.

"By making you an offer you can't refuse."

The Turk's tenor slid a note or two up the musical scale as he laughed. "What might that be?"

In answer, Matt moved his hand out from behind Marco's back, digging the barrel of his pistol into Marco's side and shoving him a half step forward.

Paige gasped. "Matt, no!"

"Quiet." The muzzle of the Turk's weapon nudged behind her ear. "I could kill her where she sits and take what I want."

Matt's face tightened measurably. "You touch her and I'll kill Angelosi. You'll never find your Magic then."

Silence reigned for several long seconds. Matt stared at the Turk, never flinching. She assumed the Turk stared back.

Oberas finally broke the silence. He spoke to the Turk. "Go ahead and do her. I can take him before he gets Angelosi."

"Not unless your gun hand is faster than your brain," Paige bluffed. Oberas might not be too bright, but Matt was still outnumbered. Marco was cuffed, and she was unarmed. If it came to a gunfight, they were doomed.

The Turk shifted behind her. "Don't be so hasty, my dim-witted friend. Let's hear what the good sergeant has to say."

Matt spoke up. "You let her walk away. When she's out the door, I'll send Angelosi over to you."

"Just like that?" The Turk waved the gun barrel, then

settled it back against her neck. "You're just going to let me walk away with him."

Matt nodded.

"You're a cop."

"You think I care what happens to him, after what he did to my sister?" Matt stepped up to Marco and jammed the gun to his neck. "You kill him, you're saving me having to do it myself."

"Matt!"

"All I want is my sister," Matt said. He pushed Marco forward another step. "He's yours."

"And all your cop friends," the Turk said. "They feel the same?"

"I can't exactly ask them now, can I? Because then I'd have to let on that my sister lied about him being dead. That she covered for a thieving, lying piece of—"

"Tsk, tsk," the Turk interrupted. "And I thought they said cops always stuck together."

Matt glared at Marco. "He's no cop. Not anymore."

"You have a point there." The Turk stroked his chin a moment. "All right. She can go."

"Come here, Paige."

The Turk held her down with a hand on her shoulder. "After you put your gun on the floor and kick it this way."

Matt didn't look happy, but he leaned over.

"Matt, no!" She leaped from the chair, tears blinding her as she pulled out of the Turk's grasp and ran to Marco.

"Easy," Matt said. "Easy." She heard his gun skid across the cement as she flung herself against Marco's chest.

She squeezed her eyes shut, clinging to Marco's shirt, shielding him and trying to make herself small at the same time. Waiting for the eardrum-shattering report of gunfire.

When no shots rang out, she opened her eyes. Matt stood as rigid as a broad tree trunk, hands empty. Risking a glance over her shoulder, she saw the Turk lower his gun marginally.

"Looks like you have a problem, big brother. The lady doesn't want to go."

Matt snagged her arm and pulled her toward him. "She'll go."

She yanked her wrist from his grip. "The hell I will."

"Dammit, Paige, get over here."

"What do you think you're doing, Matt? You're a cop, for cryin' out—"

"Paige." Marco's quiet voice cut her off. She looked up into dark, unreadable eyes. "Go."

"No!"

"You have to go."

"I'm not leaving—"

He cut her off with a kiss. His mouth descended on hers almost violently, crushing her lips, demanding a response. And respond she did, their audience be damned. This was Marco. She could no more stop herself kissing him back than she could stop a freight train.

She wound her arms around his back, surrendering to him, acknowledging how wrong she'd been about him and how sorry she was for it. The moment her hands flattened against his spine, she realized that's what he'd wanted. The kiss was a guise. A very convincing, erotic guise, but a guise nonetheless.

Marco's cuffed hands took hers, guided her fingers around the rim of the steel bracelets. Very loose steel bracelets. Then he pressed her palm over a bulge at the small of his back that could only be a pistol tucked neatly out of sight.

He released her lips, but a long moment passed before Paige could breathe. Slowly he lifted his head, pulling her hand away from the gun. She questioned him with her gaze and got a quirk in one corner of his mouth for an answer.

Damn Marco and her brother both. They were in this

together. And they were doing it again. Making her a puppet in their performance.

"Now go," Marco said.

"Mmm." The Turk laughed. "Maybe I should send the rest of you away and keep her. She looks like she could be quite…entertaining."

Marco's eyes flashed black fire. "You let her go or you'll never get your damn drugs."

"Yes, yes," the Turk sighed. "I'm afraid my financial backers will be quite unhappy with me if I don't recover the Magic soon." Smiling like a loon, he tweaked his fingers at Paige. "Bye-bye."

She thought about pulling Marco's gun herself. Actually wrapped her fingers around the butt, but Marco warned her off with a dark look and a glance at Matt, who stood unarmed in front of two cold-blooded killers.

She could have gotten off a shot at the Turk, she was sure. But who would Oberas kill before she could fire again?

Which man that she loved was she willing to lose?

The answer was neither. As always, Marco was in complete control. She had no choice but to do what he wanted. She just hoped he knew what he was doing.

Her stomach quivered at the thought. She was very much afraid he knew exactly what he was doing.

Just as he had on the bridge.

Matt captured her elbow and backed them both out of the warehouse. As soon as the door closed behind them, she wriggled out of his grasp. He snagged her wrist before she could dart back inside.

"Matthew James Burkett, what do you think you're doing? I've got to get back in there!"

"You go for help. I'll go back in."

"Forget it. I've got to help Marco."

"Just hold up a second. I—"

"Let go of me." Frantically she pried at his fingers, but

it was like trying to peel Teflon from a frying pan. "We've got to help him."

"I know." He stepped away from the door, pulling her along.

"Then what are you doing?"

"Getting you out of here," he said, panting with the effort of restraining her.

"No!"

"Paige! One of us needs to go call for backup."

"I'm not leaving him."

"He's got a gun. And the cuffs are—"

"I know. He made sure I knew. He knew I'd never walk out otherwise. But it's still two against one."

"Not exactly."

She wasn't sure what Matt meant, but she couldn't take time now for riddles. "I'm going back in." She twisted, breaking free from his grasp.

His footsteps were surprisingly light for a big man as he hurried to keep up behind her. He got hold of her again just outside the door. "You aren't even armed."

"Neither are you." Matt's pistol still lay on the warehouse floor where he'd been ordered to drop it, and the weapon Marco was carrying was probably her brother's backup. "Maybe I can...I don't know, make a distraction or something while you go for one of the guns."

"Aw, Christ." His desperate tone made her turn. He wiped his free hand on his jacket as if he'd stuck it in something slimy. "You really do love him, don't you?"

"Yes," she said without hesitation.

"After what he's done?"

"All he's *done* is try to protect me, and those men in there are about to kill him for it." Anger pushed her voice above a safe whisper and she had to force down a breath to calm herself. The vehemence with which she defended Marco surprised even her, considering she was still furious with him. Poor Matt looked absolutely shell-shocked.

She didn't approve of everything Marco had done. But he was in that warehouse about to give his life to protect hers. How could she not love that? "Are you going to help me or not?"

Matt's wide brow furrowed and she knew she'd won. He nodded, but before they could get back inside the warehouse, a gunshot startled them both.

A single gunshot, followed by silence.

All the angry protectiveness in Matt's green eyes flew away and sympathy settled slowly in its place, landing softly as a snowflake in the grass.

"No," she whispered. Her bones ached deep inside from a sudden loss of heat. Marco's heat. The fire he'd brought to her life snuffed out too soon.

Damn him, he'd finally found a way to be just like his father.

Chapter 15

Marco crashed to the cold cement floor behind a wooden packing crate, Oberas's gunshot still ringing in his ears.

He'd led the Turk and the goon out of the office. Paige had left Bravo tied to a forklift out on the warehouse floor. On the way into the building, Matt had untied the dog, just in case Marco needed a little help getting out.

And Marco definitely needed help.

As soon as Marco got near the dog, he dived, pulling out of the handcuffs and drawing his gun at the same time.

Seeing the weapons leveled at Marco, Bravo had immediately attacked. Oberas had gotten off a shot, but the volley went wild, and Bravo jumped before the man could re-aim. From the agonized sound of Oberas's screams, the dog still hadn't let go.

That left the Turk for Marco. Unfortunately, the crime boss had the advantage of being on his feet, while Marco rolled on the floor to avoid Oberas's shot. The Turk kicked the gun from Marco's hand. Without missing a beat, Marco pushed himself upright and lunged.

The tackle was perfect—shoulder to midsection. The Turk grunted on impact. His gun skidded across the cement. Together they rolled down the aisle. Both of them punched, kicked, gouged, trying to gain the upper hand, but the struggle stayed even until Turk got in a few blows to Marco's bruised ribs. The pain and the lack of breath disabled him momentarily, and the Turk seized that moment to drag him into a choke hold.

Marco flung his heels and his elbows behind him, but the blows glanced away. He pried at the thick forearm crushing his trachea. Every fiber of his being strained with the effort, but the strangulation weakened him.

His face was hot. His chest ached awfully. His eyeballs felt like they'd expanded to twice their normal size, yet his field of vision narrowed to a dark red tunnel. Death was only a matter of time now. Very little time.

No time to tell Paige how he really felt.

A humorless laugh died inside him, lacking the air to come to life. Maybe he'd been a bit hasty in sending her away. He could use her help about now. Her and that sumo-wrestler brother of hers.

As if he'd conjured her with some voodoo spell, Paige appeared, swooping down the row of crates, a warrior's expression on her face.

She skidded to a stop fifteen feet away to pick up one of the dropped pistols. Myriad emotions—joy, relief, fear and anger—played across her features as she leveled the gun at them. She would have fired, Marco had no doubt, but she didn't have a shot. He was all tangled up with the Turk. Too close.

White spots danced before Marco's eyes. The Turk struggled to his feet and backed up a step, dragging Marco's nearly dead weight along with him. The tunnel that was Marco's vision was closing, fading, shrinking in on Paige's face. Not a bad choice for the last thing he ever saw, he figured.

The Turk backed another step, then stopped suddenly, expelling a hiss.

Marco heard the hammer of a gun being pulled back very near his ear. So near his ear, in fact, that it had to be right behind him. Right next to the Turk's ear.

"Let him go." *Matt.* In all the commotion, he must have picked up the other discarded gun unnoticed. "Let him go," he ordered again, this time in a take-no-prisoners voice, "or he's gonna be wearing your brains."

The pressure on Marco's throat eased, and he slumped to the floor, choking through a giddy smile. The next thing he knew, Paige's arms closed around him, and he thought he'd never felt anything so wonderful.

When he was able to take a breath—a short breath, at least—without coughing, he opened his eyes. Paige's face floated above him, blurry but beautiful.

"Hey, gorgeous," he joked, but the words sounded more like a croak. He wondered if she'd even understood him.

Her grip almost crushed him. "Don't try sweet-talking me, you idiot."

He smiled. And coughed. Bright spots danced in his vision. "What's wrong?"

"You're what's wrong. Making me leave when you knew they were going to kill you."

"Worried about me?"

She made an exasperated noise. "You weren't wearing a vest this time, Angelosi."

No. This had been the real deal, and he knew it. "I had something better," he said, lifting his head to look around her. Across the floor, Bravo stood by while Matt handcuffed Oberas. The dog drooled over his prey as if the man was a T-bone and he hadn't eaten in a week.

Paige chuckled through her tears. "I thought you didn't like dogs."

"Who, me?" He let his head fall back into her arms. "I love dogs."

She drew him tight against her warm, soft breast, where e would have been perfectly happy to stay forever. But hey didn't have forever. They didn't have more than a few noments. Not judging by the sound of sirens—lots of si-ens—converging on the warehouse. Matt must have called rom the phone in the office.

The giddiness Marco felt at seeing her, at being alive, aded. In its wake came the pain. His ribs were battered, nis face bloodied. His throat felt pulpy as an overripe ba-nana. But he couldn't take comfort from Paige any longer.

"Maybe you'd better go help your brother," he said.

Her fingers tightened in his shirt. "What?"

He struggled to sit up. "It won't do your career any good to be seen with me. Not like this."

"I don't give a damn about my career."

"I do."

When she wouldn't leave, he got up, took two of the most difficult steps he'd ever taken—away from her—and sat on a packing crate.

"Marco, you don't have to do this. We can prove ev-erything that happened now. All we have to do is show them the pottery. It's pure Magic, Marco. The marijuana stashed inside was a diversion, like throwing a guard dog a steak so the burglar can climb the fence. Plant some cheap pot for the dogs to find, then send the cocaine—in the flow-erpots—right on through the system."

"I'm sure if we check the records for the government auctions of confiscated goods, we'll find that the Turk, or someone in his organization, has been buying them back."

"We can get the records. We can prove everything."

"Not if we can't prove those pots were made of Magic."

"We can. Just tell me what you did with the flowerpot from my car. The one you took the marijuana from."

He shook his head.

"What do you mean, no?"

"There was no flowerpot in your car, Paige, just the weed."

"There had to be...."

He shook his head again. "I'm sorry."

Her expression crumbled. Her lips quivered. Shifting uncomfortably on the rough wooden crate, Marco peeled his gaze away from the torture in Paige's eyes as the full impact of what had happened here tonight set in. If the Turk didn't have the Magic, and Marco didn't have it, then this wasn't over. None of them were safe.

"We can still fight," Paige said, but her voice held less confidence than before.

"No, Paige. We can't."

She stared at him, her eyes pleading.

"Don't you see? If the Turk doesn't have the Magic, and I don't have the Magic, then there has to be someone else. An inside man. One ballsy enough—or stupid enough—to double-cross the Turk." He shook his head, impatient with himself. "Hell, I should have seen it before. The rumors were right about a dirty cop on the task force. They just had the wrong cop pegged."

"We can find out who."

Marco glanced toward Matt, who was watching them from across the room with a pained expression on his face and a pair of handcuffs in his hands. "I don't think I'm going to be doing much investigating where I'm going."

"Then I'll do the investigating."

"No," he said. "You leave this alone."

"I can protect myself."

"From both the bad guys and the cops?" He lurched to his feet. "Paige, if you take my side in this, whoever stole the Magic won't be your only problem. The department will assume you helped me all along. They'll file charges. You'll lose your badge."

Disbelief settled slowly on Paige's face. "So that's it? You're just going to quit?"

He looked away.

"I should have known." She made a derisive noise and crossed her arms over her chest. "Like father, like son."

Unable to stop himself, he snapped his gaze back to hers. "What is that supposed to mean?"

"You're a quitter, just like you said he was."

Marco's heart stuttered. "He—he wasn't a coward."

"You said he gave up. He let himself die. You were angry with him for it."

"I was angry because I loved him. But—" A decade of guilt and rage bubbled inside him. "But he was a hero."

"How do you figure?"

"Most people with Lou Gehrig's disease live only five or six years after they're diagnosed. My father hung on for eight and a half, even though he couldn't afford the medicine he needed, even though it humiliated him to be taken care of like a baby."

"Why?" she challenged, not backing down when he loomed over her? "Why did he hang on?"

Marco's mind whirled, reliving the last agonizing months of his father's life, the grief of his death. "To make sure I finished school, I guess."

Her eyes flashed like brass daggers. "That's not it."

The rage exploded inside him. He saw red, but a voice inside him kept him from letting it all pour out. *Liar,* it said. He raked a hand through his hair. "Hell, I don't know. I guess he knew I needed him."

"Exactly!" she said.

Marco blinked. "Exactly what?"

"He lived longer because you needed him, and he loved you. No matter how bad things got for him, he fought through the pain. He did it for you. Your father didn't die for you, Marco. He *lived* for you—long past the point when he could have escaped the suffering. He lived until you were old enough to make it on your own.

"Don't you see? Love isn't about what you give up, it's about how tight you hold on."

Marco's feet were trapped in clay. His heart thundered like stampeding buffalo. He wanted to deny what she'd said, but he couldn't. He couldn't speak at all, because a lifetime of misplaced anger and guilt clogged his throat.

Paige waited. He knew she wanted him to say he'd hold on to her. That he'd fight for her. But he couldn't give her what she wanted. Despite what he understood, or didn't understand, about his father's choices, there was still someone out there who could hurt Paige.

The sound of tires screeching outside permeated the warehouse walls. It sounded as if a whole flock of cops had just landed. Matt strode over from where he'd secured Oberas and the Turk on the floor.

Marco's head hung. The tendons on the back of his neck stretched taut. His self-control stretched tauter. Trying not to think about returning to jail, he turned his back and offered his wrists to Matt.

Paige's gaze fixed on the handcuffs dangling from her brother's fingers. "Matt, no!"

"He's still a fugitive, Paige."

"You know he doesn't deserve this."

"It's for his own safety," Matt grumbled, clicking the first bracelet in place. "There's a whole herd of nervous cops about to storm this place, and he's still wanted. When they come in, I want them to be real clear this situation's under control."

Matt closed the second bracelet around Marco's wrist. "I'm sorry," he said.

Beside him, Paige had turned her head away.

Shouted orders and reports sounded from outside the warehouse door. Matt lingered a moment before going to greet the troops. "I'll do what I can for you with the judge."

Marco shook his head. "Just make sure Paige is okay. We still don't know who's really behind all this."

Matt clapped a hand on Marco's shoulder, his eyes grateful. "You'd better get down," he said quietly.

Marco looked at Oberas and the Turk, lying on their stomachs. He knew what Matt wanted. Knew Matt was right, and that he had to comply, even if it meant giving up any dignity he had left.

He'd been through this drill once before. He could do it again.

As Matt walked away, Marco forced himself to one knee.

"You're right about your father. He was a hero," Paige said.

Marco paused just a second to look at her one last time. Her brassy stare had softened beneath a fan of dense lashes. Tearing his eyes away before he lost his resolve to go through with this, he stretched out on his belly.

"You're the one who's a coward," she said, her words almost lost in the shouts of the sea of cops who flooded the building.

His jaw clenching so hard his teeth ached, Marco turned his head away and rested his cheek on the cold concrete floor.

With Bravo on the floor beside her, leaning on her leg, Paige sat on a crate, willing herself not to cry. Not to feel anything. The Turk was being detained in the warehouse office, whining about calling his lawyer, or so she'd heard. Tomas Oberas was on his way to the hospital to have his dog bites treated.

Marco sat outside in a squad car, waiting to be taken back to jail.

Paige couldn't wrap her mind around what he was doing. All she knew was she couldn't let him do it. Somehow she had to stop him.

Not out of love. No, she could never love a man who

would turn his back on her the way he had in the warehouse. She would find a way to get Marco—and herself—out of this mess, because she didn't want to be indebted to him.

And she certainly didn't want to be the altar at which he made his sacrifice to his almighty father's memory.

Bravo picked up his head. His ears pricked forward. A moment later Paige heard footsteps behind her. She ignored them. Maybe whoever was there would go away.

No such luck.

She jolted when a hand was clapped on her shoulder. "Jarvis," she said, looking back.

"Officer Burkett." He propped his hip next to her on the crate. "I'm happy to see you in one piece."

"I'll bet," she grumbled, shrugging his touch off her shoulder. Her initial surprise at seeing the assistant district attorney here faded beneath the strength of her usual distaste at being anywhere near him.

"Just because we don't live together anymore doesn't mean I want to see you hurt," he said, leaning close, as if afraid someone might overhear him.

She hopped to her feet, her temper rising. "What do you want?"

"I came to take your statement, of course. I'll be prosecuting this case personally." He stood and straightened his suit. "Both Angelosi and whomever else charges might be brought against."

Her fingernails dug into her palms. Bravo stood and whined. She flashed a signal to sit, and the dog plopped down at her heel. "What are you saying?" she asked the A.D.A.

He smiled charmingly. "Angelosi had to have help to pull this off. Whoever helped him committed a crime. That's all."

"Are you accusing me?"

The A.D.A. put on a shocked face, but Paige saw right

through it. Jarvis Bickham had never been a very good actor.

"Go to hell, Bickham." She spun on her heel, but he stopped her with a hand on her arm. Bravo stood, his stare fixed on the man holding his mistress, and growled. Though she would have loved to let the dog have his way with the A.D.A., she ordered Bravo to back off.

After Bickham let go of her arm.

"I'd like to do that," he said, still eyeing Bravo warily. "But I need to hear your story first."

Paige's stomach quivered. For the first time, the possibility that she could be in trouble for her actions seemed real. Undoubtedly the A.D.A. already knew exactly what had happened here in the warehouse tonight. It was what had happened before that which worried her. She wouldn't lie about her role in Marco's resurrection from the dead. She couldn't. But if she told Bickham the whole truth, then she'd be confessing to a felony. There wasn't much she could do to clear Marco if she was in jail herself.

"It's late," she finally said, stalling for time to figure out what to do. "I'll make an appointment with your secretary tomorrow."

"I'd rather do it tonight, while events are still fresh in your mind."

"You mean before I have time to make up a story."

"That, too." His smile sickened her stomach. "I never would have thought Angelosi was your type, Paige. He's a renegade, and you...you were always so cautious. Always played by the rules. I hate to see you make a fool of yourself over him."

"But you didn't mind when I made a fool of myself over you." It wasn't that she cared what Bickham thought of her. On the contrary, it was the sudden knowledge that she'd let him set the *rules* in her life far too long that made her snap. She was tired of playing by his rules. Maybe some of Marco had worn off on her. She'd become a renegade.

At least Bickham had the grace to look sheepish. "That was different."

"Was it? How so?"

The A.D.A.'s eyes turned feral, his cheeks reddened. "I didn't try to walk away from the scene of a crime with five kilos of marijuana—from your bust—under my coat. I didn't stand up in front of a gangster like the Turk and try to make a deal for drugs I didn't even have."

How—? Paige bit off the question before she voiced it. How did Bickham know Marco didn't have the Magic? Marco wouldn't have told him, and she doubted he'd had time to interview Matt yet.

When she looked up at him again, looked really close, she knew. She just knew. Bickham had known about Marco's undercover assignment to find the dirty task-force cop. And framing her fit right in with Jarvis's history. He'd used her before; why not again?

Of course, even he couldn't have known Marco would take the drugs rather than see her face charges. No one could have predicted that.

"Are you going to throw your life away for a drug dealer and a thief?" Bickham asked, oblivious to the revelation that had struck her like lightning.

"No," she answered, still somewhat dazed. She wasn't throwing anything away. She was taking a calculated risk, for Marco's sake and for her own. Surprisingly enough, it didn't feel like she was giving anything of herself up. It felt…liberating.

Her heart trebled like a singing bird as a plan coalesced in her mind. If only she had some way to let her brother know…

Then again, it was better he didn't know. He had enough problems, with the shadows of the son he'd lost and his soon-to-be ex-wife never far off his shoulders. She didn't need to involve him in her troubles, too. What needed to be done was hers to do alone.

"I'm not throwing my life away for anybody," she said, feeling as if she'd shed a great weight she'd carried for too long.

Slyly, she raised her gaze to Bickham's and smiled. "You're right. We really should talk about this tonight." She reached up to press a wrinkle from the lapel of his suit coat. "I have a lot to tell you. But I'd rather do it somewhere a little more...private?"

Bickham's nostrils flared. He studied her hand on his chest. "My car's outside. Let's go."

Matt opened the car door beside Marco.

"'Bout time," Marco said. "I'd like to get out of here." He was tired of all the sideways looks he'd been getting from cops who used to be his friends.

"Slide around," Matt told him. "I'll take the cuffs off for the ride in."

Marco grinned weakly. "It's against regs."

"Just shut up and turn around," Matt muttered.

As the lock on the steel bracelets clicked open, Port Kingston's third canine squad officer, Riley Townsend, walked up to the car. Riley gave him an unfriendly look, then spoke to Matt. "You want me to take him in, Sarge?"

"No, I'll do it." From Matt's expression, Marco guessed Matt wasn't too thrilled about taking him to jail. Paige had probably coerced him into it. Incarceration could be an ugly process, but Matt owed Marco one. Paige would count on her brother not to make it any uglier than it had to be.

"You find Paige and make sure she gets home okay," Matt said.

Riley looked surprised. "She's gone already."

Both Matt's head and Marco's snapped toward the uniformed officer.

Riley's gaze swiveled between Marco and the sergeant. "She got a ride with the A.D.A."

"Bickham?"

Riley nodded.

"On second thought, you take Angelosi in. I'll take care of Paige," Matt said, looking disturbed. Marco didn't blame the man; he wasn't too happy with this turn of events, either.

Marco almost sighed in relief when the big man walked away. He glanced at Riley as the officer opened the trunk to stow his gear, and smiled. He was getting out of here, but he was glad Paige's brother wasn't the one he was going to have to run over to do it.

Marco poked his head out the open car door. "Mind if I stretch my legs a minute?" he asked, climbing out.

"Yeah, I do." A good cop, Townsend was around the hood before Marco had both feet on the ground, but it was too late. Marco aimed his head for Riley's midsection and surged forward. Leaving the man on the ground gasping for air, he grabbed the keys and climbed into the patrol car. A second later the lights and siren were on and he was screaming down the street toward Paige's house.

Chapter 16

"Now, what was it you wanted to tell me?"

Paige took a languorous sip from her coffee, making Bickham wait. Once, when she'd been young, naive and in love, he'd taken advantage of her. But she wasn't naive any longer, though she was doing her best to look it tonight. Her feet were bare, her face unmade up. The flimsy skirt and V-necked blouse she'd changed into covered too much skin to be called provocative, but showed just enough to titillate the male imagination, she hoped.

Jarvis had used her once, but she'd learned from the experience. This time, she was using him.

He sat in an antique wing chair and she positioned herself in its mate, next to him.

"It's about Marco," she said, twisting toward him and leaning forward until Jarvis's gaze dipped below her neckline. "He told me some things in Oklahoma that I think you should know."

"What things?"

"About the drugs he took."

Jarvis shifted on his seat.

"He didn't take them from the warehouse. He took them from my car."

"What?" Jarvis feigned surprise. "The bastard. He's lying, of course, trying to get himself off by throwing suspicion on you."

"He's telling the truth."

"You can't believe that. The son of a bitch, he brainwashed you. It's that…that kidnapping syndrome. Your dependence on him made you start to sympathize with him."

Paige drew a steadying breath. Now came the hard part. She was about to confess to multiple crimes—to the county A.D.A. "I didn't sympathize with him at all," she said. "But I did sleep with him."

His face reddened. He lurched to his feet, not even seeming to notice when he sloshed coffee across the leg of his Armani suit.

"And I helped him fake his death in front of those Feds," she added.

"Why in God's name would you do that?"

She held up her hand to stop him, exaggerating the slow stretch of her legs as she uncrossed them. He shoved his hands in his pockets and rattled change.

Standing in front of him—close in front of him—she unwound the knot from his tie and tugged on the silk ends, pulling him down to her as she whispered, "Because I thought he had the Magic."

"What Magic?" His breath fanned her cheek. She smelled French roast and fear. Power surged inside her.

"The Magic the pottery was made out of. The Magic you took when you put the marijuana in my car."

"I didn't— I never—"

"You were working for the Turk, weren't you? Feeding him information about the task force?"

He tried to pull back, but she held him captive with the tie. "I—no."

''You told him that Marco was on the case, and he told you to set me up in order to get rid of him.''

''That's preposterous.''

''You put marijuana in my car, then kept the Magic for yourself. You set Marco up, too, tipping him off that he could find drugs in my car that morning. You thought he'd bust me for the marijuana. The Magic would be missing, and the Turk would think Marco took it for himself.''

A sweat broke across Jarvis's forehead.

''Marco almost blew it for you, walking off with the marijuana without busting me. That's why you dragged me and Bravo over to talk to him that morning. You wanted me—needed me—to find the drugs before he walked away. You knew Bravo would nail him.''

''You've lost your mind.''

She brushed her lips across the base of his neck, felt his pulse kick. ''Shh. It doesn't matter. What matters now is what we do with it.''

''D-do?''

''We can be...partners again.'' She watched his eyes dilate as she slipped her hand inside the unbuttoned top of his shirt. ''Just like the old days.''

''Partners.''

She nodded, standing on tiptoe to nip at his chin. ''I changed after you left, Jarvis. I learned the lesson you taught me. I don't always play by the rules anymore.''

Clumsily he pulled his hands from his pockets and wound them around her back. ''Exactly what sort of arrangement did you have in mind?''

''Besides this?'' She skimmed her knee along the inside of his leg until she met the arousal straining against his fine trousers.

Eyes closed, he made an affirmative grunt.

''You have connections with smugglers. I have a drug-sniffing dog. I'm sure someone you know would be willing to pay to have cargo…overlooked during the course of my work, yes?''

"Yes.'' The single syllable was more a hiss than a word. He crushed her mouth with his own. Angling his head, he thrust his tongue into her mouth. Plundering. Pillaging. Taking what he wanted, what she willingly gave, though the feel of him, the taste of him sickened her.

She had the bastard. All she had to do was get him to admit it out loud. The tape from the voice-activated recorder she'd hidden behind the couch while he'd been in the kitchen might not be admissible in court, but it would be enough to convince the men and women of the Port Kingston PD that one of their own had been set up. Once they knew that, they wouldn't rest until they had the evidence that would set Marco free.

Jarvis raised his head, nuzzled her neck. She angled her chin, giving him better access and swallowing the bile that rose in her throat. While his left hand held her close, his right hand closed over her breast. She gasped.

''You like that?''

''Yes,'' she lied, covering her reaction. She ducked her chin into the crook of his shoulder and squeezed her eyes shut against the torment. She couldn't give up now. ''Where is the Magic, Jarvis? You haven't sold it yet, have you?''

His hand went still. ''My, my. Greedy little thing, aren't you?''

She looked up at him, dead honesty painting her expression. ''If I'm going to sell my soul, I want to see what I'm getting for it.''

He flicked his wrist and a blade pressed against her breast. She sucked back, but the hand behind her held her in place.

''You mean I'm not enough for you?'' Jarvis scraped the point of the blade upward along her sternum, leaving a thin red line in its wake. When he used the tip to push aside the gauzy neckline of her blouse, she realized he was looking for wires. As he probably had been when he'd touched her.

The bastard.

Lamplight glinted off his silver blade as he twisted it under her chin. Insanity glinted in his eyes.

Panic tore at her with icy claws. "I can get you more Magic."

Rage mottled his face. "More? What would I do with more? I can't sell what I've got. I thought I could use the money to finance my campaign for district attorney—God knows my wife won't give me a dime of her funds. But I can't fence the stuff. No one will buy drugs stolen from the Turk, even with him in jail. The way he went after Angelosi, they're all afraid of him."

"You made the Turk believe Marco had the Magic."

"Yes, yes. He believed it. He believed it so much that he killed two prison guards trying to get to him so he could get it back."

"All that trouble for a million bucks' worth of dope?"

"It wasn't just the money. The Turk's Colombian contacts don't like slipups. They were going to make an example of the Turk to make sure no one else in the organization messed up the way he did."

Relief flooded through Paige like a warm bath. She had it—a confession. Now she just had to live long enough to get the tape into the right hands.

Pursing her lips, she whistled for Bravo and made her move.

Vaguely, she realized someone was pounding on her front door. By the time the pounding ended with the crack of splintering wood, and she recognized Marco's voice, roaring as he charged through her entryway, with Matt right behind him, Paige had the A.D.A. down on the floor, curled into a fetal position and crying like a baby.

* * *

Paige opened her bedroom window and looked out into the night. A stream of warm April air swept over her like the touch of a hand. Summer had come early to south Texas.

She wondered if Marco was out there somewhere, enjoying the clean breeze. She imagined he was. Cooped up inside would be the last place she'd expect to find him on his first night of freedom.

For eight weeks the legal system had churned, grinding its way toward the truth, and justice. Eight weeks of hearings and depositions, motions and pleas. To Paige, the process seemed to drag on interminably.

Until this morning, when Marco had walked away a free man.

Oberas had traded information for a reduced sentence, and all charges against Marco related to the prison van wreck and escape had been dropped. Somehow the fact that he'd assaulted Riley Townsend had gotten lost in the paperwork shuffle. Paige didn't have any proof, but she suspected Riley himself was responsible for the loss. Even the original convictions for theft and evidence tampering had been overturned.

Threatened with a long sentence in a maximum-security penitentiary filled with men he had helped put there, Jarvis turned over the Magic and had copped a plea for putting the marijuana in Paige's car. Since Marco was undercover investigating the possibility of criminal activity within the task force at the time, and since an attempt to frame Paige could be viewed as an attempt to derail that investigation, the judge found Marco within his rights and duties to remove the evidence.

The judge's call raised a lot of eyebrows in city hall and at the police station, but hey, she wasn't complaining. He was free, that was what mattered.

She hadn't seen him since the night of Bickham's arrest,

/hen Matt had hustled him out of her house before they'd eally had much chance to talk. She wasn't sure he would vant to see her after what she'd said at the warehouse be-ore that, calling him a coward. But as she watched him tep through the chain link prison gates, she laughed and cried at the same time. She ate up his presence, starved for he sight of him.

He'd tilted his head up to the sky, as if in thanks, taken a long look up and down the street, shaken hands with Matt, who offered him a ride, and set off down the sidewalk on foot.

Paige didn't know where he'd gone after that. Didn't want to know. The temptation to go to him would be too great. Just knowing he'd been vindicated was satisfaction enough.

Still…she wondered.

Chastising herself, she left the window and snapped off the light. If he wanted to see her again, he would have come by, or called already. He knew how to reach her.

She imagined he was busy putting his life back together, anyway.

As she slipped into bed, the white curtains fluttered, set aglow by a full moon. When the first pebble knocked against the window, she knew it was him. Two more clinked against the glass before she could pull her robe on and meet him in the driveway.

He had his hips propped against her car. His feet jutted out in front of him, crossed at the ankles, and his arms were folded across his chest.

"This yours?" he asked, glancing down at the Miata.

"Yes," she answered, wondering where he was going with this.

He raised his eyebrows, studied the car more closely. "Looks new."

"No." She bit her lip to keep from smiling. "I just washed it today."

"Ah," he exclaimed. "Clean as new, then."

She laughed, despite the nerves squawking in her chest like a flock of hungry gulls.

"What do you say we put the top down and take her for a spin?"

Her laughter fading, she pulled her robe tight across her chest. They couldn't turn back the clock, no matter how much either of them might want to.

"It's late," she said.

He smiled. "And the breeze is warm and the stars are out. So what's the problem?"

Was he orchestrating this to torture her? To remind her of the first time they'd played out this scene?

She pulled her lower lip between her teeth. "I'm not dressed."

He reached for the lapel of her robe, just as he had the first night, but she stepped back. "The last eight months can't just be erased, Marco. Not even by a warm breeze and starlight."

The twinkle of humor in his eyes flickered out. "Fine. You want to talk here?"

She nodded.

"All right. You were right about my father."

In his eyes, she caught a glimpse of the pain it caused him to admit it.

"But you were wrong about me. I'm not a coward."

Suddenly even the warm April breeze felt chilly. She pulled her robe tighter around her. "I know that."

"It's just that I wanted you so bad, but you said you didn't want me, and then things kept going from bad to worse and—"

"I said I know," she interrupted.

He stared at her. "You do?"

The fluttering in her chest calmed with the truth. "Yes."

She stared at the ground, afraid that if she looked at him, she'd be drawn inside those angel's eyes of his, and wouldn't be able to say what she needed to say. "I was wrong," she said.

After a speechless pause, Marco folded his arms across his chest and rocked back on his heels. "Well hallelujah. Paige Burkett just admitted she was wrong."

She raised her head, ready to snap at him, but her anger faded away in the warmth of his smile. He opened his arms, and she stepped into them. Burrowing her cheek into his chest, she inhaled. He smelled clean and strong. His strength gave her courage.

"I was afraid, Marco," she said.

His arms stiffened around her. "I know I used you. I'm sorry."

"No." She pulled her head back so that she could see him. "I wasn't afraid of you, or of being used. I was afraid of *myself.* I was— I was afraid...."

He took a deep breath, held her tight.

"I told you love isn't about giving up. But I was wrong about that, too. Love is about giving up. It's about giving up fear and power and control and putting your life—your heart—in someone else's hands. You gave up so much for me, Marco. I was afraid that I would never be able to give that much back."

There, she'd gotten it out. Her soul felt a thousand pounds lighter for it. Feeling as if she was just going to float away if he didn't say something, or do something, she waited for his response. It was a long time coming, while he studied her somberly. Finally his fingertips came to her cheek and wiped away a tear she hadn't realized she'd shed.

"He did this to you, didn't he?" he said. "Made you afraid to give anything of yourself away."

Some of her euphoria dissipated. "You knew about Bickham and me?"

"I'd heard a few rumors."

"Then you know how stupid I was." She stared at the ground between them. "How naive."

"I know some people don't deserve the kind of love you have to give."

"I would have done anything for him. I was a sophomore in college when we met. He was in his last year of law school. He moved into my apartment within a week. We didn't have a lot of money, so the next year, I dropped out of school to support him. I worked two minimum-wage jobs to pay the rent, buy the groceries, put gas in the car, while he ran around with his buddies instead of studying. I postponed applying to the police academy because it upset him to see me doing something I loved while he failed the bar exam three times. And then when little Suzy-what's-her-name came along with connections at city hall and old family money, he dumped me like a carton of sour milk. I was so...lost and hurt and embarrassed. I could hardly stand to show my face in Port Kingston. I would have left if all my family hadn't been here. Even then I might have left, except I...I couldn't let him run me out of town on top of everything else."

"Bickham is the one who should have been embarrassed—not you." Marco's hands dug through her hair. "The son of a bitch is lucky he's in prison, where I can't get to him." Then he smiled. "But I don't have to, do I? You already kicked his butt in a major way. That ought to make you feel better."

"Revenge is not something I'm proud of."

He grinned. "Fine. I'll be proud for you."

He pulled her closer to him and cleared his throat. "You know, I went to prison to try to keep you safe, then you put yourself right back on the line to get me out. We could have both ended up with nothing."

"Or everything." He squeezed her tighter. "Dammit, you scared the life out of me, letting him take you home. He could have killed you."

She sniffed, wiped her nose on his sleeve. "So you decided to steal a police car and come after me?"

"I decided to stop running and start fighting, like you suggested."

She laughed through her tears. "I'm not sure Riley Townsend appreciates the timing of that particular decision."

Marco put on an innocent face. "I didn't hurt him."

She cocked her head accusingly.

"Too bad," he amended.

She laid her head on his chest, content to listen to the steady boom of his heart.

"There's something else you should know," he said. She tipped her head up, questioning him with her gaze. "I'm not through fighting, yet. I don't want to let you go, but I've got to be sure you know I'm not like him. I won't force you into something you don't want."

Gently, almost regretfully, he set her back from him and squared his shoulders. "I love you, Paige." His voice cracked on her name. She watched, shocked to her toes, as he visibly restored his composure.

He cleared his throat. "But I'm not going to try to manipulate you or coerce you into loving me back. If you want me, you're going to have to come and get me. I need to know that it's what you want, not just what I want. I need you to be the one to ask me to stay."

He waited one heartbeat, two, while she stared at him as if her brain had been surgically removed from her head.

Suddenly he wheeled around with military precision. Before he marched off, he fired a parting shot. "You know, if you let the way Bickham treated you keep you from ever loving anyone again, then he's won. He'll be using you for the rest of your life."

With a clarity so sudden she could swear it had been endowed upon her by angels—or maybe just an Italian-American cop with angel's eyes—she saw the truth about herself. She saw a strong woman with a big heart, but a woman who had held on so tightly to her independence that she'd nearly squeezed the best part of life right through her fingers.

Love.

He'd almost made it to the sidewalk before her feet started moving. Running. Her robe tangled around her calves. Her bare feet slapped against the rough blacktop. Pebbles bit into her soles. She shut out all thoughts of where she was going, or what she was going to do when she got there.

She'd almost caught up to him. He had to have heard her steps, but he didn't turn. Maybe he slowed his gait a half step. Or maybe it was her imagination.

She didn't care which. She didn't slow a beat. Instead she picked up speed, ran right up behind him, leaped onto his back and threw her arms around his neck.

He staggered, stumbled, caught his balance and her, too, locking his arms under her thighs and hefting her up, piggyback style.

Rich, throaty male laughter filled the night air.

She buried her face in the musky crook of his neck, giggling and crying. "I love you, too. I love you, too."

"Then ask me to stay."

She dropped a necklace of kisses around his throat. "Stay. Please stay."

Breathing harder than she thought necessary for the exertion of carrying her, Marco took her back to the Miata and lowered her backside to the hood. Blowing out a breath when she traced the curve of his spine with one fingertip, he turned around, pushed her knees apart and stood between them.

Finally, with a palm planted on the car on either side of her, he kissed her. His tongue swept through her mouth like a summer storm, crashing, whipping, igniting lightning in her blood. She fisted her hands in his shirt, riding the lightning, but like most summer storms in Texas, the tumult was over as fast as it had begun, leaving everything in its path heavy and wet.

He raised his head, licked his lips. "Before we get any deeper into this, there're a few more things you need to know."

"More?" She'd heard enough. He'd said he loved her.

"More," he said firmly.

She looked at him expectantly, breathlessly.

"One. I am never going to stop trying to protect you."

She opened her mouth to protest, but he hushed her with a finger on her lips.

"But I won't ever keep the truth from you again. Whatever happens, we decide what to do about it together. All right?"

She nodded after only the slightest hesitation. The way that big, broad chest of his and that narrow little waist kept distracting her, she wasn't sure she understood what he said. But whatever she was agreeing to, it couldn't be that bad, could it?

"Two. I want a permanent arrangement. I want you to marry me."

She heard that one. Stunned, she looked up into his dark eyes. "What are you doing tomorrow morning about nine?"

He looked confused for a second, then grumbled, "Uh-uh. We're going to do it right. A church. Flowers. Photographer. Limo. Honeymoon. That will take a little time to plan."

She raised her eyebrows.

He pressed a quick kiss to her forehead. "Just make sure it doesn't take any longer than absolutely necessary, okay?"

"Okay," she agreed. All this commitment was getting tedious.

"Three—"

"Aren't you through yet?"

"No. Three—"

"Don't I get to make any demands?"

He eyed her suspiciously. "What kind of demands?"

"One." She chewed on her lower lip. "You have to let me help you until you get your affairs straightened out."

He was quiet a moment. "Financially?"

She saw in his eyes that he understood what it cost her—the trust she had to have—to make the offer after what she'd been through with Bickham.

Marco pulled her palm from his cheek and held it between his hands. "Thanks, but that won't be necessary. I can support myself."

"What are you going to do?"

"I went to see the chief today." He shrugged. "I guess I got lucky. He didn't boot me out of his office."

She circled her arms around his neck. "You got your old job back?"

He grimaced. "I said he didn't boot me out, not that he was thrilled to see me. Our good chief of police wasn't quite as forgiving as the judge. I'm busted back to patrol for the time being. But it beats the chain gang."

She planted a quick kiss on his chin. "Maybe we'll run into each other sometime."

"No doubt about it, since he also assigned me to canine training."

"Canine train—" She laughed. "You mean you get to play bad guy in the bite suit?"

She tried to picture him, bustled up like the Michelin man in the padded suit they used to train the dogs to attack. She wondered how she'd ever get Bravo to bite him, even if it was just for practice.

"Um-hmm. So, any other demands?"

"Just one."

He waited for her to explain.

She brushed her hands over his sides, down his hips and around behind. Explanation enough, she was sure.

His eyelids fell shut, his lips closed. "Ahh…" His eyes popped open and she smiled at his struggle for control. "What do you say we take that ride now?"

"What do you say we skip the ride and go upstairs?"

Hours later, Paige lay beside Marco in her sturdy four-poster bed, using his shoulder as a pillow and drawing patterns in the crisp hair on his chest.

He groaned. His wrist flopped over his eyes. "No more. You're killing me."

She grinned and kissed his collarbone. If nothing else, this night had proved to her that she need never fear giving up control to Marco Angelosi. Yes, she was vulnerable to his bottomless eyes and tender touch. She could no more resist him than a salmon could resist spawning upstream.

But she would always have as much control over him as he had over her. More, if the way his legs shifted restlessly in the tangled sheets and his hips gyrated as her imaginary patterns followed the narrowing band of hair down over his abs meant anything.

He lifted his wrist and opened one eye. "You're insatiable, you know that?"

She grinned. "Guilty."

"Aren't you even going to defend yourself?"

"Hmm. I guess I could plead insanity?" She enjoyed watching his one exposed pupil grow large as she toyed with him. "I'm crazy in love with you."

He smiled, but strain lines fanned out beside his eyes as he rolled over her. Blue veins bulged on his biceps where they supported his weight on either side of her head.

She only had to tilt her hips a fraction to understand the strain his body was under. Returning his smile with a beam of her own, Paige opened her legs and took him inside. His dark eyes smiled down on her. They moved together, one body, until neither of them could move at all.

Lying half on top of him, she snuggled deep into his

embrace. Her body felt languid, but her mind had never been clearer. "Marco?"

"Hmm." The scrape of whiskers tingled on the nape of her neck.

"You never told me what number three was."

"Three?"

"Your list of demands, remember?"

"Ah, yes. Three."

His dark eyes suddenly turned serious. "That would be children. I want children, Paige."

Her heart tripped. The memory of Marco somberly handing a wooden airplane to a dark-haired boy brought mist to her eyes.

He cupped his palm over her navel. "I want to touch your belly and feel our baby swelling inside. I want to put pillows behind your back and rub your feet and bring you ice cream at midnight."

The moment was so precious to her it was painful. A tear slipped over the rim of her lashes. He brushed it away with his thumb.

"Oatmeal," she said, needing to lighten the mood before she totally lost control of her emotions. "My grandfather told me both my grandmother and my mother wanted oatmeal at the oddest times when they were pregnant."

"Oatmeal it is then. It's healthier, anyway."

"Oatmeal." She smiled. "Yuck."

He crushed her to him until her heartbeat became sluggish and her eyes drooped, then eased her back to her side and curved himself around her as they burrowed under the covers.

The chime of twelve bells lulled her to sleep. Her last thoughts were of oatmeal, Marco holding her like he would never let go, and nursing babies with angel's eyes.

*   *   *   *   *

Coming in October 2001 from

ChildFinders, Inc.

HEART OF A HERO

by

The latest installment of this bestselling author's popular miniseries.

Former Las Vegas showgirl Dakota Armstrong was desperate when her son was stolen from her. She thought she knew who had taken the child, but she had no hope of recovering him by herself. Then ChildFinders' handsome and dedicated Russell Andreini takes the case, encountering more danger—and more desire—than he had ever bargained for.

Available at your favorite retail outlet.

Where love comes alive™

Visit Silhouette at www.eHarlequin.com   SIMINC2

Feel like a star with Silhouette.

We will fly you and a guest to New York City for an exciting weekend stay at a glamorous 5-star hotel. Experience a refreshing day at one of New York's trendiest spas and have your photo taken by a professional. Plus, receive $1,000 U.S. spending money!

Flowers...long walks...dinner for two... how does Silhouette Books make romance come alive for you?

Send us a script, with 500 words or less, along with visuals (only drawings, magazine cutouts or photographs or combination thereof). Show us how Silhouette Makes Your Love Come Alive. Be creative and have fun. No purchase necessary. All entries must be clearly marked with your name, address and telephone number. All entries will become property of Silhouette and are not returnable. **Contest closes September 28, 2001.**

Please send your entry to: **Silhouette Makes You a Star!**

In U.S.A.	In Canada
P.O. Box 9069	P.O. Box 637
Buffalo, NY, 14269-9069	Fort Erie, ON, L2A 5X3

Look for contest details on the next page, by visiting www.eHarlequin.com or request a copy by sending a self-addressed envelope to the applicable address above. Contest open to Canadian and U.S. residents who are 18 or over. Void where prohibited.

Our lucky winner's photo will appear in a Silhouette ad. Join the fun!

HARLEQUIN "SILHOUETTE MAKES YOU A STAR!" CONTEST 1308
OFFICIAL RULES
NO PURCHASE NECESSARY TO ENTER

1. To enter, follow directions published in the offer to which you are responding. Contest begins June 1, 2001, and ends on September 28, 2001. Entries must be postmarked by September 28, 2001, and received by October 5, 2001. Enter by hand-printing (or typing) on an 8 ½" x 11" piece of paper your name, address (including zip code), contest number/name and attaching a script containing 500 words or less, along with drawings, photographs or magazine cutouts, or combinations thereof (i.e., collage) on no larger than 9" x 12" piece of paper, describing how the Silhouette books make romance come alive for you. Mail via first-class mail to: Harlequin "Silhouette Makes You a Star!" Contest 1308, (in the U.S.) P.O. Box 9069, Buffalo, NY 14269-9069, (in Canada) P.O. Box 637, Fort Erie, Ontario, Canada L2A 5X3. Limit one entry per person, household or organization.

2. Contests will be judged by a panel of members of the Harlequin editorial, marketing and public relations staff. Fifty percent of criteria will be judged against script and fifty percent will be judged against drawing, photographs and/or magazine cutouts. Judging criteria will be based on the following:

   * Sincerity—25%
   * Originality and Creativity—50%
   * Emotionally Compelling—25%

   In the event of a tie, duplicate prizes will be awarded. Decisions of the judges are final.

3. All entries become the property of Torstar Corp. and may be used for future promotional purposes. Entries will not be returned. No responsibility is assumed for lost, late, illegible, incomplete, inaccurate, nondelivered or misdirected mail.

4. Contest open only to residents of the U.S. (except Puerto Rico) and Canada who are 18 years of age or older, and is void wherever prohibited by law; all applicable laws and regulations apply. Any litigation within the Province of Quebec respecting the conduct or organization of a publicity contest may be submitted to the Régie des alcools, des courses et des jeux for a ruling. Any litigation respecting the awarding of a prize may be submitted to the Régie des alcools, des courses et des jeux only for the purpose of helping the parties reach a settlement. Employees and immediate family members of Torstar Corp. and D. L. Blair, Inc., their affiliates, subsidiaries and all other agencies, entities and persons connected with the use, marketing or conduct of this contest are not eligible to enter. Taxes on prizes are the sole responsibility of the winner. Acceptance of any prize offered constitutes permission to use winner's name, photograph or other likeness for the purposes of advertising, trade and promotion on behalf of Torstar Corp., its affiliates and subsidiaries without further compensation to the winner, unless prohibited by law.

5. Winner will be determined no later than November 30, 2001, and will be notified by mail. Winner will be required to sign and return an Affidavit of Eligibility/Release of Liability/Publicity Release form within 15 days after winner notification. Noncompliance within that time period may result in disqualification and an alternative winner may be selected. All travelers must execute a Release of Liability prior to ticketing and must possess required travel documents (e.g., passport, photo ID) where applicable. Trip must be booked by December 31, 2001, and completed within one year of notification. No substitution of prize permitted by winner. Torstar Corp. and D. L. Blair, Inc., their parents, affiliates and subsidiaries are not responsible for errors in printing of contest, entries and/or game pieces. In the event of printing or other errors that may result in unintended prize values or duplication of prizes, all affected game pieces or entries shall be null and void. **Purchase or acceptance of a product offer does not improve your chances of winning.**

6. Prizes: (1) Grand Prize—A 2-night/3-day trip for two (2) to New York City, including round-trip coach air transportation nearest winner's home and hotel accommodations (double occupancy) at The Plaza Hotel, a glamorous afternoon makeover at a trendy New York spa, $1,000 in U.S. spending money and an opportunity to have a professional photo taken and appear in a Silhouette advertisement (approximate retail value: $7,000). (10) Ten Runner-Up Prizes of gift packages (retail value $50 ea.). Prizes consist of only those items listed as part of the prize. Limit one prize per person. Prize is valued in U.S. currency.

7. For the name of the winner (available after December 31, 2001) send a self-addressed, stamped envelope to: Harlequin "Silhouette Makes You a Star!" Contest 1197 Winners, P.O. Box 4200 Blair, NE 68009-4200 or you may access the www.eHarlequin.com Web site through February 28, 2002.

Contest sponsored by Torstar Corp., P.O Box 9042, Buffalo, NY 14269-9042.

SRMYAS2

If you enjoyed what you just read,
then we've got an offer you can't resist!

Take 2 bestselling
love stories FREE!
Plus get a FREE surprise gift!

COMING SOON...

AN EXCITING
OPPORTUNITY TO SAVE
ON THE PURCHASE OF
HARLEQUIN AND
SILHOUETTE BOOKS!

*DETAILS TO FOLLOW
IN OCTOBER 2001!*

YOU WON'T WANT TO MISS IT!

PHQ401